T0315556

UNIFORM DOLL

'Not too hard, Jade,' she said.

'You need it quite hard,' I told her, 'but don't worry. It'll be good. Trust me, you don't know the meaning of hot until you've been given a proper spanking. I'm going to warm you, and make you come, and when I've finished I'm going to make you get down on your knees and lick my pussy. While you're licking you can think about how bad you've been, and how hot your bum is as a result.'

'I haven't been bad!' she wailed.

'No?' I demanded. 'Wanking off cab drivers to get out of paying your fare? Letting other girls pick you up in bars? You're a dirty, smutty little bitch, aren't you, Zoe?'

'Yes,' she sobbed.

'And you deserve to be punished?'

'I'm not –'

'Yes, you do, and you know it, so if you can't take your spanking like a big girl you've got to have the gag. Now open up!'

Why not visit Penny's website at
www.pennybirch.com

UNIFORM DOLL

Penny Birch

This book is a work of fiction.
In real life, make sure you practise safe sex.

First published in 2002 by
Nexus
Thames Wharf Studios
Rainville Road
London W6 9HA

Copyright © Penny Birch 2002

The right of Penny Birch to be identified as the Author of
this Work has been asserted by her in accordance with the
Copyright, Designs and Patents Act 1988.

www.nexus-books.co.uk

Typeset by TW Typesetting, Plymouth, Devon

Printed and bound in Great Britain by Clays Ltd, St Ives PLC

ISBN 0 352 33698 6

*All characters in this publication are fictitious and any
resemblance to real persons, living or dead, is purely
coincidental.*

This book is sold subject to the condition that it shall not,
by way of trade or otherwise, be lent, resold, hired out or
otherwise circulated without the publisher's prior written
consent in any form of binding or cover other than that in
which it is published and without a similar condition
including this condition being imposed on the subsequent
purchaser.

The Random House Group Limited supports The Forest Stewardship
Council (FSC®), the leading international forest certification organisation.
Our books carrying the FSC label are printed on FSC® certified paper.
FSC is the only forest certification scheme endorsed by the leading
environmental organisations, including Greenpeace. Our
paper procurement policy can be found at
www.randomhouse.co.uk/environment

MIX
Paper | Supporting
responsible forestry
FSC® C018179

One

Samantha picked up the scissors. She thanked the barmaid, smiling, and took a pull from her drink. My wrists tensed against my bonds automatically. I felt my tummy muscles jump. She met my eyes, held up the scissors, opened them and snapped the blades shut with a click.

'Not my bra, Sam, please!' I begged.

'Your bra, Jade. I want you bare.'

'That's not fair, Sam! I have to have them specially made, you know I do! This one was forty quid! Sam, no! Sam! Bitch!'

She'd done it. As I'd spoken the blade had slid up under my armpit, beneath the material of my bra strap. She'd cut. I'd heard the material part and felt the tension go. It was done, my right boob hanging heavy in her ruined cup, my flesh spilling out around the lace.

'Bitch,' I repeated.

'That's not a very clever thing to say, is it, Jade?' Samantha answered. 'Not when you're tied to a cross. Now let's have them out, right out.'

I just hung my head, unable to answer as she set to work, cutting off the remainder of my bra. The left side went. My boobs lolled forwards, more out than in. One shoulder strap went. The cup went slack, held up only because the lacy material was sticking to my skin. The second went and it fell, exposing me.

Samantha pulled the wrecked bra away. I was showing, topless in the flickering candlelight, red and orange shapes dancing across my flesh, my tight nipples rich brown, then crimson. They felt huge, really blatant, great fat balls of flesh sticking out, with everyone staring at them. Well, they are huge, I suppose.

My breathing was deep, my skin prickly with sweat. I could feel the wet in my knickers, and the hot, heady smells of the orange and cinnamon incense, mixed with my own excitement. My wrists hurt a little, my ankles too, the thick rope taut against my flesh. It didn't matter. It was all part of what she was doing to me.

'Aren't they just the fattest?' she said, and reached out, taking one of my breasts in her hand. 'I do adore a little, fat, baby dyke.'

I moaned as she lifted my boob, her thumb brushing across the erect nipple. She was smiling, her eyes full of excitement, and bright with reflected candle flame. Her thumb came back, teasing my nipple. She pinched it, hard, and I cried out.

'Panties,' she said firmly, and dropped my boob. 'I want to see if your cunt's as fat as your tits.'

All I could manage was a weak sob. I looked down, watching as she pulled out the side of my knickers. The scissors went under, snip, to the other side, snip, and it was done. My ruined panties were twitched away and I was naked. Someone in the audience giggled. Another remarked on how hairy my pussy mound was. I looked up.

They were looking at me, twelve women, each with her eyes fixed on my naked body. Samantha was gloating, well pleased with herself. She was aroused, on tying me up, on ruining my clothes, on exposing me. So were the others, butch and femme alike, the couples cuddled close together, the singles pleased, maybe jealous.

Samantha returned the scissors to the bar, bending across to pass them to the barmaid. The motion pulled

2

her top tight to her back, her trousers to her bottom, showing her sleek, tight muscles. She was so neat, almost masculine, her bare midriff sleek and firm, her buns small and pert, stretching out the leather into twin balls of shiny black. I wanted to kiss it, down on my knees, with my own big, wobbling, girly posterior stuck out, bare.

She bought another Pils, paid, but went on speaking, leaned close to the barmaid. I saw her point, up, and my stomach knotted in real fear. The barmaid smiled, stood up, on tiptoe, reaching for one of the long, scarlet ostrich plumes. I was shaking my head even before Sam turned back, babbling out pleas, my body quivering. She just grinned when she saw the state I was in, took a sip from her bottle and stepped close.

'No!' I screamed, but too late, as the feather was drawn across the flesh of my tummy, to make my muscles knot and twitch.

'What a baby!' one of the butch girls remarked, and laughed.

It was the last thing I heard at all clearly. Sam was merciless. She drew the feather over my tummy again, and back, across my boobs, right on the nipples, tickling crazily. I just lost control. I was writhing in my bonds, babbling for her to stop, giggling stupidly, squirming, my muscles jumping. She didn't stop, doing my tummy, my boobs, my armpits, my thighs, until I was screaming for mercy and the audience were hooting with laughter.

My legs were wide on the cross, the tuck of my bum vulnerable. That's the worst bit, just where my cheeks come together, over my bottom hole. I was helpless. I couldn't cover it, and I knew she wouldn't let me off. She didn't. For a moment she paused, just enough to let me get my breath back, holding the awful feather up to my face. She ducked down, and in it went, between my legs, onto the sensitive skin on my inner thighs, higher, towards my pussy, towards my bum-cheeks, touching,

3

pulled slowly forwards, tickling an inch from the little dirty hole between them. I screamed, out loud. Every muscle in my body knotted, hard, my thighs, my bottom, my tummy. My boobs were wobbling, my whole chest jerking to my desperate, uncontrollable panting, my tummy jumping, my pussy twitching.

It just happened. I couldn't help it. I can't when I'm tickled, and Sam might have realised. My bladder burst, full across her chest, an explosion of pee that I had absolutely no way at all of holding back. I heard her angry yell, and the barmaid's, gasps of shock or delight from the watching girls, a giggle.

The tickling stopped immediately. My pee didn't, gushing over the floor and over Sam, who'd jerked back, but not far enough. I let it all go, shaking and sobbing as my bladder emptied. Sam stood up, mouth open in disgust, skinny top plastered to her breasts, the feather trailed from her hand, limp and wet. She was dripping pee, the fabric of her top stuck tight to her little braless breasts, showing their outline perfectly, and the small, hard nipples at the tip of each. It was on her jeans too, drips running down the perfect black leather, and a little had gone in her face. Worse, she'd dropped her bottle when my stream had hit her, and it had spilled on her boots. I'd peed on them too.

All I could do was stare at the mounting anger in her face, still with pee trickling down my leg. The barmaid was looking too, at the big puddle under the cross, which was rapidly soaking into the carpet. She vanished out into the main room, the music stopped. The owner appeared, looking like thunder.

'Out,' she ordered, jerking her thumb towards the door.

I wasn't too happy about being barred from Whispers. After all, it was Sam's fault I'd wet myself, not mine. I'd told her how ticklish I was, especially near my bumhole.

Anyway, if they didn't want rude things happening in their bar, they shouldn't have set up the back room for us to play in.

None of my arguments worked, and nobody stuck up for me, so I ended up being pushed out onto the street, in jeans, boots and top, but with no underwear. Not that anyone seemed to mind, in Soho, or even really notice, but it was a long way back to Turnpike Lane. I got stared at, most of the way, with a couple of boys leering at me and nudging each other on the tube.

It's all very well for girls like Sam to go around with no bra, but with boobs like mine it's no good. I just look rude, which is fine if I'm in the mood, and a pain if I'm not. As it was, I didn't know what I felt. I was really pissed off about being treated so unfairly, but it had been good being put on the cross. Having my bra and panties cut off had got to me, but I couldn't afford it, and Sam hadn't even asked. She'd tickled me too, which I hate, but I knew that if she'd taken me all the way the climax would have been something else. So I didn't know if I wanted sex or not. Either way, I certainly didn't want a couple of teenage boys mauling my boobs while I jerked their little cocks off, so when one finally plucked up the courage to make a pass I just ignored him.

There wasn't really enough time anyway, not even for a decent frig. Sam had been after me since we'd left work, and it had taken her quite a while to talk me onto the cross. She'd only known I was into other girls because we'd been in Whispers at the same time, and I usually try to keep my sex life out of the workplace. Not that I care what other people think, especially when I'm in a new office every few weeks, but it can be a hassle.

I was supposed to be at Uncle Rupert's by eight, and it was nearly seven when I got back to the flat. Not that he'd mind, but his company was just what I needed to cheer me up, and I hadn't seen him in a long while. Rupert is cool, very cool for a forty-year-old man, laid back and decadent and about the most open-minded person I know. If it hadn't been for him I would never have had the courage to come out, and the more fun I had, the more grateful I felt. I could talk to him, and I knew that we'd soon be laughing over what had happened at Whispers. He'd make me describe it in detail too, and when I'd gone he'd go upstairs for a sneaky wank over the thought of Samantha dripping with pee. Unlike me, she never goes with men, and she'd have hated it, which was a good revenge, if a bit abstract.

By the time I got to Highgate it was eight-thirty. Uncle Rupert didn't say anything, but then he never wore a watch, so he may just not have noticed. He had a bottle of champagne open and two glasses in his hand as he opened the door to me. I joined him in the little walled garden behind his house, which had been one of my favourite places since childhood.

It's no more than fifty yards from a busy street, but it has to be one of the quietest and most private places in London. The walls are high, and topped with clematis and Russian vine, while the house is at the end of a row and overlooks the valley. Nobody can see into the end part at all, except from the windows of his house. It had always seemed to be magical, a secret place of my own, a sanctuary, somewhere I knew I was always welcome and where I could find absolute peace. I had the key to the house, and spent a lot of time there when Rupert was away, alone, often naked, but I never brought lovers there. It was too special.

He poured champagne and climbed into his hammock, leaving one lanky leg hanging over the side. I settled into a chair, drank, and felt my stress start to slip away as the cool wine ran down my throat.

'How was India?' I asked.

'Hot,' he answered. 'Dry, dusty, crowded.'

'You got your coffee contracts?'

'Yes. My hosts were ever so hospitable. And I had the sweetest little whore in Meerut.'

'You have no morals at all.'

'To the contrary, I am morality itself. What I gave her will feed her and her family for a month, while if she didn't enjoy what we did then she is the most remarkable actress.'

'Tell me about her then. I know you're dying to.'

'Absolutely. She was dark, for a start, that lovely dusky tone you sometimes get with Indian girls, yet deeper than most. Huge eyes, fine face, tiny waist, broad hips, heavy, spankable bottom, titties like melons. It took a bit of persuasion to get her across my knee, but once her bum was warm she loved it, giggling and shaking it to make me carry on . . .'

'You spanked her?'

'Naturally.'

'Pervert.'

'It would have been a crime not to spank her. Some girls cry out for it.'

'No, what you mean is that some girls have figures you can't resist. That's your fault, not theirs.'

'I disagree. Any girl with a truly glorious bottom is sure to understand that men will want to smack it, just as any girl is sure to learn where men want to put their cocks.'

'It's not the same thing. It's just your dirty mind.'

'This coming from a girl who enjoys being tied and whipped in lesbian clubs?'

'Yeah, well . . . Anyway, I wanted to talk to you about that. I've been barred from Whispers.'

'That was your favourite, wasn't it? With the back room you were telling me about?'

'That's the one. This girl, Samantha, Sam, who works at the place where I'm temping, she put me on a cross.

7

I was in bra and panties, but she cut those off, then tickled me. I wet myself, all over her.'

'Magnificent. Tell me. Omit no detail.'

I did. He lay there listening, his eyes shut, his mouth set in a contented smile. Occasionally he would take a sip of champagne, but he never said a word, or touched himself, although I could see the bulge growing in his trousers. When I finished he was thoroughly pleased with himself, and with me. We went in, and I was left to myself as he busied himself in the kitchen.

There has always been an understanding between us, a mutual respect. I knew he might well want to come after listening to my story, just as he never came out into the garden if I was sunbathing nude when he came home. So I went upstairs to his library, leaving him the space to do it if he needed to.

I'd visited often enough, while he'd been in India, but I hadn't been into the library. It had changed, and in a way it was impossible not to notice. The shelves were the same, with their ranks of books on every subject and in every type of binding, from an early Bible in iron clasps and blackened leather to his garish collection of pornographic art, with every cover showing girls in lewd positions. So were the two well-stuffed armchairs, with their studded green leather upholstery and highly polished wood.

What was different, and out of place, were two mannequins. Both were female, and dressed in uniforms – one an air hostess, one a waitress. I was immediately fascinated, and went to take a closer look, wondering what Rupert was up to. They were immaculate, complete too, while a quick peak revealed that they even had underwear. They also had legends, on little stands which had been hidden when I first walked in, a photograph and some text. Both showed the same uniform that was on the mannequin beside it, but being worn, or rather half worn.

I was open-mouthed with delight, and a little shocked too. The air hostess was bad enough, with a pretty Indian girl taken against a bank of brilliant pink flowers, beside a stone bench, with her skirt twitched up and her panties held down to show her bare bum. She looked shy yet pleased with herself, both excited and embarrassed, feelings very familiar to me.

The waitress was worse. The photo had been taken in some anonymous hotel room, and must have been done automatically, because it showed a pretty if slightly tarty blonde in the uniform, bent across my uncle's knee. Her little pink skirt was up, her panties were down and there was a definite red flush to her bottom. She was getting a spanking and, from the pained look on her face, a hard one.

I just stared. I knew he liked girls' bottoms and spanked them if he could, but to actually see evidence of it was something else, especially with the uniforms there. It was genuine as well, because in both cases I could pick out little marks that left no doubt that the uniform in the photo was the same one as worn by the mannequin. He'd always enjoyed his stories, and I knew that in his room there was a drawer of girls' panties donated by various girlfriends across the years, or just stolen. This was different.

Naturally I had to ask. As soon as a decent interval had elapsed I went downstairs, finding him chopping shallots, a glass of red wine by his side. If he had wanked himself off there was no evidence of it, not even a tissue in the bin, which he usually left, just to show that my story had done its job. Feeling ever so slightly put out, I asked him about the uniforms.

'Ah ha, so you have seen my collection,' he said. 'If two items warrant the title of a collection.'

'A collection?'

'Just that. The start of one anyway.'

'So who are the girls? Are you collecting female uniforms? What happened? Did you pinch their clothes?'

'Please, Jade, dear, a question at a time! To answer the simplest question first, yes, I am collecting female uniforms, or rather I intend to do so. I think I need four or five to really call it a collection . . .'

'But what happened?' I interrupted.

'Patience.' He laughed. 'I will tell you over dinner.'

'Now.'

'Very well, since you insist, but don't interrupt. You saw the two, the waitress and the Air Delhi stewardess?'

'Yes.'

'The waitress was the first. It was some years ago, in a motel outside Boston. It started normally enough, with the girl, Sally, fascinated by my accent and manners, which is a not uncommon occurrence in the States. She was half my age, so naturally I was flattered, and did my best to talk her into bed. Not that it was difficult. She was as keen as I, and kept saying she'd heard the English were kinky, and asking if it was true. Well, no girl teases me like that and gets away with it, so I took her back to my room and spanked her bottom for her, bare, over the knee, in the best English style.'

'I saw the photo. She doesn't look too happy about it.'

'She wasn't. There was a bit of a misunderstanding there, you see. She thought I'd want it done to me, and was a bit shocked when I put her over for fifty hard ones on the bare. She really howled, as it goes, but I didn't see why I should stop, not when she'd wanted to do the same to me. Anyway, she was fine once her bum was warm, and I let her use a hairbrush on me, just to even things up. After that we had a fine time.'

'I bet you did!'

'Without doubt. I particularly remember her riding me, with her back towards me and her reddened bottom stuck out. A fine view. Anyway, she had come over to my room after leaving work, with her ordinary clothes in a bag. In the morning we woke late, and she was in a rush, and forgot her uniform. I suppose she must have realised and come back quickly enough, but by then I was gone, with the uniform – her bra and panties too.'

'You stole them! You bastard!'

'*Mea culpa.* I couldn't resist it. You know I like my trophies, and I had asked if I could keep her knickers. She had a spare pair, a bra too, and – well, I decided to take the lot.'

'Poor girl! I mean, you spank her bottom for her when she's not expecting it and, if that isn't bad enough, you pinch her clothes!'

'You make it sound as if I left her naked in the street! All part of the rough and tumble of life, my dear, nothing more.'

I gave him a disapproving tut and poured myself a glass of the red wine. Not that I approved of what he'd done, but it was impossible not to feel a thrill. It had been naughty, like going without panties – like having sex with other girls for that matter. Just listening had left me flushed, and I could feel the prickling sensation across my chest and face. Rupert saw, and chuckled.

He began to cook, all the while smiling to himself in a self-satisfied way. I sipped wine, waiting impatiently for him to tell me about the other girl, and knowing that if I tried to hurry him it would only make him tease me. He didn't even start when we were seated at the table, each with a plate of the complicated pasta dish he'd been making in front of us. We ate and drank, one bottle, then another, and it was when he had that open and our glasses full that he began.

'It was after my air hostess that I decided to start collecting,' he began. 'That was last week, somewhere called Jammu, right up towards the mountains. The aircraft was stranded overnight, so the crew had to stay over. I imagine they had some sort of accommodation arranged, but by then I'd already persuaded my little Induma to accept my hospitality. Her name, Induma,

11

means moon, and does she have one, so round, so feminine. But you saw?'

'I saw the photo, yes, with her holding her knickers down to show off her bum. It's really smutty, the sort of rude photo the boys used to show round at school.'

'And why not? A pushed out, bare female bottom speaks directly to the male libido. But you agree she has a beautiful bottom?'

'Yes, I suppose so.'

'Undoubtedly, and she knew it. It was by a combination of flattery and bribery that I talked her into taking her knickers down. In a secluded spot in the hotel garden, by the way. She let me have a feel too, and I'd have had her there if she'd let me. Spanked then fucked, bent over that stone bench in the picture.'

'Lecherous old goat! How old was she?'

'It's very impolite to ask a lady's age.'

'Oh, right, but it's fine to pull down her knickers and spank her on the bare bottom?'

'Naturally. True ladies seldom resent a spanking. It is in the female nature.'

'Uncle Rupert! I thought you were a liberal, not a chauvinist pig!'

'I am a liberal. That doesn't alter the fact that to receive a spanking is very much part of a woman's nature. But I know your views. Let us not argue the point. Induma did not share them in any case, taking the attitude that she should do her best to please her man, and that if that included having her delectable bottom spanked, then she was prepared to accept it.'

'So she wasn't actually into spanking?'

'Patience, patience, let me explain. After taking the photo in the garden, I steered her politely but firmly to my room. There I explained that I intended to spank her as a prelude to sex. She was nervous, and giggled a lot, but she accepted it, including keeping her uniform on for the performance.'

'I didn't know you had a uniform fetish.'

'I don't, and I hate that word. A sexual fetish is something that has become inextricably linked with sex, an object or practice without which pleasure is impossible. That is a sorry state to get into, very sorry indeed. I like uniforms, yes, they enhance a woman's body, and add a nice touch when undressing her, a rude touch, as if to cock a snook at whatever authority the uniform represents. This is an important element of my desire to collect, but I shall come back to that later.'

'Yes. Tell me what you did to poor Induma, you dirty old goat.'

'What did I do to her? I indulged myself, to the full, that's what I did. I sat myself in a convenient chair, and took her down across my knee, with that divine little peach stuck high and her thighs well parted. I then prepared her. First, I undid the buttons at the front of her uniform dress and pulled out her breasts, which I often think is good for a woman being spanked.'

'Why?'

'To take away her modesty, as if you didn't know. Bare breasts are important for a punished woman, if less so than a bare bottom. Never, ever, let a girl keep her knickers up during a spanking, let alone anything else. Covering allows her to retain a measure of pride that no amount of beating will erase, even with a cane or tawse. No, pull them down, and let her know her fanny is on show to the world.'

'You really are terrible!'

'Induma didn't seem to think so. She was quite happy with it, giggling as I pulled her titties out and had a good feel of each, even when I tugged up her uniform skirt and pulled down her panties. No, it was the actual spanking she couldn't handle.'

'No?'

'No. Well, you see, I hadn't been entirely honest with her, and what with her English, or rather lack of it . . .

13

She expected her body exposed, yes, and to be fondled, maybe to have her buttocks patted. I don't think she actually expected it to hurt.'

'But you did it anyway, didn't you?'

'I did, I'm afraid, quite hard. She liked it at first, with me stroking her bum and playing pat-a-cake on her bottom-cheeks. That had her giggling, and I suppose she thought that was all there was to it. She was even sticking her bum up, and when I saw those glorious dusky cheeks pull apart and got my first whiff of her sex, well, I just couldn't hold back. I took her around her waist, which was tiny, and cocked up my knee, making her bottom come fully open. I could see her fanny-lips like that, brown and smooth, the sweetest little purse, her bottom hole too. She had a pretty bottom hole, the same milky coffee as her skin, not even a tone darker, but quite fleshy, like a pursed mouth.'

'You didn't bugger her, did you?'

'Patience, Jade, patience. So there she was, her long black hair spread out over the floor, her glorious titties hanging out of her dress, her silk panties halfway down her legs, her divine bottom stuck up in the nude. So I spanked her properly.'

'And she didn't expect it? Did she cry?'

'Oh, yes. She absolutely howled. She was in tears almost from the first smack, as soon as she realised that I wasn't going to stop. I do spank hard, it's the best way, and, of course, I couldn't stop, because I had to get her over the pain barrier. Not that she understood that, of course, and I could hardly explain. So I just let her howl, and I think it was as much frustration as pain. That's often the way, when they really make a fuss. She certainly did, kicking like anything, until her knickers fell off. That let her get her legs wider apart, and I could really smell her sex, which was as wet as anything. I was ready for her too, with my cock rock hard against her tummy. She must have been able to feel it, and she knew full well where it was going.'

14

'You can be such a bastard.'

'No. It was for her own good. Partially at any rate. It took about five minutes of hard spanking to get her ready, but by then she'd stopped blubbering and was breathing really deeply. Her legs were cocked wide open, and she was sticking her bottom up again, and mumbling in her language. I gave her another fifty for luck, mainly on her sweet spot, to see if I could make her come. She didn't, but she scrambled onto the bed quickly enough when I let her go.'

'What did you do?'

'Why, I fucked her, of course. From the rear first, so that I could stroke her little smacked cheeks while I was up her, and tickle her bumhole.'

'That would have sent me through the roof!'

'She liked it. It seemed to get her really urgent. She wanted to touch too, to feel her smacked cheeks, as if she couldn't quite believe what had been done to her, or how good it felt.'

'I know the feeling.'

'She kept doing that, all the while as I put her through her paces, except when she was on her back, of course, then she'd feel her titties. She never said a word, all the time, not in English anyway, just doing as she was told, one position after another, and sucking my cock in between. Before long she'd started to get eager, adopting her own poses, and dirty too, rubbing at herself while I fucked her, with one finger on her bottom hole. That was her favourite, lying on her side with one leg cocked up, so that I could get into her and she could touch herself front and back. She came like that, and she made nearly as much noise as she had during the spanking. By then she had a finger up her bottom, deep in. I'd nearly come when she did, but I didn't want to risk her getting pregnant, so I'd held back. After I saw that her finger was up her bum I just couldn't hold back any longer.'

'You came up her pussy?'

'No. That's when I buggered her.'

'You utter bastard. Tell me.'

'She pulled her finger out when she'd come. I withdrew and she rolled over onto her front, sticking her bottom up. She was looking back, smiling, with that perfect coffee-brown moon lifted to me, the cheeks flushed dark from her spanking, her bottom hole moist and a little open, the ring still pulsing a little from her orgasm. I think she wanted me to put my cock back up, and it was tempting, with her fanny puffy and wet with juice, the hole so open that I could see up her. I think I would have, only she reached back to take hold of her smacked cheeks, clutching them and pulling them apart. That made her bottom hole stretch, and, well, I couldn't resist it. So I got on her, and put my cock between her cheeks, to her anus. She gasped when she felt where it was going, and said something, but I don't know what.'

'Probably calling you a dirty bastard.'

'Maybe. Anyway, she took it well enough, just grunting a little and making these odd little mewing noises as I pushed the head of my cock in up her hole. She was tight, but pretty moist where juice had run down from her fanny, so I got up easily enough, right in. I could feel my pubic hair between her bottom-cheeks and my balls were lying on her fanny. She was moaning by then, and had a hand under her tummy to frig with. I took my time, holding her by her tits and just keeping my erection firm up her bottom, until she started to come. I felt her ring go tight, and with that I really jammed it in, clutching her to me as I buggered her, with her hole clamping on my cock, until I did it up her, while she was still coming.'

'That's enough. I need the garden.'

I just ran. It was too much for me, the whole thing, what Sam had done to me, then Rupert with his dirty stories. I needed to masturbate, and I needed to do it in my special place. He chuckled as I fled the room, knowing perfectly well where I was going, and what I was going to do. Not that he was any better, as the last thing I heard as I went was the sound of his zip being pulled down.

My head was spinning with wine, or maybe I'd have thought twice about what I did. As it was, I just needed my clothes off, to feel the cool night air on my body. I stripped then and there, on the back step, naked, peeling off my top and bra, pushing down my jeans and taking my panties with them. Of course I had to sit my bare bum down on the rough concrete to get my boots off, but that just added to my delicious feelings of exposure.

Stark naked, I ran down the garden to the hammock. I climbed in, settling the rug beneath me, but with my bum against the rope so that I could feel the mesh pulled tight into my flesh. My thighs came wide, one over each side, and I was spread, my sex agape to the night, wide and wet. Wet was right, soaking, so that I managed to slide three fingers straight in. They went to my mouth, so that I could taste myself while I did it, then back.

I began to rub, flicking at my clitty and one nipple as the rude thoughts ran through my head – of exposure and punishment. I thought of having my bra ruined so that Sam could show how big my boobs were to the girls in the bar. I thought of the girls Rupert had held down across his knee, shivering in their humiliation, their bottoms bare, their bottoms spanked. Not just spanked either, but spanked and then fucked, spanked and then buggered in the case of the poor stewardess.

Men are so filthy, so crude, putting their cocks up girls' bottom holes, where the shit comes out, and they just don't care, so long as it's hot and tight and feels good on their gross cocks. Rupert had buggered Induma, spanked her and then buggered her, with his cock up her bottom hole, in her rectum, in her dirt box. He

17

wasn't even ashamed of it. He was proud. He was pleased with himself, pleased that he'd seduced some hapless girl into sex, spanked her until she cried, fucked her until she was too high to hold herself back, then buggered her.

That was too much for me, just the thought of a man's penis going up a girl's bottom hole. Cocks are ugly, really gross, and what men want us to do with them is just so filthy. Not fucking, so much, but sucking, in our mouths, till they spunk and force us to swallow their disgusting sperm. Worse, up our bums, deep up our nice, clean little holes, in and out, until we're not clean any more, until I'm not clean any more.

Not clean no, anything but, slimy and sweaty and dirty, soiled, with a big, fat cock stuck up my dirt box and a fat, hairy belly slapping at my bottom. It would happen one day, I just knew it. Some bastard wouldn't accept my preference for girls. They'd push, teasing me into experimenting, into taking their ugly great cock in my hand, in my mouth, up my pussy, and at last, up my bottom hole, and that's where they'd come.

Which was what I had done, crying out my ecstasy softly to the night, naked, wet with sweat, my body shaking with reaction to my filthy fantasy.

Not that I was ever, ever going to admit to getting off over fantasies of being buggered by men, much less let it happen. That was private, from everybody.

After I'd come I went back indoors, feeling rather embarrassed, and he explained about his uniform collection. The morning after sleeping with Induma, he had tried to explain that he wanted her panties as a trophy. She hadn't really understood, partly because they were something she only wore with her European-style hostess uniform anyway. Instead she had thought he had wanted the whole uniform, a misunderstanding that had sparked the idea in Uncle Rupert's head. She had been reluctant to give it up, not surprisingly, but in the end had sold it to him and pretended she'd been robbed when she got back to the aeroplane.

So Rupert had his uniform and, by the time he'd returned to the UK, he had the whole thing worked out. It was typically obsessive, and typically male, with rules and everything, just as if he'd been collecting rare pieces of china or old paintings. The most important one was that the uniform had to be genuine. It had to represent some form of institution or business for which the woman worked, or belonged to, or had done. Theatrical wear, or buying something and dressing a girlfriend up in it, definitely did not count. There had to be a photograph too, of the woman wearing the uniform, and at the least in a cheeky pose, preferably an actively rude one. If necessary he could pay for the uniform, but the women weren't allowed to know what was going on. It had to include her underwear too.

I wasn't at all sure if I approved. After all, it seemed pretty mean to go around pinching clothes from hard-working professional women. He was also seducing them under false pretences, which I didn't feel happy about either. Not that I was all that worried, because I couldn't actually see him being very successful. He had the front for it, and I could see him offering a pretty traffic warden or nurse fifty quid to flash her bum and a hundred for her uniform. That wouldn't have been in the spirit of the game, though, and I knew how important that was to him. When I explained my reservations he just laughed, telling me that my generation were far too soft.

That was it, and our conversation drifted onto other topics. By then I was feeling mellow, and pleased that our relationship was as open as ever. That's important to me, because he had helped me come to terms with my own sexuality, and I would hate to lose any of the intimacy that had built up between us. Not that we have sex or anything like that, but he knows me better than my parents, and I sometimes think he understands me better than I do myself.

I never even met him until I was nineteen, fresh out of school and away from home for the first time, at art college in London. Naturally I'd been given his address, as the only person even vaguely related to me in the city, but not without some hesitation. He wasn't even a proper uncle, just the son of my mum's step-brother, which I suppose made him a cousin of sorts. What he did have was a serious streak of rebellion, moving to London as soon as he was old enough at the end of the seventies, as bass guitarist in a punk band. The band had flopped, arriving too late, as he explained, but probably just crap. Since then he'd done well, becoming head buyer for a major coffee concern, and very cultivated, but I'd never heard his name mentioned without a hint of disapproval, even despair.

Not surprisingly, I'd been fascinated, and had arranged to visit him almost as soon as I'd got off the train. We'd got on well from the start, with his laid-back lifestyle and total lack of respect for anything that smacked of authority was just what I wanted to emulate. He had supported me when I'd decided to give up college, after two failed relationships with boyfriends, and when I finally decided that I preferred girls. He'd even stood next to me while I phoned my mum to tell her I was a lesbian.

That had been a year previously, and by then I'd had a spare key to his house, which I could use as long as I respected his wishes and privacy. I was good about his wishes, as I had no intention of sharing my secret place with anyone else. I wasn't so good about his privacy, investigating his library and his bedroom, and shocking myself quite badly.

It had been hard to take at first, not so much his obsession with the naked female form, but his clear, uninhibited delight in girls' bottoms, and in spanking them. Perhaps, fortunately, I'd had my first CP scene a few days before my discovery. I'd been very drunk at a club, one where fetishists hung out, and leather dykes, which made me feel it was a cool place to be. After watching a girl whipped, I'd let two big, butch dykes talk me into trying it. They'd been careful, warming me until I was nearly coming, and only really laying in when I was actually at climax. Afterwards I'd been taken into the toilet to lick them, one at a time, but I was used to that by then. What did surprise me was the state of my bottom the next morning, with long, dark bruises across both cheeks. I'd had no idea they'd done it so hard.

So it wasn't so shocking to learn that my kind Uncle Rupert was a secret spanker. I knew that girls could like it, and it seemed reasonable to assume that the girls in his pictures were either into it, or being well paid. I'd swallowed it anyway, because by the time I'd been browsing his huge collection for an hour I was too turned on to care. I'd masturbated, right there on his library floor, with my jeans and panties around my knees and my top and bra pulled up.

Having done it once, I couldn't hold myself back. Just knowing that the collection was there was too much for me, just the same way I used to be unable to resist climbing up to the cupboard Mum kept the sweets in. It became a compulsion, and I'd do it at every opportunity. The thing was, unlike ordinary dirty pictures, each spanking picture seemed to tell a story. One or another could always be guaranteed to trigger a fantasy, with me as the victim.

Eventually Rupert noticed – or, rather, eventually he felt he had to say something, because he probably noticed fairly soon after I'd started. He spoke to me about it, very casually, one day when I was visiting for tea. I was hideously embarrassed, guilty too, and upset,

21

because I felt I'd betrayed him. I would have run from the house, but he quickly made it plain that the only reason he hadn't wanted me to know was because he felt sure I'd be down on him for it.

We talked for hours that night, until the birds had begun to sing. When I finally went up to his spare room for some sleep, I found an album of spanking pictures laid discreetly by the bed, underneath the latest *Metropolitan*. I read it, and masturbated over a wonderful fantasy about being spanked in a girls' dormitory, in front of all the others. He knew, I'm sure.

It never occurred to me for a moment not to trust him and, sure enough, he never tried anything on, or even asked to watch. Over the next few months it became a regular occurrence, not always happening, but as often as not. Meanwhile, my sex life grew wilder, with my reputation for enjoying punishment spreading rapidly among those who liked to dish it out, until the day I got myself thrown out of Whispers.

Two

After a couple of months I'd put Uncle Rupert's uniform collection to the back of my mind. The two mannequins were still there, but he'd failed to add any more to the collection. I'd had other things to think about as well, like how to carry on enjoying my sex life without being able to go to my favourite baby dyke bar. Everyone seemed to know about my accident too, which was well embarrassing. I got teased mercilessly whenever I went out to clubs, and made to do it on the toilet while some of the butch girls watched.

I'd moved on to a new job, and I didn't see Sam again until I went to a festival out near Farnborough. It wasn't really a gay thing, but there was a dyke band playing, and I'd been given a spanking by the drummer once, so I went. It was good, in a huge field, with everyone drunk or high or just really chilled out. I knew lots of people, and was wandering through the crowds, just chatting and kissing and knocking back bottles of Bud.

Sam was with a group of friends, all dressed much the same: polished boots, tight leather trousers, skinny tops or leather bras, along with plenty of body jewellery. I could just have ignored them, but there's a self-destructive impulse in me – or, rather, a self-chastising impulse. So I threw myself to the wolves.

'Hi, Sam,' I managed, trying not to sound too cheeky.

They turned to look at me, all five of them, all taller than me, all cool and poised and dominant.

'This, girls,' Sam announced, 'is the one who pissed herself when I had her on a cross. Say hi to the girls, Jade.'

'Hi,' I said, smiling weakly as Sam's arm came around my shoulder.

'All I did was tickle her,' Sam went on, 'and she lost it. Such a baby. I was going to use a tawse across her fat thighs, maybe her boobies. What would you have done then, Jade, shit yourself?'

I went scarlet as they answered her with laughter. My tummy was starting to knot, and I felt terribly helpless with Sam's arm around my shoulders, far too helpless to try to pull away.

'She pissed on your boots, didn't you say?' one of them asked, the tallest, a girl with cropped hair dyed almost white.

'That and spilled beer on them,' Sam answered her.

'She spilled beer on your boots?' the blonde demanded. 'What did you do about it?'

'Nothing,' Sam answered. 'She got thrown out of Whispers –'

'You should have made her lick them,' the blonde cut in.

I could see how it went. Sam sounded a lot less confident talking to the blonde girl, who was obviously someone they looked up to. I wasn't surprised. Her body was really hard, with long, smooth muscles showing under her skin, even across her tummy. She had some serious tattoos as well, stark black-and-white designs, and plenty of piercings, with a big silver female symbol on a chain around her neck.

'You're right,' Sam said. 'I should have.'

'Do it, then,' the blonde told her.

'Here?'

'Why not?'

They were all looking at Sam, and I knew she was going to do something. I could have run, maybe, but a moment later she'd tripped me and I was sprawled on the muddy ground. Sam squatted down, taking me by the hair as the others moved into a ring around us. Nobody else made the slightest effort to interfere as my head was dragged close to her boots.

'Lick,' she ordered.

I did it, without hesitation, poking my tongue out to taste the leather and polish, then kissing, one toe cap, then the other. One of the girls standing over me gave a little snort, of contempt, of amusement. Another kicked my bottom.

'Pull out her tits,' the blonde ordered.

It was done, hands reaching down to snatch my top up, then my bra, the cups jerked off my boobs to leave them hanging in the warm mud. I scrambled into a kneeling position, with my bottom swelling out my green combats, stuck out right at the blonde. I was being bullied, badly, but all I wanted was to have my bottom smacked, right there, in public.

Already it was good, licking Sam's boots while they laughed at me and prodded at my body, kicking my thighs and buttocks, even my breasts. All it needed for perfection was to have my combats pulled down, along with my knickers, showing off my big bottom to everyone. Then they'd have spanked me, hard, taking it in turns, until I was grovelling, red-bottomed in the mud, sore and punished, my pussy gaping to the crowd as I rubbed myself to climax . . .

They didn't have the bottle. People were starting to stare, and not all of them in approval. Sam announced that I'd been put in my place, and I was told to get up. I struggled to my feet and ran, frantically trying to cover my muddy boobs, full of confusion and arousal. Only when I was well away from anybody who might have seen me degraded did I stop, to sit panting on a bank.

I was so turned on that my head was spinning. I didn't know what to think, at all. Part of me was wishing they'd punished me properly, but another part just wanted to burst into tears over what had been done to me. Again, part of me wanted to get as far away as possible, another to go back and ask Sam if she'd like to take me into the bushes, or all five of them for that matter.

They'd really humiliated me. I'd licked boots before, and nude, not just topless, but always at clubs or in the back room at Whispers. This was different, in broad daylight, somewhere that people had come to listen to music, not for sex, and worst of all, with men watching. Beforehand, only five men had ever seen my boobs bare. Now it was thirty or more, six times as many, in the space of seconds.

In the end I went to get another beer, which helped to calm me down a bit, although I was still shaking. I was a bit of a state too, with mud on my trousers and in my bra, which was really uncomfortable. One or two girls were topless, but none with boobs like mine, and I knew that to do it would just make my arousal worse, and my feelings of vulnerability.

What I did do was take my bra off under my top, which left me looking pretty rude, but not so bad. People still starred, and my nipples were showing really badly, but that tends to happen anyway, because they're so big and they go hard so easily. People stare anyway.

Three Buds later I was back on the bank, and drunk enough to be seriously considering going off into the bushes for a sneaky frig, or else trying to pick someone up to share it with. That was when I saw her, walking towards me out of the crowd. She had no piercings, no tattoos. She didn't need them. Just in boots and combats she was as butch as they come.

For a start she was huge, and I mean huge. No taller than Sam's blonde friend, but twice the weight, easily, and most of it muscle. She was shaved too, or nearly so, with no more than a millimetre of black stubble covering her scalp. That, and her strong, broad face, gave her a look to put Sam's leather dyke friends to shame, and it wasn't all. Her legs were huge, but still looked long, rising to massive hips, but without an ounce of fat. Her torso was better still. The camouflage vest she was wearing hardly covered anything, with her great solid boobs sticking out, firm and high under the thin material, with a massive bra to support them. That was enough to have me staring, but it was her arms that really made me gape. I'd seen less muscle on girl's legs, on some men's legs.

She wasn't coming over to ask me the time. I was smiling and blushing before she even reached me, not sure where to look. She showed no such uncertainty, sitting down beside me and passing me one of the beers she'd been carrying.

'I saw you,' she said, 'getting made to kiss that girl's boots. Nice.'

'She was . . . she was punishing me,' I stammered. 'For . . . for spilling beer on her boots.'

'I heard. Pissing on her too. You do that on purpose?'

'No! It was an accident.'

She gave a grunt, halfway to laughter. Her voice was really deep, masculine, but the rich, hormonal scent of her body was anything but. I could feel myself melting.

'Would you . . . would you like me to lick your boots?' I asked.

'I'd like you to lick my cunt,' she answered. 'Come on.'

She stood up, taking me by the hand. I went, mesmerised. I was expecting to be used, thoroughly used, right there in the bushes at the back of the field, probably where other people would see. Instead I was taken to the car park. She had a jeep, genuine old-style army, with a cover over the back. I was lifted in, just so easily, and she followed, doing up the flaps behind us.

It was cool and dim under the cover, a soft, brown-green light, with bright patches where the sun shone through the eyelets. There were sacks of clothing or something, soft anyway, which I lay against, watching her. She didn't waste time, kneeling up to undo her trousers and pushing them down, taking her huge blue knickers with them. The scent of her sex became suddenly stronger as her pussy came on show, the plump mound shaved to stubble, just like her head, but with a triple chevron of bare skin. I giggled at the sight, wetting my lips.

'Like it?' she said.

I nodded.

'Well, I'm a real sergeant, if that makes it better for you,' she said. 'now get licking.'

That was it. No preliminaries, no foreplay. She hadn't even told me her name. Her trousers came down to her ankles and she leaned back against the tailgate of the jeep, her massive thighs spread wide. I crawled over, pulling out my boobs on the way, and buried my face in her sex. She was musky, and already wet, with a slight tang of pee, which I quickly licked up.

She held me by the head as I licked at her, pulling me in and moving me to make me pay attention first to her pussy hole, then to her clit. That was big, a firm bud of flesh, poking out from under a fleshy hood. I kissed it, sucking it in between my lips, nipping gently with my teeth. She moaned, pulling me in harder still as I fed on her clitoris, sucking and mouthing until she came with a grunt, her thighs locking firmly around my head.

'Nice,' she said. 'You're a good cunt-licker. What's your name?'

'Jade.'

'Mo. Well, Jade, seeing how you lick so well, I'm going to give you what you want. Well?'

'I . . . I like to be spanked.'

'Spanked? What, across your backside? Pervert, are you?'

28

I nodded, with the blood rushing into my cheeks. She just laughed.

'So you like your backside slapped?' she went on. 'What with? My hand? A belt?'

'A belting might be nice.'

She gave a shrug, and a look that suggested I was mad. I was, because for all my arousal I could just imagine how much it was going to hurt, with those huge arms and the great, thick leather belt which had been holding her trousers up.

'Get them down then,' she said, nodding to the sacks, 'and over those. There's enough room in here, I reckon, just about.'

I went, trembling hard as I undid my combats and pushed them down over my hips. My bum felt huge. Well, my bum is pretty huge, I suppose, though I tell myself that's just the way it looks because my waist is so slim. As it came on show, she reached out, taking a big pinch of one meaty cheek, to make me squeak.

'Soft,' she said. 'You need to tone up.'

I didn't deny it, pulling two sacks out of the pile and putting one on the other, with my hands shaking as I did it. She watched, fingering her belt, which she had pulled free, as I laid myself over the improvised spanking horse, to leave my boobs hanging down, squashed out on the cold metal floor, and my bum right up high. She chuckled at the sight.

'Modest, are we?' she said, taking hold of the waistband of my knickers.

'No,' I answered. 'Pull them down.'

She did, immediately, just tugging them casually off my bum, as if it was no big deal at all. It was, for me, the intimate exposure of my bottom for punishment. I knew what I'd look like from the rear as well, with my pussy wet and puffy between my thighs and my cheeks far enough apart to hint at the dark crevices of my bottom hole. It felt rude and exposed, stripped of my

29

modesty, ready for whipping. I could even smell myself, hot and urgent, mixing with her scent, a greasy smell and the tang of sweat from the bags. I looked back to find her grinning down at my nude bum.

'Would I like to get a few of the girls like this,' she said, and brought the belt around.

It landed on my bum with a crack, jamming me forwards, squealing, my meat shaking to the blow. It stung crazily and I was panting immediately, but I held still, just whimpering a little as I waited for the next. She gave it, lower, a hard smack right on my sweet spot, sending ripples of flesh across my bottom and leaving me gasping with shock and pain.

'I could get to like this,' she said, and gave me my third.

It came higher, and harder, really slamming into my poor bum. I cried out in my pain, my legs jerking apart to stretch out my knickers, my bum coming up, just in time to catch the fourth.

'Watch your feet!' she ordered, and gave me another, harder still, to make me squeal and dance again, writhing over the clothing bundles with my bottom shaking behind me.

'Tie me, then,' I managed, still breathless as I came down from the sudden pain.

She gave a pleased grunt and reached forwards to pull at one of the sacks. The neck closed with string, which I saw a moment before it was twisted around my ankles, and tied off. She wasn't finished, though. My arms were taken, pulled up behind my back and lashed together, tight, leaving me helpless for my beating. The sacks under my tummy were adjusted, forcing my bum higher, to make my cheeks part and show off the dirty little hole between them. She had a feel, stroking my hot skin and briefly poking a finger into the wet cavity of my vagina, before once more picking up the belt.

I watched, looking back, shaking as she lifted it, her face set in concentration as she took aim. It came down, slamming into my bum. I screamed, bucking in my bonds. Another followed, and a third, in quick succession, until I was panting and gasping, writhing on the sacks, my hot bottom stuck high, my boobs wobbling to the smacks.

It hurt so much, real pain, a good, honest beating, smack after smack of her horrible belt landing across my meat, making me scream and writhe and fart, helpless in my bondage and just as helpless in my pain. Again and again the belt caught my sweet spot, the fat bit where my bum flares over my pussy, where smacks really count. I was going to come, I knew it, and I found myself babbling to her, pleading for it harder, and faster, on that special spot.

She obliged, slamming the belt into my bottom, with all the force of her massive arms, full across the fattest, meatiest part of my bum. Every jolt caught my pussy, getting me closer, and closer still, until at last it hit me. I screamed as I came, really loud, with the belt smacking down on my bum in a furious rhythm, fast and vicious, beating me without mercy, just exactly the way I wanted it.

Mo went right on thrashing me, until at last it was over and I was screaming at her to stop. She did, and I slumped down over the bags, panting hard, my bottom burning, my whole body tingling, sweat running down over my skin.

'Lovely, thank you,' I managed. 'I needed that.'

'You did,' she assured me, and began to pull up her trousers.

I waited, assuming she'd tidy herself up, then untie me. Instead she just pulled up her trousers, fastened them and began to open the rear. With the gap wide enough, she poked her head out, then swung a leg over the tailboard.

'What are you doing?' I demanded.

'You think I'm passing you up on a quickie?' she answered. 'A live one like you? I'm taking you home, girl.'

'Hey! No!'

'What's the matter? You want more, don't you?'

'Yeah, but –'

'Then cut the crap, you'll get what you want, in plenty.'

'All right, but where are we going? And could you untie me?'

'Back to my accommodation.'

'Where's that?'

'Aldershot.'

'Well, okay, but I've got to get back this evening. Look, you'll put me on a train or something won't you? Please could you untie . . .'

'Shut up,' she interrupted.

I shut up, sort of. She delved into one of the bags, pulling out first a sock, then a pair of knickers, soiled ones, with a big stain on the crotch and sweat marks where they'd pulled tight to the girl's pussy and bum-crease.

'Open your mouth,' she ordered.

'No!' I protested. 'They're filthy, and smelly! Whose are they?'

'Corporal Jane Lewis,' she read from the label. 'One of my best.'

'I don't care how good she is, I don't want her dirty knickers in my mou –'

I stopped abruptly, because Mo had pinched my nose and stuffed the panties in my face. I could smell the corporal's pussy, her sweat too, stale and strong as I struggled to pull away.

I got it done to me, inevitably. I mean, I'd just been given a belting, and she was very much in charge. Despite my struggles my mouth came open in the end, and Jane Lewis's dirty knickers were forced into my mouth. They tasted horrid, of stale pee and sweat, making me grimace as Mo tied them off with two equally filthy socks.

With me gagged, she didn't even bother to cover my boobs or bum, but just left me there, lying among the laundry bags with the taste of some stranger's dirty panties in my mouth. They were really dry too, the cotton soaking up all the moisture in my mouth, forcing me to chew on them to make spit, which made the taste even worse.

The back of the cover was fastened, I felt the jeep rock to Mo's weight, and we set off, bumping across the field. She drove fast, bumping me about in the back and rolling me to one side or the other with every corner, until I was bruised and dizzy, feeling slightly sick. It seemed to go on for ever too, and all the while I could do nothing but wriggling in my bounds, trying to lessen my discomfort.

It may have hurt, but it really got to me, just being bound, utterly helpless, which nobody can understand unless they've had it done to them. My throbbing, belted bottom made it worse, as did the horrid taste in my mouth, and the nagging fear that I'd let myself in for more than I could handle. All that would have been strong, but half stripped, with my top up around my neck and my combats and knickers pulled well down, it was almost too much. I had everything showing, including a well-smacked bottom, and for all I knew we'd have to pass a check point or something, and someone would look in, probably a man. By the time the jeep finally pulled to a stop I was snivelling, close to tears with worry.

There was no check point. When Mo pulled open the flaps I saw that we were in a garage, with the door safely closed. She lifted me out easily and slung me across her shoulder, putting her hand on my bottom to hold me steady. Hanging head down over her back, with one of the laundry bags half over my head, I didn't see much, only the green stair carpet as she marched up to her bedroom, then the coverlet as I was thrown down.

Mo stood over me, grinning and nodding her head in satisfaction. I looked back, feeling small and scared, but alive with the moment and anticipation of what was to come. She reached down, her fingers going to the knots on the laundry bags. They were pulled open, my ankles, then my wrists. I was stripped, my boots and socks pulled off, my trousers and panties, my top last, leaving me nude. The gag came last, pulled out to leave me to run to the loo, where I did my best to spit out the stale taste. Mo watched me, chuckling.

I needed to pee too, and I sat down as soon as I'd had a glass of water to rinse my mouth out. She didn't move, and I realised I was going to have to do it in front of her. As I had with the butch girls in the club toilet, I swung round, spreading my thighs to let her watch it come out. I looked at her, and she met my eyes, her strong, hard gaze locked with mine, before moving slowly down, to my bare pussy. I let go, shutting my eyes as the pee spurted from my body, to tinkle into the water beneath me. There was a lot, all the beer I'd drunk at the festival. I was shaking so much that it went everywhere, on the seat, down my thighs too, so that even when I'd finished it was dripping off my pussy-lips and bum-cheeks.

'I hope you're going to clean that up?' Mo said, nodding to the patch on the seat.

I nodded back, my body trembling harder than ever as I got up and turned around. I knew what she meant, exactly. Anyway, I knew what I was going to do. I wiped myself, letting her see, then went down on the cold tiles of the floor, kneeling, my bottom stuck out with my knees set well apart. Out came my tongue, and I looked up, meeting Mo's eyes as I took hold of the lavatory bowl. She was smiling, cruel, and delighted, as I leaned slowly forwards, to poke my tongue into the little pool of urine. It tasted a bit acrid, also hormonal, very feminine. Dirty, yes, and arousing, for all that it was such a dirty thing to do, with her looking down on me as I cleaned up my own piddle with my tongue. My head was right over the bowl too, and I could smell myself, really strong.

'Do you want to see what the slovens get in barracks?' Mo asked.

'What do you do?' I asked.

'We flush them,' she said, and snatched out for my hair.

She caught it, twisting hard, and an instant later my head was down the lavatory. I screamed in shock and protest, and struggled, kicking, waving my hands in the air in blind panic. It did no good. My head went in, right in, until my hair was dangling in the mixture of pee and water and loo paper I had made in the bowl. She held me there, ignoring my entreaties and pleas for mercy, her other hand coming behind me, between my bum-cheeks, one thick finger sliding up my pussy, lifting.

I screamed again as my body came up, in surprise and horror. She upended me easily, holding me by my pussy and neck, upside down, my head as far down the lavatory as it would go, touching water, with the smell of my own pee strong in my nose. Her grip changed, clutching me around the waist, with my legs waving frantically in the air, squealing in fright and panic, babbling pleas for mercy.

I was still doing that when she pulled the chain, which was really stupid. It went in my mouth, water, pee, loo paper, everything, up my nose too, roaring around my head, sucking at my hair, even splashing my boobs where they hung upside down over the loo. I lost control, choking as I thrashed in her grip, hitting my head on the china, only to have it stuffed in deeper still, like a loo brush, as the gurgling water subsided around my ears.

She pulled me up, coughing and spluttering, and set me down on the floor. My legs went, and I sat down, hard. I was soaked, my hair drenched in dilute piddle and decorated with bits of soggy loo paper, more running down my breasts and back. I'd swallowed plenty, and my mouth was full of it, running out at the sides as I knelt there, gasping for breath. It was coming out of my nose too, with spittle and mucus running down my face, while I didn't even dare open my eyes.

I did when I heard Mo chuckle. It was just so wicked. Peering from beneath wet eyelashes, I saw her pull up her top, exposing massive boobs, as big as mine, and firmer, in a bra like a piece of armour plating. That went next, and I'll swear they didn't drop more than an inch, real bumpers, with small, regular nipples on top of each, very hard. Her boots followed, unlaced and kicked off, and her trousers, the big blue panties too.

That left her nude, and if she'd been scary dressed, she was terrifying with it all on show. I'd never seen so much muscle on a woman, or on the few men I'd seen naked either, for that matter. She was so hard, every muscle outlined beneath her skin, with her close shaved head and the sergeant's stripes in her pubes giving that final touch to the image. Just to see her made me shiver with fright as I peered up from under my pee-soaked, dripping fringe. As she stepped towards me I was already sticking my tongue out to lick her sex.

Kneeling, my head barely reached her pussy, and I had to come up a bit. She took my head, pulling me in, only not to her sex, but lower, trapping my head between her huge thighs, clamped tight as her hand twisted hard into my wet hair. I realised what was going to happen an instant before it did.

She pissed on my head, and all over my body, a great torrent of hot, steaming fluid gushing out from her sex onto my crown. It went everywhere, down my arms and back, over my bottom-cheeks, into the crease between them to soil my anus and pussy. Some even went down the front to cascade from my nose, filling my eyes to make them sting crazily, and my mouth, spilling from the edges to splash over my boobs and the floor.

I thought she'd let it finish before she made me lick her, but no, not Mo. Her stream was still coming, hard, when she suddenly changed her grip, jerking my head back and pulling me hard into her crotch. Piddle exploded into my face, more going in my eyes, then up my nose as my mouth was forced to her sex. I couldn't do it, not without choking, but I tried, lapping and gulping down urine as it sprayed into my face. It took her about five seconds to tire of my pathetic efforts, before she started to use my face to masturbate on, rubbing my nose over her big clitty, up and down, with the pee still gushing out.

It was too much for me, running down my front, hot and wet, over my boobs, to drip from my nipples, down my belly, and over my pussy. That was the final straw, when the warm, wet trickle found its way between the lips of my sex and onto my clitty. I put a hand there, masturbating in her pee as she rubbed my face against her sex, both of us filthy with it, our bodies slick with fluid, soiled and dripping.

I was coming almost before I knew it, thinking of what Mo had done to me. She'd bog-washed me, the term they used at school for sticking a girl's head down a lavatory, pissed on my head and, last of all, made me lick it up as it sprayed, hot from her pussy. I would have screamed if my mouth hadn't been full of piddle, and as it was I nearly choked myself, swallowing my mouthful just as my muscles tensed in the most glorious orgasm.

Suddenly I was gagging, my climax breaking, as I went into a frantic coughing fit, sputtering pee all over Mo's pussy and thighs. She took no notice, none at all, grunting as she came on my face, jerking my head up and down, hard, until it hurt. My nose was bumping over and over against her big clit, piddle still spraying out, my senses swirling in a haze of ecstasy and pain, until at last she was satisfied, and let go of my hair.

I sat back down, indifferent to the wet feel of the pee on the floor as my bottom settled into it. Getting up was beyond me. All I could do was squat there, utterly spent, in a big puddle of pee, with the steam rising from my skin. Mo was made of sterner stuff, and stood back, one leg shaking a little, but her breathing barely faster than it had been before. She was well pleased with herself, though, grinning wickedly as she folded her arms across her chest.

That was just the beginning of our night together. She had leave until noon the next day, and we made the best of it, every minute. I wasn't allowed to leave, as simple as that. Instead I was made to phone the friends I had said I'd meet and put them off. I didn't really mind, because I knew that what I was going to get from Mo would be better than anything that was likely to happen in London.

She was rough with me, really rough, and not that worried about whether or not I wanted exactly what she did. That was what made it so good. I never had to ask, not after the first time, when I'd admitted to liking spanking. After that she just assumed that I was a dirty slut, and would soak up whatever she could dish out.

After she'd pissed all over me we showered and she made me clean up, scrubbing the floor with my combat top while she watched. Only when I'd reduced my nice top to a filthy, pee-soaked rag did she start to be less demanding, fixing coffee and biscuits, which we ate as we talked, both still stark naked.

What she wanted to do to me was basically what she couldn't do to her recruits, but fantasised over. In reality she was cautious, being a lesbian in charge of so many nubile girls, including some pretty young recruits. Even the bit about flushing their heads down the toilet wasn't true, news which filled me with an odd mixture of relief and regret.

So to make up for her frustration, she made a habit of picking up baby dykes, sometimes for what she called quickies in the back of her jeep, sometimes for more. She seemed to be successful, and with her image I wasn't surprised. There's nothing we submissive girlies like more than a big, strong woman to dominate us. She showed me some photos, of various girls in army kit, or some army kit anyway. Some were being made to drill with no tops on, or no bottoms, others nude except for boots.

That was what she liked best, dressing her conquests up and working them into the ground, then pissing on them as they licked her pussy. Spanking them was rarer, although I wasn't the first. Gagging them with dirty panties was a favourite. She was responsible for the laundry at the camp, which made it easy, with a ready supply of kit, both clean and dirty. She was senior enough to get accommodation outside barracks too, shared, but with a housemate who enjoyed bringing more boys home than the army would have approved of.

By the time she'd explained all this to me, and shown me nearly a hundred photos of pretty, half-naked girls being ritually humiliated, I was ready for more. I'd been well spanked, back in the jeep, so that was out, but I was ready to try her drill fantasy. I was thinking of something else as well and, with more mischief than guilt, my Uncle Rupert.

Mo dressed up in something she called her number two dress uniform, a smart khaki outfit complete with sergeant's stripes and various insignia. Skirt, jacket, shirt, tie, stockings, boots, cap, all of it was immaculate, far neater than anything I'd ever worn, even for a job interview. It made her look older, and very stern – not just a brute, but a calculating, sadistic brute. With her dressed like that, and me still naked, I found myself feeling incredibly small and vulnerable, craving a spanking despite what she'd already done to my poor bottom.

I asked, and got it over her knee, without a stitch, my big bottom visible in a wall mirror, wobbling and bouncing to the smacks. It stung, but I took it until my whole bottom was warm and glowing, pink all over, covered with goosepimples, with the angry belt-marks clear in the middle. I love the sight of myself after a good punishment, or during it, and this was no exception. She took a photo too, with the camera on a tripod and set to automatic. It was nicely posed, looking back with my bum lifted high and the cheeks wide, so it showed my face and my pussy at the same time.

Now fully turned on again, I was given a choice of uniforms, although Mo pointed out that any girl recruit with my figure was going to get given some serious physical training. I retorted that I wasn't overweight, just voluptuous, and asked how many of her girls could boast a twenty-two-inch waist. She just laughed at me, and told me to hurry up.

I chose to go bottomless, which always leaves me feeling more vulnerable. That meant boots and socks, adding to the feeling of exposure of my lower body, along with a khaki blouse, jacket, a tie in deeper brown and a hat, the private to Mo's sergeant. It felt good, kinky and irreverent too, making me appreciate what Uncle Rupert had said about authority and having sex with a girl in uniform.

All of it went on, although the blouse was tight over my boobs, leaving my nipples poking out, even with them packed into one of Mo's bras. It looked all right though, especially after Mo had straightened it up, but being bottomless in it was simply wonderful. It looked so lewd, so humiliating, with the immaculate uniform on top, and my pussy showing between the sides of the blouse. Better still was the rear view, with the tuck of my spanked cheeks just peeping out from beneath the hem of the jacket.

She made me drill like that, thoroughly, using a swagger stick to adjust my body and to smack my bum or thighs every time I made a mistake. That was often, because I didn't understand any of her instructions, and in no time both my legs were hot with bruising and my pussy damp enough to leave a smear of moisture between my thighs. Mo noticed and pushed the stick in between my lips, rubbing it on my clit to bring it up wet with juice.

'Look at it,' she said. 'Disgusting. Suck it.'

I opened my mouth obediently. She pushed the stick in and I sucked, tasting my own sex, with my lips pursed around the slim wooden shaft. It was good, and I shut my eyes in pleasure, revelling in the taste of my own excitement.

'Like that, do you?' she snapped. 'Well, let's see if you like this. Across the bed.'

I went, bending down to make my bottom the highest part of my body and sneaking a look in the mirror. My rear view was great, two chubby pink cheeks sticking out under my shirt-tails, red from spanking, and parting, with my little plump lips showing and the shadowy crease between my cheeks. It just made me want to lick myself.

'Eyes front!' Mo shouted, and I found myself moving instinctively, with a pang of real fear.

The swagger stick caught the back of my thighs, hard, leaving a long red welt. I yelped, gasping, and got another one for my trouble, up under the tuck of my bottom.

'Silence!' she snapped, and I felt the tip of the swagger stick touch my pussy.

She slid it up, deep, until I felt a dull push against my cervix. For a moment she worked it in and out, until my breathing started to quicken, stopped, and pulled it free. It was put to my face, sideways, the smooth shaft sticky with thick white juice. I licked it up obediently, only to catch another swat for being so eager.

41

'You wait,' Mo said. 'You wait until I say. Until then you do nothing. Do you understand?'

'Yes, sir,' I responded.

'Not sir, sir is for officers. Yes, Sergeant!'

'Yes, Sergeant.'

'Better,' she said. 'Well, as being made to taste your own cunt doesn't seem to have any effect on you, perhaps we should try something else. Backside up, pull that back in!'

I obeyed, feeling my bum-cheeks spread as I dipped my spine. I knew what was coming, or I thought I did, and my lower lip was already shaking. Sure enough, the swagger stick was put to my flesh again, between my legs, pressing to my pussy mound. Slowly she moved it back, my trembling growing stronger as the rounded tip traced a slow line between my sex-lips, making me jerk and gasp as it touched my clitty. For once she ignored me, moving higher still, to slide the stick back into my vagina, wiggle the tip and once more pull it out.

My hole closed with a rude noise. The stick touched me again, slimy with my juice, full on my anus. A little sob escaped my lips at the thought of what she was about to do, then a gasp as my bottom hole was penetrated. The rounded end of the stick twisted past my greasy anus and up into the cavity beyond. I screwed up my face as it went up, well up. She began to poke the stick around up my bum, a truly disgusting feeling, buggering me. I knew she was watching too, her cruel eyes glued to my poor little ring as the wooden shaft slid in and out.

She took her time, really enjoying my bumhole, before pulling the stick slowly out. I knew exactly where it was going next, but I just couldn't look. Screwing my eyes up tighter still, I opened my mouth, with my brain screaming at me that I was a disgusting little slut. That didn't stop me, or Mo. The stick went in, the tip poked against my tongue, and I could taste my bottom. I closed my mouth, sucking on it, my body trembling with reaction, my stomach knotted tight. Mo chuckled, and pushed it deeper in, making me take the full length of what had just been up my bottom. I tried, but started to gag as the tip prodded the back of my throat, at which Mo pulled it out, laughing. Again it was put to my mouth, sideways, to let me kiss and lick at it.

'I thought so,' she said. 'A dirt sucker. You disgust me.'

That was so unfair, and I stifled a sob as she pulled the swagger stick away. It went back up my bum and was left there, sticking obscenely from between my cheeks. Mo went for the camera and took a whole series of photos of me like that – such a dirty pose, bent, bare bottom, with the stick in my bumhole. She even took a close-up, just inches away, of no more than the stick and my poor little hole. At last she tired of the game, pulled it back out and once more stuck it in my mouth.

'Suck on that,' she instructed. 'I think that fat arse could take a little more.'

'Please, sir . . . Sergeant, I can't!' I protested instantly. 'I'm too bruised!'

'Who said I was going to beat you, pervert?' she answered me. 'And don't speak unless you're spoken to. Stay there.'

She left the room. I stayed still, sucking on the swagger stick and wondering what she was going to do. My bottom felt so exposed, and so big, sore too, and I was fairly sure I was going to get something up it, something bigger than the swagger stick. She had gone downstairs, and I was imagining her in the kitchen, picking out a big, fat courgette, greasing it with butter, stuffing it rudely up my poor, straining little bumhole, just like some fat, ugly cock . . .

It was worse, it was a cock. A rubber one, maybe, but just as ugly and just as big – bigger maybe, at least bigger than any of my boyfriends. It was black and bumpy, designed for a pussy, never a bumhole, not mine, but I knew that was where it was going. She had a tube too, toothpaste, and that proved it. She was holding it up and staring at my bum, nodding thoughtfully to herself. I could only whimper, shaking at the thought of the hideous thing up my bottom hole, and wondering if I could even take it.

'Up on the bed,' she ordered. 'Kneeling, arse high, back in.'

'Yes, Sergeant.'

I scrambled up. Mo knelt down on the bed, beside me, one brawny arm wrapping around my waist. I shut my eyes, biting my lip. She held me tight, keeping me in place as firmly as if I'd been in secure bondage. There was a rude noise, like a little fart, and I felt the cool toothpaste touch my skin, right between my cheeks. She laid it down between them, a long worm, starting right up where my cheeks began to bulge, all the way down to my anus. Her finger touched my skin in the crease, smearing the toothpaste down, making a fat blob, pressing to my hole. It went up me, into the little dirty ring, taking the toothpaste with it. I sighed at the feeling, with my hole cool and greasy and open. A second finger invaded me, and a third, stretching my now juicy hole wide, to make me gasp.

That was when it started to sting. There was just a warm feeling at first, nice really, but it grew hotter, until it was burning, turning my anus to a ring of agonising fire. I cried out, my feet kicking, my mouth coming open to the sudden pain. Mo responded by jabbing a toothpaste-smeared thumb up my pussy, rubbing it into the mouth, up between my lips, over my clit. For a moment she fucked me, in both holes, as I gasped and wriggled. It hurt so much, like a cut, my whole rear burning, my anus so open I was sure I'd soil myself, as she stuffed her fingers deeper and deeper up the hole.

She stopped, chuckled, pulled out her fingers. I was panting, my eyes shut, my mouth wide, a piece of spittle hanging from my lower lip. The dildo touched me, round and firm against my anus. I was open, wide open, but I still felt my ring stretch as the great bulbous knob was forced up me, stretching me until I cried out in pain. She eased it out a little, pushed again, and again. On the third my anus popped, with a sharp stab of pain, then an awful, bloated feeling as it went up, filling my rectum with fat, rubber cock, until the whole obscene thing was up my bottom.

It hurt, my anus burning, my pussy too, my rectum bloated so much I felt I would burst. I was wiggling my toes, biting my lips, drooling down my chin, and as she began to move the awful thing about up my bum I was crying too. I just couldn't stop myself, it was simply too much for me, everything, from being clothed except for my legs and my great, fat bottom, to being held helpless in my pain and exposure, to being buggered. Big, oily teardrops were rolling from my eyes, down both cheeks, to splash on the bed cover beneath me. I was sobbing too, little, broken sounds, so miserable, so pathetic.

Mo just kept right on buggering me, pulling the dildo slowly in and out of my aching hole. Sometimes it came right out, only to be shoved up again into my gaping cavity. After a while her hand found my pussy, curled under my tummy to cup the plump mound, with her longest finger on my clit. She began to frig me, rubbing the toothpaste over my swollen, inflamed clit, adding to my pain, and to my awful, helpless frustration too. Before long I was gasping, with the tears running freely down my face, but in helpless, uncontrolled ecstasy.

I was going to come, I couldn't stop myself, whimpering and snivelling, well in tears, begging for mercy. She just went faster, rubbing hard at my clitty, jamming the dildo in and out of my straining bumhole. The pain became unbearable, my legs kicking out, the saliva running free down my chin. I was screaming, blubbering and screaming, my whole rear on fire, in burning pain as I was sodomised and masturbated, brought to orgasm with my anus full of rubbery cock and a big woman's fingers on my sex.

Did I scream, so loud, until Mo had to make a snatch for my discarded panties and stuff them in my mouth to shut me up. That didn't stop me coming, and I chewed on them as she finished me off, rubbing at me with the dildo jammed to the very hilt in my back passage.

That was it, for me. Of course I was made to suck the dildo, and lick her out again, a favour for a favour. We ate after that, with me serving her, still bottomless under my uniform. There was more sex afterwards, drilling and humiliation for me, photographed in a dozen lewd poses for her album, most of them focused on my smacked bottom.

We slept, eventually, and when I woke it was bright sunlight Mo was already dressed, in a different uniform to the night before. There was another woman there too, a sergeant like Mo, who had just come off duty. I could have done with coffee and toast, maybe something more substantial, but Mo was pretty off-hand with me. I was left to fend for myself, wandering around in my top and panties while she tried to hurry me up.

Up until then I hadn't been certain, but I just couldn't resist it. If she'd been cuddly and sweet I wouldn't have done it. I couldn't have done it. It was all there too, her full number two dress uniform, or whatever she'd called it, her bra and panties too. I even had the photograph, or at least I did once I'd pinched the film. Her housemate had gone straight to bed, so I didn't even have to worry about her. I just gathered up Mo's clothes, stuck them in one of the laundry bags and walked out.

Three

I didn't feel bad about pinching Mo's uniform. In fact I felt it was pretty fair. She had made a real mess of my bottom, with almost the whole surface bruised, and the hole too. My cheeks smarted for days, and I couldn't even walk properly, let alone sit down in comfort. My anus was worse, and I began to understand why girls whose boyfriends bugger them resent it. After all, it's not just the indignity and sheer filthiness of taking a cock up the bottom, but having to waddle about like a duck for days afterwards.

That didn't stop me taking the uniform to Uncle Rupert, as soon as I'd had the photos developed, discreetly. He noticed, of course, and I saw his sly smile as I put a cushion on my chair in the kitchen. Not that he said anything, but he knew. I had the uniform in a bag, and I put it on the table, sitting back.

'That's a pressie for you,' I told him. 'Open it.'

'A present? How kind,' he answered, taking the bag and peering inside.

He pulled out the jacket, looking puzzled, until he saw the insignia on the sleeves. His expression changed to astonishment, then delight, as one by one he took out the pieces of Mo's clothing, her skirt, her blouse, her tie, her huge bra, her stockings, her panties.

'You didn't?' he demanded, holding the huge blue knickers up.

'I did,' I answered, and threw the pack of photos on the table.

He pulled them out, his hand shaking visibly as he looked at the first, of me taking my spanking across Mo's lap.

'I'm, er ... not sure I should be looking at these, Jade,' he said weakly. 'Good God!'

Whatever his moral qualms it hadn't stopped him looking at the next. His mouth came slowly open, until he reached the close up of my bumhole with the swagger stick up her, when he put his hand over his eyes and passed them back. I couldn't help giggling.

'Choose one,' I said. 'Maybe the first, where I'm only being spanked.'

'And the uniform is for my collection?' he asked.

'Of course,' I said. 'It counts, doesn't it?'

'Certainly it counts – I can't imagine why it wouldn't, so long as you didn't break any of the rules.'

'No. She's a genuine army sergeant, stationed at Aldershot, even if she is only responsible for the regimental laundry. As you can see, that's the uniform she wore when we had sex. One of them anyway.'

'I see,' he said weakly, taking up the picture of me across Mo's lap again. 'By God, but she's a monster!'

'I like them big.'

'So I see. Well, thank you then, and yes, I'll use the picture of her spanking you to confirm the trophy. But you must see what I have achieved myself!'

That slightly took the shine off my satisfaction, but I followed him eagerly upstairs, taking the uniform with us. I'd guessed he'd got another himself, immediately, and sure enough, there it was, an immaculate uniform, on a new mannequin, a familiar uniform.

'A Girl Guide?' I managed. 'Uncle Rupert!'

'A Girl Guide leader, thank you, Jade,' he responded. 'And aged a respectable twenty-six. Allow me some morals.'

'Hang on,' I said. 'They abandoned these uniforms while I was still at school.'

'Not at the more respectable girl's public schools,' he answered, grinning.

'Was that where you got it?' I asked, reaching out to touch the crisp blue fabric.

It was perfect, the blouse blue-grey cotton, the skirt darker, and wool, with the sweet little neck-tie in the same colour. There were even badges on the sleeves, an association one, a school one, and another for her rank as adult-leader. With mischievous pleasure I reached down to lift the skirt, revealing demure white cotton panties stretched tight across the mannequin's bottom.

'Come on,' I demanded. 'What happened? When?'

'The day before yesterday,' he replied, 'but it wasn't easy. It took weeks, and no, sadly, I never actually visited the school in question.'

'You surprise me, you dirty old goat. So how did you do it?'

'In due time, my dear. First I want to hear about your army sergeant, in detail.'

'Fair enough,' I answered, but moved to look at the photo of Uncle Rupert with his Guide.

She was pretty, dark-haired, petite, with an air of insecurity about her that I knew would have appealed to his instincts. Not that it was surprising she looked insecure. In the photo she was bending to touch her toes, with her long blue skirt hoisted up onto her back and her little white panties down around her thighs, along with her tights. Her bum was small and neat, her pussy so hairy I could only just make out the lips. Not just that, but she was outdoors, in a field by the look of it. I could imagine exactly how she would have felt.

'You really are a bastard,' I told him. 'Imagine making her pose like that. In the open!'

'It was actually rather secluded,' he said. 'She went bare later.'

'You've got to tell me everything.'

'Certainly, over a bottle of wine, and you are to go first. I insist.'

We went back downstairs to drink red wine in the kitchen. I told him about Mo, leaving out only the very worst bits. He listened, nodding and sipping his wine, the look of amusement on his face growing slowly more intense. By the time I finished he was grinning like a schoolboy.

'Splendid!' he declared. 'You put my efforts to shame.'

'I'm sure I don't,' I answered. 'Now tell me about your Guide leader. What was her name?'

'Sarah. Miss MacKinley to her charges.'

'And how did you meet?'

'Using the wonders of modern technology, an Internet dating service to be exact. I use several, mainly for spanking partners, and while most of the replies are from professional ladies angling for trade, a few have proved worthwhile. Sarah isn't into spanking though – or, at least, she wasn't.'

'Dirty old goat!'

'If you say so. I'd like to think she's grateful. Now do stop interrupting, unless you have a sensible question, or want more description.'

'Okay.'

'The agency she was listed on wasn't a spanking one. It wasn't even necessarily a sexual one. Sarah's was one among many, and inconvenient because she was right down in Cornwall, near Fowey. Nevertheless, I was drawn to it, mainly by her photo. As you can imagine, she was irresistible to me. Such a delicate face, so earnest, so sweet . . .'

'So vulnerable. That was it really, wasn't it?'

'Perhaps, yes. A vulnerable look on the victim's face does improve the pleasure of dishing out a spanking. Now, no more interruptions, please. She looked vulner-

50

able, yes, but what she did do, which is unusual, was stress her academic qualifications. That intrigued me, and also made me wonder if I couldn't come away with a nice Oxford BEd gown. They're very fine, you know, with a green silk hood.

'So I went through the motions and, rather to my surprise, she replied. She was guarded at first, shy too, but after an exchange of emails I persuaded her to meet me for lunch, and even suggested bringing a friend.'

'Lunch? In Cornwall?'

'I was hooked. She was so sweet. Intellectual, but very unsure of herself. How could I resist?

'So I drove to Cornwall at the weekend, booked in at a rather nice hotel, right on the coast, and the next day met her for lunch. She had brought a friend, a suspicious and man-hating virago by the name of Carla. Fortunately I managed to turn that to my advantage, with bruised innocence when it was suggested I was only trying to get Sarah into bed. Aside from that, I managed to hold up my end of the conversation on art, philosophy and architecture, if I was a little weak on local history. I paid the bill too, the awful Carla included. What I didn't do was attempt any intimacy with Sarah, except to kiss her hand as I left, which I hoped would be taken as a gesture of charming eccentricity. She accepted a date for the following weekend, *sans* Carla.

'And so it went. We kissed for the first time the next weekend . . .'

'You make it sound like something out of one of those soppy romance novels Mum used to read.'

'Far from it. Shy she may have been, but she was no innocent, certainly no virgin. Like I said, we kissed, after lunch, on a pretty clifftop footpath. The next thing I knew her hand was down the front of my trousers, squeezing my cock. I responded, which wasn't hard, and we barely got in among the trees before her knickers were down and she was stuck on my cock – up against a tree, if you please. It was a bit unexpected, but I did my best, even though I'm not really keen on sex standing up.'

'Hard on the knees, I suppose.'

'It's not so much that. You can't see the girl's bottom.'

'You can have a good feel though.'

'True, and I did, even tickling her hole, which she didn't seem to mind. She was really urgent, actually, clinging on like anything and writhing herself against me. She came just by rubbing herself on me, and I very nearly did it up her, but I had the sense to pull out and rub off on her stomach.'

'She was bare?'

'No, in a dress, which she'd pulled up, right up to her neck. She still had her knickers on, just pulled aside, and her bra, with the cups turned up. A very nice sight it was too. I do adore dishevelled female clothing.'

'But no uniform?'

'No. I was working on that. We got on perfectly after sex, and while she was certainly liberal, she didn't seem kinky. Hot and straight seemed to be her style, with no real sense of naughtiness. Not that she was a prude in any sense and, when we made love the second time, she was happy to bend across a convenient rock for me. We were nearly caught by this old couple walking their dog along the beach, and that was what gave me my idea. Unfortunately it didn't come to me until I was halfway back to London on the Sunday night. But I did have another date.

'The idea was this. She liked being nude outdoors, for the feel of the air on her skin and the sense of freedom it gave her rather than for the sake of exhibitionism. People's disapproval didn't particularly turn her on, but it did make her feel resentful, her feelings being that she had a perfect right to go nude or partly nude, and that it was none of their business. What I was going to do was suggest that she wear her academic gown with nothing underneath, leaving her other clothes in the car. Then I could simply have forgotten to return it, nipped up to Ede and Ravescroft for a replacement, and all would have been well. Panties I could add if she'd bothered to wear any.'

'In a gown and one of those funny hats, in Cornwall? She'd have looked weird!'

'Yes, I realise that, and I was still trying to think of a way to justify doing it, other than simply for the sake of being kinky, the next time I saw her. She was late, and when she did come, I forgot all about her academic dress. She'd been doing something with the Guides, and she was still in her uniform. It was so beautiful, so demure. I had to have it.

'I wasn't entirely sure how to go about it, but I was going to give it a bloody good try. First I needed the photo. I had the camera, naturally, and I made sure she had plenty to drink at lunch time. I gave her the old line about needing something to remember her by during the week, which was true enough, and I soon had her posing.

'She was giggling like anything, really showing off, but shy, and it still took a bit of persuading to get a good rear view. As you saw, I succeeded. By then she was ready for sex, and game for just about anything. I got her to do a striptease, one article at a time, which had me so hard I thought I'd come then and there. She made me chase her through the woods too, with her in just shoes and socks, which I must say looked charming. She couldn't really run, bare, and I soon caught her. I was too excited to really think, too drunk as well, to be honest. I just put her across my knee, standing, with my foot up on a rock, and gave her a bloody good spanking.

'Well, at first she yelped like anything. They usually do. It got to her quickly though, or I think that would have been the end. After twenty slaps or so her bottom was nicely red, and she was sticking it up, and thanking me for doing it to her. I do adore that, when you spank a girl's bottom and she's grateful for it. So I carried on, until she was red and hot, and really panting. It was wonderful, with her lovely round bottom-cheeks dancing in the dappled sunlight, and the little cries she was making, quite romantic really. My cock had been hard all the time, just from what I could see, and what I was doing, and as soon as I stopped she was on me, sucking my cock while she diddled her fanny.

'She came, still with my erection in her mouth, and let me do it in her face. Afterwards, she was full of excitement, chattering away, about how she'd never realised that having her bottom smacked could be pleasurable, and thanking me for doing it to her. In fact, I think she thanked me fives times in all. She is now a confirmed spankee.

'Still, I didn't have the uniform. Now, it hadn't really come into our sex, although I had complimented her on how pretty she looked in it. I imagine she thought I was just trying to be nice, because before she had dressed up rather smartly for me, and she was a little embarrassed. Maybe that was why the idea of staying nude appealed to her. She did it anyway, and was quite bold about it, if a little nervous.

'I don't know if you have visited that part of the country at all, but it's mostly slate, with small creeks cutting in from the sea, steep, and heavily wooded. There was a footpath at the bottom of the slope, a busy one, but we stayed firmly in the deep woods. Every time we heard a human voice she'd get that little bit more excited, biting her lip and ducking down among the ferns, and constantly throwing me little nervous smiles.

'Didn't she want you to strip?'

'It didn't seem to bother her. She just liked being naked herself, and showing me her smacked bottom, which was very rapidly too much for me to resist. I had her again, on a ledge among some ferns, with her uniform for a bed. She was stark naked but for the shoes and socks, me with just my cock out of my trousers. That's always good for a spanked girl, to be in the nude while the man who's punished her stays dressed.

'Not that she'd have thought any such thing, but I did, all the time I was in her. She went on her knees first, with her pretty pink bum stuck up for my attention, so beautiful. I spanked her as I did it, and she diddled herself again, coming while I was up her fanny. I put her on her back after that, and sideways, with me kneeling up, so that I could see every detail as my cock went in and out of her. After that I was ready to come, so I had her cuddled up to me, sucking my cock as I stroked her bottom, feeling the hot cheeks and tickling her between them. As I got nearer I put the tip of my little finger up her bottom hole and another one in her fanny. She stuck her bum out, to get more in, and that was too much for me. I did it in her mouth, she swallowed, and licked up what she'd spilled on my balls, ever so dutifully . . . Look, perhaps a minute alone?'

'No, just get it out. Keep talking.'

'In front of you? Here? Look, Jade . . .'

'Just do it, I don't care.'

'We shouldn't, I . . .'

'Bollocks. We're not even blood relatives. Just get your cock out. I'm going to toss you off while you talk.'

'Jade . . .'

'Do it, Rupert, for me.'

He swallowed, hard, and his hands went to his fly. It came down, his hand went in, to pull out a thick, very pale cock, already erect. I came round the table, sat by him, took it, fighting down that little hit of revulsion I always get when I touch a man's cock. He sighed, and I started to wank.

It felt so odd, with my uncle's penis in my hand, but I knew it had been coming. Every story session had got that little bit ruder, that little bit more intimate. Yet he'd never tried anything, not even watching, although he could have, easily. That was the key, that he'd let me do what I wanted to, and that was why his erect cock was grasped firmly in my hand.

He just sat back, eyes closed, enjoying it. I was so horny, thinking of him and the girl, with her bum all red and his fingers up her holes. I was thinking of the picture too, of her bending over in her Guide uniform, panties down, bum bare, showing her pussy off, and just before her virgin spanking.

My free hand went up my skirt, onto the front of my panties, pushing the damp cotton down between my lips. I found my clit, began to rub, all the while jerking at his cock. It wasn't enough, and I stuck my hand down the front, onto bare flesh, finding my clitty once more. I focussed, thinking of Sarah, delicate, sensitive, thrown across my uncle's knee in the nude, and spanked, in shock as her ripe little bottom was slapped up to a glowing red, gasping out her pain and astonishment, furious, humiliated, until her bum began to warm and she realised exactly why she was being beaten.

I came, thinking of that little rounded bottom, all red with the pussy-lips showing from the back, so lewd and so vulnerable. I'd stopped wanking Rupert, just squeezing onto the cock which had been in her body as my climax ran through me. As my orgasm faded I began again, tugging slowly, faster, and faster still, when he groaned, jerked, and suddenly my hand was covered in thick, sticky, male come.

'Thank you,' he sighed. 'Thank you, Jade, darling.'

'My pleasure,' I answered, cheekily, trying to hide the emotion in my voice.

He blew his breath out, his hand shaking as he reached for his wine glass. I stood, crossing to the sink and twisting the cold tap on with the hand that had been down my panties.

'So what happened with Sarah?' I asked, rinsing the sticky mess off my hand.

'Well,' he answered, 'by then I really didn't feel right about it. She was so lovely, so open. There was no barrier between us, no pretence, no calculation.'

'Except that you wanted to pinch her Guide uniform.'

'Exactly, so I felt bad. I was close to deciding not to do it.'

'So how come?'

'Patience. I'm coming to that.'

He'd put his cock away, and that was that. There was no mention of what we'd done, no guilt, no moral discussion. He'd needed it and I'd given it to him, help, as he had given me so many times. There was nothing to say, and I certainly didn't want to.

'Sarah was incredibly eager,' he went on, 'so animated, as if she was releasing an immense amount of pent-up emotion, all at once. Perhaps she was. She still wanted to stay nude, and she couldn't keep still, either. We moved on, both knowing that we'd have sex again as soon as I was ready. Unfortunately, the slope became steeper, with less undergrowth, until we could see the path below us and were having to scramble across patches of loose slate. We could hear voices too, and a dog, coming up from behind us.

'She had to dress, and of course her clothes were wet and covered in leaf mould because we'd used them as a bed. That made it hard to get them on, and she only just made it, with the dog snuffling up to us just as she was fastening her skirt. She was giggling crazily, and really bright-eyed, full of mischief. There was no question of stopping, but we needed privacy, so we moved on to the head of the creek.

'It looked perfect, because the footpath continued up the valley, but the far side of the creek was even steeper than where we'd been, with ledges of shale coming right down to the tide line. The tide was out, but it didn't look easy, so it seemed likely that the head of the little point between there and the next creek would be about as lonely as you can get. We tried anyway, holding hands and laughing as we tried to avoid stepping in the thick mud of the creek. It got harder, until I was hanging onto a root with one hand and Sarah with the other, which is when I let go.

'She went right in, bottom first, but just about everything got its share. The mud was thick, really thick, and she fell right over backwards, so her hair had gone in and her skirt had flown up. Her thighs were open, wide, and it did look sweet. There was a moment, as she lay there in the mud, her legs wide apart and the dirty stain creeping slowly up the front of her white panties, when I could happily have mounted her, or perhaps just relieved myself over her . . .'

'What, pissed on her?'

'No, my dear. Although after your monstrous sergeant I could see why you would think that. I meant hand relief, a rather old-fashioned term admittedly. Wanked over her? Is that better.'

'But you didn't?'

'No. I would have done, but we might have been seen from the path across the creek, and I'd come twice in the space of just over an hour anyway. So I helped her out. She was filthy, absolutely bedraggled, with her hair plastered around her head, her uniform soaked and filthy, and even her panties soaked with dirty water. It was smelly too, a real reek, but to my amazement she saw the funny side of it, giggling and joking as we made our way back to the car.

'She was in such a state, and very understanding about my leather upholstery, so she agreed to get into my robe, which naturally was in my suitcase, and to come back to my hotel to clean up. Even getting her changed in the car park was quite a thrill, with people coming and going while she was muddy and naked behind my car. She made a fair job of cleaning up, and I bundled the dirty uniform into a bag, bra, panties and all.

'From there it was simple. Into Fowey, where she sat in the car while I bought clothes for her. Back to my hotel, where we had an excellent dinner followed by a night of more conventional lovemaking. Sunday spent in walking, talking and more sex. Back to the hotel for a tearful goodbye, only to find that the maid had removed the dirty uniform for cleaning just before going off duty, or so the under manager claimed in return for a tenner. And so back to London, trophy on board.'

'Poor Sarah! Seduced, abandoned, just so that you could get your dirty little mits on her Girl Guide uniform!'

'Not at all. I am seeing her this weekend.'

I had to admit he'd done better than me, which was a bit of a downer. I'd been really proud of pinching Mo's uniform, and as he hadn't said anything I'd assumed he'd failed or even given up. Instead he'd been carefully seducing the delectable Sarah, who I had to admit was cuter than Mo, if not so much my type. The uniform was better too, rarer for one thing and more feminine.

I was thinking about it on the bus home that night, about what made a good trophy. Rarity was obviously important, as unusual uniforms would be hard to get. Rupert had also made it clear that he rated formal uniforms over more casual ones, and ones with a long history over recent inventions. Then there was the question of how risky it was likely to be obtaining them.

The least impressive would be, perhaps, a supermarket checkout girl, with a common uniform, modern and casual in style, with minimal risk to pinching it. Rupert's waitress fell into much the same category, while his air hostess better and my army sergeant better still. Sarah's Girl Guide outfit topped the list, but there had to be better.

I could think of several, but the most satisfying was a really senior policewoman, say a superintendent. There weren't many, for a start, while their uniforms were very traditional and very formal. The risk was high. In fact the risk was seriously high.

It was a lovely fantasy. To reach that sort of rank in the police a woman has to be really competent, intelligent, stern, mature, in control. In short, just the sort of woman I like to dominate me. All I needed was one with a secret lesbian streak, and who fancied small, curvy girls who enjoy being tied up and punished. How we'd meet I wasn't sure, but once we did there'd be no barriers. She'd belt me, like Mo had done, really hard, with me strapped down tight over a chair or a trestle. She'd keep me in her house, like a pet, nude, or in nothing but high heels and collar. I'd be kept in a kennel, made to eat dog food, walked in the nude in her garden, crawling on all fours behind her. She'd take me down to a state of utter degradation, doing things to me most people wouldn't think of doing to a real dog. Occasionally she'd take photographs, and even more occasionally she'd be in them, so one day, after a really tough night of whippings and buggery and worse, I'd pinch her best dress uniform, the photos too, and run for it.

I snapped out of my fantasy because a couple of women further up the bus were giving me very peculiar looks indeed. It was only then that I realised how hooked I was. Rupert's fantasy had me completely drawn in, so that for the rest of the journey I couldn't see a woman in uniform without wondering how to get her out of it. Not that I minded. It was fun, naughty too, and I could see that plotting was going to do a lot to lift the boredom of working as a temp.

I'd made plans to go to a bar called Betty's, which a lot of the girls had talked about. It was more glam than dyke, but I like to dress over the top now and then, and there seemed to be a good chance of a pick-up. That was what I wanted, after talking dirty to Rupert for so long – some cool, sharp leather dyke to take me home and fuck with me until the morning.

Dressing wasn't easy. I was in a cheeky mood, and would have gone for no skirt, thong panties and black fishnet tights, to make the best of my bottom, only the bruising was really too much. Not that I mind a few marks, just to show I'm spankable, but it had been under a week since my belting from Mo, and my cheeks were still a mess.

After spreading half my stuff out on the bed, I decided to go for a colourful look instead, with a brilliant yellow PVC outfit I'd picked up at the Fetish Fair. The jacket was short, with just one button. It had never been designed for a girl as busty as me, and left my boobs high and proud, squeezed together and bulging out at the front. It was totally over the top, even a bit embarrassing, but I knew a few Buds would deal with that, while the girls would love it. It made the best of my waist too.

The skirt was cheeky, showing my bottom if I bent over, but not otherwise. I'd had to put a tuck in it to make it fit both my hips and waist, but that was hidden under the jacket. All the yellow needed a contrast, so I went for the thong and fishnets after all, these great yellow boots with five-inch stack heels, bunches in my hair, tied up with yellow ribbon and some serious make-up.

I was a hit, straight off, with even some of the gay guys wanting to bury their faces in my cleavage. That was fine by me, but what I needed was a nice butch leather dyke, who were a bit thin on the ground, at least until Sam turned up. She wasn't alone either, but with her tall blonde friend and another girl, with purple hair.

The first I knew about it was when they surrounded me at the bar, where I'd been unsuccessfully trying to get a drink. Sam's arm came around my shoulder as she pushed in next to me, the blonde and the third girl coming close on my other side. Immediately the trannie barman who had been deliberately avoiding letting me catch his eye came over.

'Miss AJ! Fab look!' he said, addressing the blonde. 'What can I get you?'

'Four beers, Bud,' she answered, almost shouting above the music. 'She's paying.'

She jerked her head in my direction. I nodded, passing him the fiver I'd been holding out.

'This won't get you very far, love, not here,' he said, and turned back to the blonde. 'Get her, with the dumplings. Doesn't it just make you want to spit? Four Bud, here we are.'

He had taken the beer from a fridge under the bar. I paid.

'Dumplings,' Sam said. 'That's good. That's her name, eh, girls?'

The blonde laughed and reached down, quite casually cupping one of my breasts, squeezing, then pushing up. Abruptly she took hold of my jacket, pulling the top wide to spill out my boobs, both of them. I squealed in shock, my heart jumping at the sudden rough treatment.

'Dumplings it is,' the blonde said. 'Keep them out.'

I could really feel my emotions building up, and took a swig of my beer in a vain attempt to cover them. About a dozen people were staring at my bare boobs, every one of them enjoying the view and the way I'd been so suddenly stripped. I didn't dare put them back either, not with the three of them around me, looking at me – the blonde, AJ, especially.

'Is her arse as big?' the barman asked, as he came back for someone else's beer.

'Just about,' Sam answered, and her hand closed on my bottom, squeezing.

'Ow!' I protested. 'Sam, that hurts!'

'Hurts?'

'Yes. I'm a bit bruised.'

'Bruised? Been whacked, have you? Show us.'

'Not here, there are too many men looking. Take me in the loos.'

'No, here,' AJ ordered.

'No, not here!' I squealed, but they'd already got me by my arms, and the purple-haired girl was lifting my legs.

I did fight. I tried to, but it didn't do any good. I was hauled up onto the bar, my boobs squashing out into a pool of beer and fag ash. Sam got my arms, twisting both into the small of my back, the purple-haired girl coming up between my legs, forcing me to spread them. The barman laughed at me, others too.

'Please, not here!' I begged as AJ began to turn up my skirt. 'Please, don't let her, Sam! Not here!'

'Shut up,' Sam answered, and my bottom was on show, my big cheeks straining out the fishnets.

'Okay, you can see!' I babbled. 'Just don't pull down . . .'

I broke-of in a mew of despair, a noise that sounded pathetic even in my ears. AJ had put her hands up under my skirt, taking hold of the hem of my tights. They came down, slowly, peeled off my big, fat bottom, all the way, down to my knees, to leave me shivering with humiliation, my bruised cheeks stuck up, bare.

Everyone was laughing at me, without an ounce of sympathy for my plight. AJ took hold of my bottom, squeezing my cheeks and pulling them wide, to show off the crease, with the thin strap of my thong barely covering my bumhole.

'Pull them down!' someone called, a man.

'Yeah, strip her!' another demanded.

'Shut up,' AJ said. 'Well, Dumplings, you have been whacked, haven't you? What with, a tawse?'

'A belt,' I said miserably, as she continued her inspection of my bottom, prodding my bruises with her fingers to make me wince.

'I'd have tawsed you,' she said. 'Maybe I will.'

'No, please,' I begged. 'I'm not ready. I couldn't take it. Let me up, please, I'll lick you, all three of you.'

'You will,' she answered.

'Come on, tall girl, pull down her pants!' a man called. 'Show us her cunt!'

'Piss off,' AJ answered. 'All right, Sam, Naomi, let –'

'She ain't got the guts!' a voice sang out, derisive, mocking.

'Stop,' AJ ordered. 'I haven't got guts? Watch this.'

'No!' I wailed, but it was too late.

My thong was down, jerked suddenly off my bum. Naomi pushed my legs wide and it was showing, all of it, my pussy, my bumhole, gaping to the leering, clapping crowd. I fought like anything, writhing and struggling in their grip, squealing like a pig, my boobs sploshing around in the pool of dirty beer. They took no notice, AJ slapping my bottom to set the cheeks quivering, then pulling them wide, stretching out my bumhole to the audience.

'Please!' I begged, but it did no good.

Something touched between my cheeks, cool and wet, hard too. I gasped as cold fluid splashed on my skin, beer, running down my crease and over my pussy. The bottle neck touched in my crease, hard and cold, moving slowly down and my eyes and mouth went wide in agonised realisation of what was being done to me. It touched my anus, bumped over the tight bar of flesh between my holes, to my pussy, and up, the cold beer gurgling into my hole as she stretched it down to let the air out. I gasped, panting as my vagina filled with beer, still struggling faintly, in an agony of humiliation and exposure, my head burning with the thought of all those gloating male eyes on my big, fat bottom, my dirty little bumhole, my stretched pussy.

AJ pulled the bottle out. I sprayed, unable to hold back, a fountain of beer erupting from my pussy to the sound of laughter and catcalls, also Naomi's gasp of shock and disgust as it hit her full on. AJ smacked my bottom again, took me hard by my hair and pulled my head around. The bottle was pressed to my lips and I drank, tasting my pussy as I swallowed what little beer was left.

'Do put her down, AJ darling,' the barman said suddenly. 'Management.'

I was on my feet in a second, my skirt tugged down to hide my bare bum. A man appeared beyond the crowd, totally out of place in his dark suit. Sam smiled at him and he gave us an odd look, but moved on.

'Toilets,' AJ said. 'You wanted to lick me, Dumplings, now's your chance.'

She took me by the hair again, her hand twisted into one of my bunches, to drag me behind her as she marched off, the others following. I was held low, forced to walk sideways, with my head close to AJ's leather-clad bottom. I did want to lick her, badly, the others too, but I knew it didn't matter. I was going to have to do it anyway.

They took me to the girls' loo, a long, brightly lit room painted vivid pink. To my horror there were as many transvestites there as real women, but AJ didn't seem to care. She chose a cubicle, one with the floor wet with pee, casually pushing down her trousers to bare a neatly rounded bum, small and tight, so different from my own wobbling posterior. I'd thought she would sit, but she didn't, kneeling on the seat, her bum stuck out as I was pushed down to my knees by Sam and Naomi.

Everyone was crowding round to watch the show, girls, transvestites, even a couple of ordinary men. My cheeks were burning with humiliation, but when AJ reached back and snapped her fingers, pointing at the puff of white hair visible between her thighs, I went willingly enough, crawling forwards through the pool of piddle, until my face was inches from her bum.

I could smell her, rich and feminine, her pussy swollen and wet, with beads of moisture hanging from her lips, along with two silver rings. For a moment I hesitated, swallowing, only to have Sam take me firmly by the head and push my face into AJ's bottom. There was laughter, and someone pointed out that my nose was pressed right against her bumhole. It was true, the little sweaty ring splaying out against my nose tip, with the smell of her strong in my head.

I began to lick, lapping at her piercing rings and clitty, rubbing my face in her crease. As I did it, Naomi took hold of my skirt, hoisting it up over my still bare bum. Sam let go of my hair, and they began to feel me up, fondling my bum and boobies as I licked at AJ's sex.

It was awful, but it was lovely too. There were men staring at me, and it was impossible not to think of their cocks growing hard over the sight of my near-naked body. I had my face in a girl's bum though, a lovely, dominant girl, and I do adore licking pussy. I don't even mind licking a bumhole, if I'm feeling dirty, or if I'm made to, by a woman who's dominant enough. AJ was, and I licked hers, with my tongue poked right up, as far as it would go, to the sounds of delight and disgust from the women looking over the top of the stall.

She was frigging by then, so I kept on rimming her, jabbing my tongue in and out of her now sloppy little hole with her firm cheeks spread out across my face. The others were feeling me openly, squeezing my boobs, with my bum held apart, to show off my pussy and bumhole to the audience. I heard AJ groan, starting to come, and as she did a finger slid up my pussy, a second, pulled out, back, and my vagina was gaping to a fist.

AJ's bumhole tightened on my tongue. She gave a single, choking grunt and pulled away, even as my pussy stretched out on the invading fist. It was Sam, grinning as she forced her hand up my hole, deep in. AJ moved, and I went forwards, down over the lavatory, panting as Sam twisted her fist inside me. Naomi took my jacket, pulling it back to trap my arms, AJ snatching at my head, to force it hard down into the bowl.

'No! Not again! No!' I screamed and the water exploded around my head as AJ shoved hard down on the handle.

They held me there, head down the loo as I was bog-washed, again, for the second time in days, and again coming up dripping and coughing, with my hair sodden and full of bits of loo paper, the mixture of water and pee dripping from my bunches and out of my nose.

'You bitches!' I managed, gagging for breath as I struggled to pull my head out of the loo.

AJ slapped my face, hard, but Sam's thumb slipped out of my pussy and found my clit. I came, almost immediately, as her thumb pressed to the little sensitive bud, flicking it as my mouth came open to the sting of AJ's slap. Naomi tightened her grip, pulling my arms back until it hurt, and forcing me to stick my bum out onto Sam's fist. I screamed in ecstasy and pain at the same instant as Sam's thumb flicked once more on my clit, and again. I was writhing, squirming in their grip, my boobs slapping on the toilet, drops of dirty water spraying everywhere as I shook my head in uncontrollable, frenzied climax. AJ slapped me again, harder, full in my face, and spat, right in my open mouth.

That was it, the final, awful detail, right at the top of my orgasm, and putting the last, perfect touch to my torture. The spit went right in my mouth, landing on my tongue and I just stuck it out, showing them all what she had done to me as my climax faded slowly away.

Four

It had been good, very good, but it had hardly been fair. Basically they'd abused me, and if they'd frigged me off, it had been more to show me up than to give me pleasure. Sam and Naomi had made me lick them too, afterwards, taking turns to sit on the toilet with my head between their thighs, before I was even allowed to clean up.

For days I would go into a fit of shaking every time I thought about it, and I lost count of the number of times I came over the memory, masturbating until my pussy was too sore to touch. That was what made me forgive them, in the end, or at least Sam, who had been the one doing the frigging. AJ too, because she had helped me tidy myself up afterwards, and dealt with the various men who thought they were going to get their cocks sucked just because I'd been easy for the girls. Naomi was the vicious one, even if she hadn't been giving the orders, so while it was impossible not to think of her just about every time I came, it was also impossible not to resent her.

In an effort to restore my battered pride, and to stop myself from rubbing my pussy red raw, I concentrated on uniform collecting. With Sarah's Girl Guide outfit proudly displayed on the mannequin, easy options just weren't going to satisfy. I wanted something good, something to impress my uncle. Given his anti-establishment views, a policewoman's uniform seemed ideal.

To really satisfy, it had to be a policewoman with some rank, preferably with pips on her shoulders. It was not going to be easy, but then nothing worthwhile was going to be easy. The first thing was that I had to meet her socially, not professionally, otherwise there wouldn't be a hope of getting her knickers off. So it was no good getting arrested for some trivial offence. Nor could I very well advertise for a lesbian police inspector on the net, as anything so obvious was certain to set alarm bells ringing.

It was the lesbianism that really put the icing on the cake and, try as I might, I could not think of anything that was even remotely likely to succeed. I tried though, and spent most of my evenings and a fair bit of time at work struggling to come up with an idea. I also avoided clubs and bars, determined to allow my bottom to return to a nice even shade of baby pink before doing anything that risked another whacking. I didn't even see Uncle Rupert, who had spent the weekend with Sarah in Cornwall. To cap it all, I came onto my period early, and by the time that was over I was beginning to wonder if I shouldn't set my sights on something more realistic.

The only even vaguely sensible thing I could think of to do was start making it known that I was into policewomen, as opposed to policewomen's uniforms. Rumours spread, and I reckoned that there was a fair chance of someone coming back down the line to me. So I began to go out again, and put a couple of carefully worded personal ads on the net, suggesting I liked to be dominated by women in police uniform but without being too specific. I'd baited my line, and it was all I could do, so I got on with work, and licking women's pussies and the other joys of life. I went to see Uncle Rupert too, to see how he had got on with Sarah, and also because I had a strong urge to take his cock in my hand again. Well, I hated the thought of the actual cock,

69

but I wanted to make him come, and if that's weird, then that's just me.

'Well?' I asked him, more or less as soon I'd walked through the door. 'How was it? I suppose she's been made a priest and you pinched her robes after the service?'

'Sadly no,' he laughed. 'Although a female cassock and dog collar would be quite a coup, assuming they differ at all from the male.'

'You'd have the photo,' I pointed out.

'True,' he admitted. 'No uniforms, I'm afraid, but we had a wonderful weekend. You?'

'Not much, other than being raped by three girls in the lavatory of a club in London Bridge.'

'You're joking?'

'Partly. I supposed I could have screamed the place down if I'd really wanted to. The trouble is I'm getting too much of a reputation for liking it hard. Tell me about Sarah, once we're comfortable.'

He said he'd fetch wine and glasses, and I went out into the garden, pinching the hammock and making myself thoroughly comfortable. When he came out it was with a bottle of champagne and two tall, slim glasses, serving before he started his story, still standing.

'Well,' he began, 'I drove down on the Saturday morning again, as she wasn't free until the afternoon. When we did meet, I had the full explanation for the absence of the Girl Guide uniform ready, but she didn't give me a chance to use it. Her hand was on my crotch before we were half a mile from the school, and she sucked me off in a lay-by on the A391, which was risky to say the least. I'm sure every lorry that passed could see, but she didn't seem to care, pulling my cock out and sucking on it as if her life depended on getting her mouthful of sperm. She got it too, within a couple of minutes, swallowing what she could and doing her usual dutiful thing by licking up the rest.

'I've never seen a woman so urgent, and I masturbated her while she did it too, with a hand up her skirt and in her panties. She was wearing stockings, which I adore, and these lovely silk panties. As I said, I came quickly, but she got there first, with my cock in her mouth as she did it, sucking really hard.

'After that, it was sex with everything. She wanted to go nude again, and to be spanked. I tried to explain the joys of keeping some clothes on, especially during a punishment, but she didn't really get it. Even the idea of having her knickers peeled slowly down off her bum as she waited for it only made her giggle. For her it's best to be nude, completely, without any concealment whatever, and to be proud of it. Also to be proud of her red bum once she's been smacked. In fact, the idea that it was a punishment doesn't appeal at all. She sees it very much as a sexual thing, and the red bottom as showing that she's desirable, wanted really.'

'Maybe you should cane her, or use a strap?'

'Maybe I should, but I'd rather not be testing her limits, just yet. I spanked her anyway, and pretty hard. She likes to lie over my knee while it's done, so I took her to a secluded place she recommended, right up on the edge of the moor, by one of the china clay pits, an abandoned one, and half full of water. It was great, hot and sultry, very quiet, with just the buzz of insects and the occasional bird call as she undressed in front of me, then the ringing echoes of my hand on her bottom and her cries. Like before, she warmed really quickly, and once she was ready she got down between my knees to suck me hard, and sat on my cock, bouncing up and down with her hot little bottom-cheeks against my thighs.'

'Lovely,' I broke in. 'Go on, take your cock out.'

This time he didn't hesitate, moving closer to the hammock to be absolutely sure he wasn't in view from any other houses and handing me his glass as he freed his penis.

'I'll watch you,' I said. 'I'd like that. Go on.'

He began to stroke himself, retrieving his glass of champagne for another sip before continuing.

'She came like that,' he said, 'sat in my lap and rubbing at her pussy while she wiggled her bottom on me. It was glorious, and I'd have come if it had been the first time, and I'm not even sure if I could have held back from doing it up her. As it was, I had her sit down and did it between her titties, which are just big enough to fold round my cock, then fed her the spunk with my finger. By then we were both hot and sweaty, so we went in the pool. Someone saw us, actually, from the lip of the pit. A few minutes earlier and they'd have caught us fucking, or me with her over my knee.'

'She'd have loved that, by the sound of it,' I put in. 'Hmm, you're getting nice and big.'

He was, with his cock almost erect in his hand and making a really lewd, meaty slapping sound as he tugged at it. It was ugly – cocks are – but I still wanted to watch. He turned a little, holding it out to me. I took it, gingerly, squeezing on the shaft to feel the silky flesh move over the hard, gristly core, which is just such an obscene sensation. I wasn't as horny as when I'd first wanked him off, so I gave him a couple of tugs to be polite, no more.

'She liked just being seen,' he went on, taking his cock up again. 'It was like a challenge to her. She even pulled herself out of the water, as if to dare them to disapprove, or to let them admire the view if they wanted to. They went away, out of embarrassment we assumed, but it really turned Sarah on. She wanted it again, and made a big show of towelling herself down, then rubbing in suntan cream. That was good, quite a show, and better when she got me to do her back and bottom. I could imagine their excitement, and jealousy, which I find quite a turn-on, but I didn't feel comfortable about actually fucking her when people might see.

'I couldn't anyway, I was so drained, not like now. I could come just over the thought of Sarah lying there, with her bottom still a little bit pink and her legs just far enough apart to show the rear of her pussy. Look, er . . . if you want to?'

'No, thanks, I'll . . .' I began, then changed my mind. 'Oh what the hell.'

I wouldn't have felt comfortable bare, so I popped open the button of my combats and slid my hand down the front of my panties. My pussy was wet, and I soon had my finger burrowed down between my lips, rubbing my clitty as I waited for him to go on. I shut my eyes, purring as I masturbated.

'Sarah was getting more and more turned on,' he said, 'and I'm sure it was because we were being watched, whatever she said. I'd put plenty of cream on her, but she didn't want me to stop, enjoying having her back massaged, her neck especially, that and her bum. It was getting to me too, two orgasms or not, but my cock didn't really want to respond.

'Her legs came further apart as I massaged her, until I could get my hand down between her thighs, to stroke her pussy. I put a finger in, and she pushed her bottom up, making the crease part with a sticky sound. Her hole was still dry, and so tempting, so neat and small, just dying to be touched. I put cream on it, and she just sighed, lifting it higher. I'd meant to wait, before really exploring her anus, but I couldn't resist. I rubbed the cream in, slowly, not sure how she'd react, circling the hole, putting the top joint of my finger in. She gave the sweetest little moan at that, a sob really, and began to tug at my cock again. I put my finger up, right up, wiggling it to open her, until her hole was sloppy and loose. By then my cock was hard.'

'You didn't . . . you didn't bugger her?'

'I did, in among some bushes. We never said a word, either of us, we just knew it was going to happen. I took

73

her hand, and led her in behind a clump of bushes. She went down, trembling like anything, with her buttocks up and that juicy, creamy little hole showing for me. I put my cock in, all the way, buggering her as she sobbed and shivered underneath me. She even cried a little, but she let me, all the way, until I came in her, Jade, up her bottom . . .

'Ah, that is good, too good . . . May I . . . please, just pop it in your mouth?'

'No . . . Yes. Do it.'

I didn't open my eyes. I couldn't bear to look. Something rubbery nudged against my lips. There was a moment of shock, revulsion too, then my mouth was open and it was going in, his cock, in my mouth, deep in, until I was sucking on the fat shaft with my head full of the taste of man. He'd got it right, judging the moment when I'd let him, and asking too.

I might have been sucking, but I wasn't going to be a good girl, like Sarah, and let him spunk in my mouth, then swallow it all dutifully down. I was going to be a bad girl, and make him do it in his hand. Then it had happened. No warning, no nothing. One moment my mouth was full of cock and the taste of man, the next a mouthful, of salty, slimy sperm had been ejaculated down my throat. Rupert groaned, trying to push his cock deeper in. I gagged, pulling back, to cough up my filthy mouthful, all over his cock, then the ground, spitting and gagging with my head hung over the side of the hammock.

'Sorry,' he said.

There was nothing to say to answer that, except to look up with what I sincerely hope was an expression of reproach, but was probably spoiled by the long stream of sperm hanging from my chin.

So he'd buggered Sarah, and was well pleased with himself. All the way home I kept getting pictures of her with her bottom lifted and the hole all slimy with suntan lotion, then with him mounted on her, his cock up her bottom. It's just such a dirty thing to do to a girl, and Sarah looked so sweet, so natural. One thing was obvious, which was that Rupert was falling in love with her. Not that it had stopped him sticking his cock in my mouth, but that's just men.

I didn't mind. There was something dirty about our relationship, wonderfully dirty, and honest too. It wasn't just that he was my supposed uncle either, but more the way we did it, his cock out, my hand down my panties, happily masturbating while we told each other filthy stories. It was so much the opposite of what women are supposed to want, the right man, Mr Perfect, who'll come along and sweep them off their feet, saving them the trouble of having to work, or worry, or think. I hate that, and anyone who tells me it's not true in the new millennium only needs to go and read a bit of chick lit. That or watch a Hollywood romance, with all those prudish, up-tight women who're supposed to be our role models. Bollocks. I want it rude, dirty, with three girls in leather holding my head down a toilet while I'm fisted and frigged off from the rear. Or, if I must have a man, then let him tell me that he wants to wank over my tits and bum, make me suck his gross cock, or stick it up my bumhole. That's the truth, after all.

After my unexpected mouthful of sperm, and not having come myself, I was in a funny mood. I couldn't stop thinking about girls taking cocks up their bums. Most men want to do it, to me anyway, and I suppose most girls end up getting it. So far I'd resisted. I intended to keep doing so, but there was a sort of horrible inevitability about it. My excuse had always been that it simply wouldn't fit, but Mo had put the dildo up me, so I knew a cock would go too.

I'd have masturbated on the bus if it hadn't been so crowded, I was that horny. As it was I did it in my flat, face down on the bed with a hairbrush stuck up my bum, imagining myself being buggered. The fantasy was simple. Greece, where I'd been on holiday, and two men talking me into a fucking when I was unable to pay a restaurant bill. Only they wouldn't fuck me. Once they'd got me tied to the table with my bikini pants pulled down and my boobs in a pool of spilt beer, they'd take it in turns up my bum.

It was a good orgasm, but left me fidgety, unsure what I should do with myself. In the end I walked down to the cyber café, on the off chance someone had replied to one of my ads. They had, two obvious time wasters and another, not a policewoman, not even a single woman, but a couple, and she was a prison warden.

The suggestion was that she dominate me while he watched. Normally I wouldn't have bothered, but a chance at a female prison warden's uniform was seriously tempting. It was fairly rare, fairly risky, and hopefully both old-fashioned and formal. It was also a pet fantasy of mine, being abused in a prison cell, which seemed to be more or less what they intended.

The message looked genuine, but I still intended to be cautious. After all, I had no evidence that she even existed, and I'd heard enough stories of girls going to meet 'couples', only to find that the female partner was conveniently indisposed. I replied anyway, sending a picture of myself holding an orange in my left hand and demanding that they did the same.

What came back sealed it for me. It showed her, in the uniform, younger than I'd expected, and pretty enough, but very severe, tall too, maybe even six foot, as well as I could judge. Her hair was up in a tight bun, adding to the image, while the uniform was great, better even than I'd imagined. It was a long dress, steel-grey, belted at the waist, with a simple insignia at either shoulder, absolutely plain and absolutely severe. She had the orange, and she also had a reproving look on her face. The text said simply that I'd earned myself a severe punishment for doubting her word.

Two days later I had the meet set up for the following weekend. They were in Stevenage, which was easy enough for me, and we were supposed to meet in a pub, as neutral ground. Still cautious, I arrived a little late, to find them sitting in the beer garden. She was casually dressed, with her hair down, but unmistakable. He was very ordinary, mid-thirties, average height, with a beard and beer belly. Telling myself that he'd only be watching, I stepped boldly forwards.

It worked from the start. She was called Andrea, her boyfriend Mark. There was sexual tension between she and I immediately, while he had the sense to let us get on with it, friendly, but not obtrusive. Within half-an-hour I knew I was going to do it, and within an hour I was back at their house, slightly light headed from the beer I'd drunk, and ready to play.

They were well into it, and had even converted their spare room into a cell, and very realistically. There was an old-fashioned bed, the iron painted the same dull grey as the walls, the mattress thin and covered with threadbare blankets. A tatty chest of drawers, a wooden chair and a sink completed the appointments, along with a huge pot pushed halfway under the bed. That was all. It was enough. It was perfect. Even the door looked authentic, while the CCTV camera high in one corner made a nice touch. It also meant I was going to be filmed.

'You're going to vid the scene?' I asked, nodding up to it.

'Sure,' Andrea answered. 'That's how Mark watches, most of the time. You won't even know he's there. There's a digicam too, there.'

She pointed to what looked like a discoloration on the wall, but sure enough, concealed a tiny lens. I'd get my photo.

'Okay,' I answered, 'but nothing on the net, not with my face.'

'We wouldn't, don't worry. You looked at our site, didn't you?'

'No, you never sent the URL.'

'You can, if you want. We do put pictures of the punishments up, sometimes, but no vid.'

'The captures aren't good enough anyway,' Mark put in. 'I like it perfect, or nothing.'

'Fair enough,' I answered. 'I'll look later. I want to see your uniform, Andrea.'

'You will,' she promised. 'Right, Mark, out, set the computer up. Jade, with me.'

We went into the next room, where she opened a big wardrobe, pulling out a plain dress in some coarse, grey-blue material and throwing it to me.

'This ought to fit,' she said. 'Try it.'

'What is it?' I asked, holding up the hideous thing, a dress, but shapeless and plain, also quite short.

'Prison clothes,' she answered.

I'd already twigged, and was staring at the thing with my glands doing their best to knock the top off my head. It had to be real, presumably pinched from the prison laundry, and just the thought of being punished while wearing it was enough to make me want to come. Not only was it going to be a truly humiliating thing to wear, but some genuine inmate would have worn it before, maybe several.

Andrea had pulled out her uniform, one from among several in the wardrobe, and was holding it up to her front. I swallowed, hard, to see in the flesh what I had seen in the picture. We dressed, hurriedly, both keen to get into the scene. I finished first, having little to do except strip to bra and panties and pull the horrid little smock over my head. For Andrea it was more complicated, with a petticoat, girdle and seamed stockings on underneath, along with big, white cotton panties. I was already picturing the ensemble on one of Rupert's mannequins.

I was already shaking as she finished, coiling her hair into a tight bun. Casually dressed, in jeans and a skinny top, with her long, dark blonde hair loose, she had looked so normal. Not now. The transformation was extraordinary, street girl to stern, sadistic warden, and if our scene wasn't real, then she was.

'Let's go,' she said, smiling and reaching out to take me by the hand. 'We need to set out our limits here. How much do you like being smacked around?'

'I can take quite a lot on my bum. I don't mind my thighs too much, or a gentle titty whipping.'

'What about your face?'

'Well . . . not really. A few slaps perhaps, but nothing to bruise.'

'Sure. You'd better have a stop word then. Make it clemency.'

'Clemency, fine.'

'Okay, like I said, we try to make it as real as possible, the whole thing. Right, Mark, we're on.'

We were in the passage, and she had called out the last remark towards another room, where I could see the pale light of a computer screen through the half-open door.

'I'm there,' he called back. 'Go for it.'

'In,' Andrea ordered, and jerked me towards the cell door.

I went, and she followed. The camera swivelled, purring, but I ignored it, in role, turning to her.

'Right you little bitch,' she snapped, and slapped me in the face.

The smack caught me totally by surprise, full across one cheek, hard. I went down, gasping, to my knees, and her hand twisted into my hair. My head was jerked back, my hand going instinctively to my cheek. She gave me another, backhanded, across the other side.

'Ow!' I protested.

'Shut up,' she snapped. 'You've had this coming a long time.'

She wrenched at my hair, sending me sprawling on the floor, my bottom towards her, my hands still up to my smarting face. Her toe caught me, a hard kick, in the fat of my bottom, and another, on my thigh. I gasped in pain, trying to roll away. The grip in my hair tightened, her boot thudding into my bottom again, twice. Her hand snatched down, jerking up my skirt, high, over my bum, and higher, up around my waist, jerked over my boobs. My bra came up with it, one cup all the way, to flop a boob out, the other halfway, to leave the flesh bulging out below the wire. Her grip twisted tighter, rolling me onto my back.

I was panting, my face burning, my bottom and thighs smarting. Andrea stood over me, gloating down at my body, her face set in a hard sneer. She spat suddenly in my face, catching my nose and one eye. My mouth came open in disgust and got spat in. I looked up at her through my one clear eye, swallowing.

She hit me in the face, a hard open slap, making me scream. Another caught me, and a third, knocking my head to one side, then the other. I cried out in pain, gasping to the sudden shocks, putting my hands up to protect my face. She laughed, and dropped my head.

'Slut! Bitch!' she swore, and set to work.

She really beat me up, slapping and kicking at my body as I rolled on the floor, always the fat bits, but hard. My bottom and legs really did get a good kicking, the toes and heels of her boots jabbing into my flesh again and again, until I was screaming and grovelling on the floor. My boobs weren't spared either, or my face, slapped over and over, until my flesh was an angry red, stinging furiously, my nipples hard and aching. She pulled both boobs out, fully, and put a boot on my stomach while she slapped them, holding my wrists in one hand, and smacking, harder and harder, mercilessly, until I was dizzy with pain, writhing under her foot. They got spat on too, repeatedly, until the hot, red flesh was running with spittle.

My face was done next, slapped harder and harder, until I was gasping with the pain, frantically shaking my head from side to side to escape the smacks. She didn't let go, pulling at my hair, calling me a bitch, a slut and worse as the stinging slaps came in, until finally it was too much and I was screaming for clemency. She stopped, immediately, gave a snort of contempt and spat in my open eye.

'Over,' she ordered, and kicked my thigh.

I went, bottom up, lifting it to what I knew was coming. She gave a harsh laugh and kicked me again. My panties were wrenched down and off, leaving me nude from boobs to boots. My hand went back between my thighs, finding my pussy swollen and wet. I lay on the floor, my breathing deep and even, and began to masturbate. My bruises hurt, my face felt swollen, my boobs too, but she'd got it right, because I was there almost as soon as I touched my clit.

Her boot settled on my back, squashing my boobs out on the cell floor. I turned my head, opening my sticky eyes to find her towering over me, the woman who'd just beaten me up, the steel-grey dress, the tight bun of her hair, the look on her face, amused, contemptuous, merciless. I locked eyes with her, rubbing at my clit and sticking my bum further up, to make the fat cheeks open and show her my busy fingers and the wet dimple of my bumhole.

She reached down, to the bed, pulling something out from beneath the covers, a whip, short, thick, the single lash made of braided leather. I gave a little whimper, genuine fear, and rubbed hard, waiting. She lifted the horrid thing, sneering, her eyes bright with pleasure, and brought it down, with all her force, full across my sweet spot. I screamed, my whole bottom jerking in agony, a line of hot fire springing up immediately. My flesh was burning, heavy and rough, my head dizzy with pain. A second cut caught me across the first and I screamed again, coming, through the pain, in agony and ecstasy as cut after tearing cut exploded across my naked cheeks, beating me into pure, grovelling, craven submission . . .

The orgasm lasted so long, on and on as she flogged my poor bottom, so, so good. It didn't stop until she did, her boot lifting from my back as the last cut bit into my bottom. I just collapsed, exhausted on the floor, my whole body burning, sweaty and sore, my fingers still in the wet mush of my pussy. Above me, Andrea began to hitch up the grey skirt, exposing her stockings, the bulge of soft flesh at the top, her panty crotch. It was wet, showing the outline of her pussy, the lips bulging out the white cotton, damp with her juice.

Her hand came down, gripping my hair. I was pulled up, roughly, struggling to my knees. Two of her fingers hooked into her panties and she tugged them aside, exposing the moist, ready flesh of her sex. I caught her scent, my mouth coming open even as she pulled my face in. I touched, tongue to pussy, and I was licking, in absolute, wonderful gratitude, lapping urgently at her clitty, determined to at least try to give her the same pleasure she had given me.

She held me there, so stern and strong, cruel too, making a girl she had just beaten up and forced to masturbate lick her pussy for her. With the grey skirt held up, just visible to me, the cell around me, and everything just so right, it was impossible to resist. I began to masturbate again, feeling my well-smacked boobs as I flicked and rubbed at my pussy. She let me, and came in my face just as my orgasm was building up, stepping back so that I finished with her juice running down my chin as I looked up at her in absolute worship. She spat in my face.

I was left, Andrea turning away without a word, slamming the door and locking it behind her. My orgasm was still tailing off, and I closed my eyes, just letting the pleasure slowly fade, aware of every sensation. I could feel my bruises, dull and aching, the prickle of sweat on my skin, the tension of my lifted dress and bra, the cool damp where her spittle was running down my cheek.

Finally I shook myself and smiled up at the camera. Nothing happened, not surprisingly, so I crawled to sit on the bed, to nurse my bruises and wait for them to let me out. She came, after about ten minutes, but with water and a plate of instant cottage pie, soggy cabbage and boiled spuds, which she put down on my chest of drawers, leaving without a word.

I ate it, wondering just how real they were trying to make it. The beating had been a punishment, and I was now confined, eating alone. I was exhausted, and my body hurt all over. What I needed was a cuddle, but I was also wondering just how far the fantasy could be taken, and I needed to get Andrea's dress. So I didn't call out my stop word, and when Andrea came back to collect my tray I was curled up on the bed, facing away from her, pretending to be beaten and miserable.

I was left, lying on the bed, just staring at the ceiling and jumping at every tiny noise from outside. It was hard to know what they were up to, but they obviously wanted something to happen. I made a big show of going over my body, nude and with the camera in mind, looking sorry for myself as I inspected my bruises. I was in a fine state, with big, dark ones all over my bum and thighs, red and black, while the whipping had made a real mess of my cheeks. My boobs were bruised, quite badly, and I was sure my face would be too, although my climax had been so good I couldn't even find it in myself to resent Andrea for doing it.

By the time I'd finished I was ready to masturbate again. I did it on the bed, with my ruined bottom stuck out at the camera, to really give them a good look at what Andrea had done to me. It was good, if less so than the other two. When I'd come I dressed and collapsed on the bed.

I meant to work out the best way to pinch Andrea's dress, but I was asleep within minutes.

When I woke up it was late afternoon. I felt a bit silly, awkward really, also stiff, sore and dry. Andrea had left the water, and I drank the lot. I needed to pee, and was going to call out, only to realise that it might be exactly what they wanted me to do. After all, there was the big potty under the bed, and they hadn't put it there for nothing.

I wasn't really in the mood, but I didn't want to spoil Andrea's fantasy either, or break the scene. Still I hesitated, only for a truly brilliant inspiration to hit me. I'd pee in the pot, and I'd make sure I was holding it when Andrea came in. I'd spill pee on her dress, accidentally, or even as part of the scene. It would have to be cleaned, and afterwards it would go on their clothes dryer, which was in the tiny garden. When I left I'd stay in Stevenage, returning at the dead of night to pinch it, a bra and panty set too, maybe even her stockings if I got lucky. It was perfect, and wonderfully mischievous.

Putting on a sour face, I pulled the potty out from under the bed. It was big, and porcelain, the real thing, and by the look of it about a hundred years old. Thinking of just how many bare bottoms must have been lowered onto it over the years, I pulled my dress up and pushed my knickers down to my ankles, bum to the camera. I squatted, lowering myself onto the pot with my rear stuck well out to give them the rudest possible view. For a moment I held on, thinking of them watching, then let go. My sigh was genuine relief as my pee squirted out into the pot, tinkling on the china, then bubbling as the pool deepened. I let it all out, relaxing completely, and only just stopping in time as my bumhole began to pout.

I glanced back at the camera, feeling embarrassed and wondering if they'd noticed. I hadn't realised I was so urgent, but I could feel the weight inside me and knew I'd have to go soon. I was sure they didn't want to watch that, so I gave my bottom a quick wiggle to shake the last few drops away and stood, pulling my knickers up.

That was enough. It had been a great fantasy, and I'd given them their pee shot, but I needed to use the proper loo, wash, and have Andrea rub some cream into one or two important places. I waved to the camera, called out my stop word, and went to the door. It was locked. I called out, but nobody answered, so I did it again, telling Andrea I needed the loo properly. Again there was no answer.

I began to get worried, wondering if they had seen I was asleep and gone to the shops or something. Banging hard on the door, I yelled out my stop word again, loud, with the first feelings of genuine unease as I felt the pressure in my bowels rise suddenly. I called again, telling Andrea to stop mucking about. She didn't answer, and I realised that they really weren't there. After all, if they'd wanted to torment me they would have come to the door, to taunt me and peep in through the spy hole. At the least I'd have heard a footfall. There was nothing.

At last I stepped back, wondering what I ought to do. I was beginning to get really urgent, but doing it in the potty was going to be horribly embarrassing, with the camera presumably still on. They'd realise too, even if it wasn't, when they came back, from the smell. It didn't bear thinking about.

I even considered trying to break the door down, as it was only plywood, for all that it looked like a genuine cell door. Unfortunately I couldn't bring myself to do it. Smashing other people's doors down just isn't on, not when you've only just met them. So I stayed still, sat on the bed with my knees pressed together, trying to ignore the growing pain in my tummy. I kept hoping they'd come back, sure I could last, my ears straining for the sound of their return.

Finally I realised that I had no real choice except for the potty. I was going to have to do it, on film, that or fill my panties. Still I struggled to hold it back, knock-kneed with desperation, clutching my tummy. The pain became abruptly worse. I gasped, gritted my teeth, clenched my bottom-cheeks, fighting it back. It was no good, it was coming. Desperately, I snatched for the pot, pulling it out to slosh pee over my sleeve. I didn't care. My skirt was half up, right up. There was a truly awful, utterly helpless feeling as I went, but my knickers were down, my bum on the pot as it all came out and a wave of utter, blissful relief swept through me.

I had come so close to filling my panties, so close. If I hadn't had a plump bottom I'd have done it. For a moment I didn't even worry about the camera, just happy not to have soiled myself and overcome with the sense of relief it gave me. It was when I heard the purr of its motor that I looked up, finding the lens pushing out into a close-up. The blood went straight to my cheeks, sending them flaming to crimson, smacked as they were, and my mouth came open in horrified realisation. They were there, and they'd watched my wriggling desperation, my panic as I struggled to get my knickers down, the look on my face as I did it. They had a prime view too, with my thighs well apart towards the camera. I hid my face in my hands, unable to cope with the thought of Mark watching me do my potty. They'd made me do it, and they were probably masturbating each other as they watched, and laughing. It was just too humiliating, too rude.

That was my undoing. I was shaking, sobbing too, close to tears. It didn't stop me. I pulled my dress up, and flopped out my boobs, increasing my exposure and vulnerability. I shut my eyes, and caught them up in my hands, feeling their weight and the roughened flesh where Andrea had smacked them. My nipples were hard, sensitive, urgent. I petted them as I finished off into the potty, the burning shame in my head slowly giving way to arousal.

One hand slipped down, to my pussy, and I was doing it, masturbating on my potty as they watched. It was good, with my little prison uniform pulled up, showing it all off, abused, punished, tricked, and now showing what it did to me. I knew there was a man watching me, a man with his ugly great cock in his hand, wanking it over one of my most intimate moments. There was Andrea too, as I pictured her, austere dress pulled up, hand down her knickers, her face set in amused contempt as she watched me.

My pleasure rose, quickly, my last inhibitions slipping away as I approached climax. I put my other hand down, under my bum, feeling the full cheeks, the skin rough from my punishment. Moving down, I touched my tuck, fuller still, no, fat, embarrassingly fat, my big, bouncy bum, which the girls always seem to want to beat, or to make me show off the wrinkled hole between my cheeks. I had to touch, and I did, despairing at my own dirtiness as I let my finger move to my slimy little bumhole. My face screwed up as I tickled it, in delight and disgust. I couldn't stop. My finger went up, poking into the hot, wet cavity of my rectum as I came to orgasm in blinding, dizzying bliss.

As I came I heard another cry of ecstasy, Andrea's, giving my climax a last, lovely nudge as the thought of her masturbating over me. There was silence, my mind and body coming slowly down from the peak as reality flooded back in. I had no loo paper, my finger was well up my dirty bottom and I wasn't at all sure I could get up without spilling the potty.

'Clemency!' I yelled. 'Andrea, help!'

She came to my rescue immediately, in just her underwear, giggling and holding her nose as she passed me a roll of loo paper. I managed to clean myself up, eventually, and emptied the potty before joining Andrea in the bathroom. She was already nude, in the shower, grinning at me as she soaped an arm.

'Thanks, that was great!' she said. 'I had a lovely orgasm watching you!'

'Thank you, mine was good too. Why no dress?'

'Mark made me take it off to suck him, after the first time. I took it in my mouth while you were masturbating with your backside in the air. He loved that!'

'I bet he did. Where is he?'

'He got beeped, poor man, right in the middle of it.'

'Beeped?'

'He's a doctor, didn't we say? He's on call.'

'So he didn't see me on the potty?'

'No, just me. He should be back soon. You can watch me suck him off if you like?'

'Well . . .'

I was going to decline, but I had to keep the scene going. Otherwise I would lose my chance at her uniform. I had it worked out too.

'Come on, he'd love to have you watching. He adores his cock, and he loves girls to see it.'

'I'd love to, sure, I was just going to ask a favour.'

'Ask away.'

'Do it in your uniform. It would be nice, to see the tables turned a bit. Maybe we could do a little scene, with Mark as the governor or something, forcing you to suck his cock in front of a prisoner?'

'Maybe, if he's into it.'

'And let him come in your face and down your front, with your boobs out. I'd love that.'

'So would he, believe me. There's nothing he likes better than soiling girls with his spunk.'

He came back half an hour later. By then Andrea was in her dress, ready, although with my own uniform wet with piddle I'd had to change into my jeans and top. As she had predicted, he was seriously randy. Andrea explained the fantasy.

'Fine,' he answered, 'but it's got to be over Jade's bum. I was so close!'

'She can bend over the chest of drawers then,' Andrea said, 'with her jeans and knicks down, as if I'd been punishing a new inmate who'd yet to have her uniform issued, or getting a last thrashing in on a girl due for release. How's that?'

'Great,' he answered. 'Do it.'

'I know . . .' I tried. 'Look, this is going to sound stupid, when you've seen everything on camera, but I'm . . . I'm not really comfortable showing my bare bum in front of a man with an erection. I know it's stupid, but . . .'

'No problem,' he said. 'I'm well into girls' bums in jeans. Keep them up, but stick it well out.'

We went to the cell, Mark running up the stairs, Andrea and I walking behind, arms around each other and giggling at his urgency. Inside, I arranged myself over the chest of drawers, bent, with my bum stuck right out. The sight nearly had his eyes popping out of his head, and he asked if he could touch while she sucked him.

It was only on the seat of my jeans, so I said he could as long as he didn't feel my pussy. He agreed, taking his cock out as Andrea got down on her knees. I shut my eyes, holding the pose and listening to the little slurping noises of her sucking on his erection as he began to stroke my bottom. It didn't take long, just minutes, before he grunted, his hand tightening on my flesh, and that was it.

I was already picturing her with come in her face and all down the front of her dress. Unfortunately it wasn't, not much anyway, but even with him babbling apologies it took me a moment to realise what had happened. He'd done it over my jeans, loads of it, right across both cheeks where they'd been stuck out for him to fondle, and especially in my crease. Her dress was clean.

Furious, I went to clean up in the bathroom. A glance in the mirror showed the state I was in. There was no possible doubt that I'd let a man spunk over the seat of my jeans. There was a great, thick streamer across both cheeks, and blobs lower down, and in the crease, a real mess. I did my best to clean up, but only succeeded in making it look as if I'd had a little accident, or at the very least sat down in a puddle. That was bad enough, but now there was no reason for her to wash her dress. After all, she'd only had it on for a few minutes, just while punishing me.

They were in the study when I came out of the bathroom, looking at the pictures from the digital camera. They were good, and I had them print several out for me, including a really heavy one of me masturbating while Andrea thrashed me, which I decided was the one for the display.

'One for the gallery that, definitely,' Andrea said as the print emerged, with my beaten bottom showing in glorious colour. 'If that's all right, Jade?'

'Go ahead,' I said. 'Anyone who can recognise my bum like that is welcome to see.'

'Show her some of the others, Mark.' She laughed.

He made a few deft clicks of the mouse and their website gallery appeared. There were several series, most of different girls, some with Mark, some without, but always with Andrea, rows of thumbnails. Mark clicked on one, bringing up a picture of a pretty blonde across Andrea's lap, outdoors, skirt turned up, panties down, her face set in an expression of total consternation. It was a classic spanking photo, the sort Rupert collected by the hundred, but it wasn't the girl's bum I was looking at, or the sorry expression on her face. Andrea was in a policewoman's uniform.

'You didn't say you were in the police before you became a prison warden,' I said, with the possibilities rushing through my head.

'Don't be silly!' Andrea laughed. 'I'm not really in the prison service! I'm an office manager.'

Five

I was not a happy bunny on the Monday morning. I hurt all over, and people kept giving me funny looks because of my smacked face. Both cheeks were bruised, and it was very obvious it had been done carefully and not in anger. I was sure everyone would guess I'd been smacked up in an SM scene, and that their response would have been angry disapproval rather than the sympathy I'd have earned if it had been for real.

When the agency rang I told them I wasn't well and turned down the job, although I needed the cash. I couldn't even bear to go over to Uncle Rupert's, not with the prospect of half-an-hour or more on a crowded bus. Not only that, but I had nothing to show him, while I was sure he'd not only have had a brilliant weekend with Sarah, but would have managed to bring off some amazing coup uniform collecting.

I rang him anyway, at work, and sure enough, he was bubbling over with enthusiasm about Sarah. He hadn't got a new uniform, which was something, and wanted to hear about my exploits. So I ended up accepting an invitation to dinner on the Friday, hoping that by then my face would look rather less like a smacked bottom and vice versa.

It did, more or less, after using up an awful lot of cream. I'd also accepted a job on the Wednesday, back at the office where Sam worked. I thought that was going to mean trouble, but it turned out that she didn't take her leather dyke attitude to work. In fact she was really friendly, making sure everyone was nice to me and even had a go at one of the male employees for using me as a coffee maid. She was also seriously keen on a date with me, which was flattering, although I didn't want her getting at me until my bottom had recovered. I didn't want to lose my chance with her either, so I explained the problem and ended up showing her my bum and legs in the storeroom. She was well impressed, and made me promise not to let anyone else punish me until she had had her turn.

That was the Friday afternoon, which left me in a pleasantly naughty mood for the evening. I was anticipating telling Uncle Rupert about Andrea and Mark, then listening to what he had done with Sarah. I was also sure I'd end up doing my duty again, which was how I thought about playing with his cock.

I didn't, nor anything of the sort. To my surprise, Sarah was there. Term had finished and she'd come to stay the weekend, so what should have been a rude evening turned into a frustrating one. Not that she wasn't nice, but she was very demure, and treated me very much as her junior if not quite as a little girl. I suppose from her point of view I wasn't much older than the senior girls at the school she taught at, but it was impossible not to resent her attitude. Sex was out of the question, with Rupert doing his best to impress her and certainly not in the mood for anything risky. The library was locked.

So I left feeling fed-up and frustrated. He'd made a remark about me being a bit of a brat sometimes as well, just because I wasn't deferential to her, which stung. Worst of all, as I sat on the bus home, I could just imagine what they'd be doing, kissing, cuddling, maybe Rupert inching up the prissy blue dress she had been wearing so that he could spank her bottom. That at least was a satisfying thought, although I'd have preferred to do it myself, with a whip.

I was also pretty drunk, as Rupert had opened some fancy bottles to show off to her. So I got off the bus at Archway and took the tube into town. I'd dressed on the assumption that I was likely to end up sucking cock, with a loose skirt, little pink panties and a top it was easy to pull up over my boobs. It wasn't exactly dyke gear, but it was going to have to do.

I chose Sugar Babe's, not really a dyke bar at all, but a hang out for pole dancers and glamour models, with a good sprinkling of baby dykes and bi-curious girls. It was also full of girls out for the thrill of pretending to be lesbian, which was why I didn't normally go there. There's not much worse than making a move on someone and then finding they're just posing.

It was a risk I was prepared to take. What I wanted to do was pick someone up and get rough with her, back at my flat. That was the mood I was in, because of Rupert and Sarah, because I'd spent half the week with a smacked face, and because everyone I meet seems to want to abuse me. With my reputation for liking to be on the receiving end it would have been hard in most places, almost impossible where my friends went. In Sugar Babe's I had a chance. I knew what I wanted too. She had to be slight, delicate, preferably with an air of insecurity, and have long, dark hair. Like Sarah.

I made my choice almost immediately. She was Sarah's height, smaller if anything, and might have passed for a younger sister. The only thing she lacked was Sarah's wholesome, country girl look. That was only because she had some serious make-up and two big, red silk flowers in her hair, and if it made her look as if she'd stepped out of a hostess bar, then she probably had.

Shy I'm not. The introduction was easy and I was giggling drunkenly with her and her male friend within minutes. She was called Zoe, and she wasn't a hostess, just a girl up west for a good time, and he was gay. That made it so easy. He spotted me for a dyke on the prowl immediately, and did his best to persuade her to go for it. After three bottles of Pils Zoe and I were snogging.

She had real attitude, as bad as me. We got so passionate that the barman told us to cool it, and she called him a boring old fart, to his face. After that we left, sharing a cab to Turnpike Lane. My boobs were out before we'd crossed the Euston Road, with Zoe sucking on them. Girls with little ones get like that over me, and Zoe was no exception. I didn't mind at all, and nor did the cab driver, sneaking glances back as Zoe suckled me. It was too much to resist.

'Keep your dirty eyes on the road, mate,' I warned him.

Zoe's head came up, her mouth wet with saliva, leaving my nipple red with lipstick. She glanced to the rear-view mirror, where the man's eyes were still fixed on us.

'Dirty old pervert,' she slurred. 'What d'you want, a toss off instead of our fare?'

He said nothing, his eyes flicking back to the road as the traffic light we'd stopped at turned green. Zoe went back to feeding, more urgently now. I'd been stroking her neck, and began to pull up her top, determined that if I was going to be showing off to some dirty old man, then so was she. She responded, pulling back to peel off her top and coming into my arms again, topless. We were coming into Camden, and there were people on the pavement, looking in. I don't think she noticed, pawing and kissing at my boobs, until finally the driver lost his cool.

'Put them away, for God's sake!' he snapped. 'I won't have that sort of behaviour in the back of my cab.'

'Yeah,' Zoe sneered, 'unless we gave you a bit. Come on, I dare you, the fare against a hand job. I mean it.'

'Just put your tits away, love,' he answered, 'and watch what you say. One day someone might just take you up on it.'

I thought that was it, and covered up. So did Zoe, and we contented ourselves with kissing and cuddling, until we reached Turnpike Lane. Instead of turning down towards my road, he pulled into the entrance of an industrial estate. Suddenly I realised that he'd decided to try it on.

'Right girls, fifteen quid or you suck my prick,' he said, leering back at us. 'Take your choice.'

'A toss, I said, you dirty bastard!' Zoe responded.

'Tits out, then,' he said.

She nodded, accepting his filthy suggestion and leaving me gaping. I couldn't admit to being scared, not to Zoe, and before I could decide what to do he had climbed into the back with us. Drunk or not, I was shaking, in a real state. I was between them too, which was not good. Zoe didn't notice, or else she didn't care. He certainly didn't. His cock came out, a thick, dark one with a really fleshy foreskin, just gross.

'Come on, girls, tits out we said,' he urged, and before I really knew it Zoe had hoisted my top up again, bra and all, and they were bare.

'Fuck me but you've got big ones,' the cabbie growled, reaching out.

'No, you don't!' I squeaked, pulling away.

'Yeah, no touching, you perv!' Zoe added. 'Come on, give me your little willy. Jade, climb across, we'll do him together.'

I moved, scrambling quickly across him to the far side. Zoe already had her top up, and she took him in her hand as I settled in place. He was getting hard, and I was hoping he'd just spunk up in her hand, really quickly. It was just so ugly, with the thick red brown shaft sticking out of his fly and the bulbous, hairy ball sack underneath. Seeing it in Zoe's pale, slender fingers just made it worse. I stared, fascinated and horrified at the same time, until she abruptly stopped wanking him and shook her hand.

'Your turn,' she said, and that was it.

My choice was to help wank him or lose her respect, and probably her company for the night. So I wanked him. My hand was shaking as I reached out to take the horrid thing, and I felt my stomach knot as I took it. It was hot, and a bit sticky, really disgusting, but I began to pull up and down, slowly.

'Jade's a lessie,' Zoe said calmly, 'that's why she's no good. Come on, Jade, I'll show you.'

Her hand folded around mine, squeezing my fingers onto his prick. She began to move, guiding my hand in a fast, jerking motion that made the cabbie grunt and gasp. His arms came around us, but she didn't stop him, so nor did I, allowing him to squeeze us to his body. Our hands were hammering at his cock, really fast, Zoe eager to make him spunk, me eager to get it over with. He was getting over-excited, squeezing me hard into him, Zoe too, until our heads were inches apart. She was grinning, her eyes bright with mischief. She let go of him, reaching out to touch one of my nipples, and leaving me to his cock. His hand folded closer, around me, to touch the side of one boob and I began to jerk at him with frantic urgency.

He came, a fountain of sperm erupting from his cock, spurting high to splash hot on my boobs and into Zoe's face. Both of us squealed in disgust, jerking back to leave him to finish himself off.

'Bastard!' Zoe spat, putting her hand up to wipe a thick blob of sperm off her cheek. 'Yuck, some's gone in my eye. Where's my bag?'

'Here,' I answered, 'have a tissue.'

We took several, cleaning ourselves up as best we could while he watched, as pleased by our disgust in getting spunked over as by the view of our boobs. Zoe kept calling him a pervert, but it just made him laugh, and five minutes later we were on the street, decent, fifteen quid better off than we would have been, but seriously humiliated. I was anyway, Zoe seemed to regard what we'd done as no big deal.

Her arm came around my waist as we started for my flat, and I responded, trying to push what we had done from my mind. The prospect of sex with her was too good to miss, and after making me toss the cabbie off, she really was in trouble. We walked, unsteadily, stopping to snog now and then, until we got back to my flat. Inside, we just fell on the bed together, pulling at each other's clothes in our eagerness.

We didn't strip, just pulled everything out. She was eager, really passionate, kissing and pawing at me, my boobs especially. I wanted her bum, and got it, pulling her down and throwing a leg across her back before she could stop me.

'This is for making me wank that filthy old git off!' I told her, and twitched up her skirt.

'What?' she demanded. 'What is?'

'This,' I answered.

Her panties were already down, just off her sweet little peach of a bum. I smacked, making the cheeks wobble, then again, harder.

'What, you're going to spank me' she said, giggling. 'Ow! Jade!'

She might have been giggling, but her squeal had been for real. I smacked her again, harder still and she bucked under me.

'Ow! Not so hard!' she protested. 'Jade!'

'It's got to be hard,' I told her, smacking away. 'It's the only way.'

'Ow!'

She lurched under me, twisting suddenly. I went over, sprawled on the bed. She came on top of me, smacked at my thigh, to catch it a stinging blow.

'Not on the leg!' I squeaked. 'On the bum!'

She took no notice, rolling on top of me in an effort to pin me down. I pushed back, clutching at her as we struggled, laughing, slapping at each other's bottoms. Tumbling together, each determined to get at the other's bum, we fought, smacking and pulling hair, but giggling and kissing too.

In no time we both had red bums, and both had our knickers off, pulled down and free in the fight. My top was up too, everything showing, sweaty and wet, flushed hot with excitement. My pussy was soaking, hers too, our nipples hard and sensitive.

It was me who lost, in the end, so far as there was a loser. I just got carried away, spanking her and kissing her bottom, with her squealing and wriggling in mock anguish. I could smell her sex, and I wanted to lick while I spanked her, but she was writhing so hard I couldn't get my face to her pussy and ended up having her bum shoved in it instead. I caught her scent and that was too much. A moment later I was licking her bumhole.

She gave a little gasp, called me a dirty bitch and stuck her bum in my face. That was the end of my wanting to be on top. Her bottom was lovely, soft and round and girlie, also warm from spanking, the most lickable of bottoms. I did it, saying sorry with my tongue, burying it right up her dirty little hole as she sighed and moaned. Before long she was frigging, rubbing at herself and telling me to get my tongue further up her hole. I tried, pushing really deep, until her anus was sloppy and open under my mouth.

I pulled round, until she could get at my pussy, frigging me as I lapped at her anus. I took over on her pussy, pushing a thumb up the hole and rubbing with my palm. Her hand went to my sex, a finger poked up my hole, and as I spread my thighs she started to slap at the tuck of my bottom, fingering and spanking as I licked her bottom out. She was in charge, punishing me, with my up tongue up her bumhole, licking in dirty, lewd submission, a little fat slut, only fit to get my nose dirty for her pleasure.

When she came she screamed and called me a whole string of dirty names, bucking her whole body up and down, her bottom stuck right into my face. I just licked and licked, until she had finished, smothering my face in her bottom. Her attention recovered, her fingers became firmer, more purposeful, and I was coming too, sucking and slobbering over her open bumhole as my muscles clenched and locked, in dirty, drunken ecstasy.

We slept together, after more or less constant sex until it had begun to get light. There were no inhibitions between us, and I got it properly after our first orgasms, at my own request, lying over her lap with my hands tied behind my back as she spanked me with my own hairbrush. She thought it was hilarious, and really went to town on my bum, indifferent to my lingering bruises. She was good too, teasing me with her fingers to make me think she would let me come, only to go back to spanking me and feeling my boobs. When I did come it was glorious, long and high and uncontrolled, with her laughing at the state she'd got me into by punishing me. Afterwards I licked her pussy, kneeling nude at her feet, my hands still tied, with her sat on a chair, looking down on me with the most wonderful expression, of pleasure, amusement and just a little contempt, all at once.

It was nearly noon when I woke up, to find her lying beside me, fast asleep, still with the red flowers in her hair. I made coffee, and by the time it was ready she was awake. We got up slowly, not really speaking much, which was good. She didn't freak about what we'd done, which was better still, and by the time we were dressed we were getting on really well.

We went shopping in Wood Green, then to a place in Barnet to get some silk flowers for my hair. That left us closer to her place than mine, so we ended up there, a big suburban house in Whetstone, where she lived with her mum and dad. They were friendly, old hippy types, leaving us to our own devices, and we were soon up in her room, looking through her stuff.

She had loads of clothes, and some seriously fancy shoes, including some zebra-stripe thigh boots I'd have given a month's wages to own. That wasn't what really caught my eye though, or any of the designer stuff, not even the leather. It was the plainest thing in the wardrobe, a knee-length skirt in green tartan with a white blouse and a bottle green tie thrown over it.

'Do you like dressing up as a schoolgirl?' I asked, pulling the outfit out.

'No . . .' she answered, with all her boundless confidence suddenly gone from her voice.

'Why not?' I demanded. 'This is cute.'

'It is not cute! It's really daggy. I hate the thing.'

'Why . . .?'

I stopped. I'd been going to ask her why she'd bought it if she hated it so much, but the penny had finally dropped. She shrugged, blushing.

'That's right,' she said. 'I'm still at school.'

'That's not a problem! You're what, eighteen?'

'Seventeen.'

'Seventeen? Have you been to bed with another girl before?'

'Yes, I have! Look . . .'

'Sorry, sorry, sorry . . . I didn't mean it to sound that way. I'm just a bit surprised, after last night and everything. I mean, you were good. You really handled me when I got into my subby thing.'

'I just did as you asked, Jade, but yeah, it was good. You're a bit pervy, but I like that. It's . . . it's like you don't give a fuck. You licked my bum!'

It was my turn to blush, but the awkward moment was past.

'So you're still at school?' I asked, eyeing the uniform.

'Marchmont Girls,' she said. 'Lower Sixth, but fuck that. I want to hear about how you got in to having your bum spanked.'

'Simple, it turns me on.'

'Yeah, I noticed.'

'Didn't you like it? I had you quite red.'

'I suppose. I don't know really.'

'It's great. Put your uniform on and I'll show you.'

'My uniform? No way!'

'Go on, it's best. It's not all physical, you see. Most of it's in your head, like you want to feel you're really being punished.'

'If any masters tried that on me at school I'd kick their balls into next week!'

'Sure, but I'll bet a lot of them would like to do it to you. Think how randy they must get. You know what dirty bastards men are.'

She nodded.

'And think how jealous they'd be,' I went on, 'to think of you getting a spanking from another girl, in your uniform.'

'They're not going to find out!'

'You'll let me, then? It'll be nice.'

'No . . . Maybe. I don't know, Jade . . . Okay, you can spank me, but not in my uniform.'

'Pretty please?'

'Oh, all right, you perve! You're worse that that old bastard of a cabbie! Lock the door, and you're not to do it hard. If you make me squeal Mum and Dad'll hear!'

'There's a way around that. Come on, get in your uniform!'

She made a wry face and took the uniform as I passed it to her. I went to lock the door, my heart absolutely hammering as I skipped across the room. I was going to get to spank a schoolgirl, a real one, and if it wasn't so very much my thing, I knew it would leave Uncle Rupert green with jealousy.

I sat down to watch Zoe dress. She stripped first, all the way to the buff. That was cute enough, with her bending to pull off her socks and treating me to a flash of her pussy from behind, but my thoughts were on how she was going to look over my knee.

For all her pretence of innocence, she knew how to be pervy. She chose white panties for a start, probably the sort she really wore to school, along with green socks, shiny black shoes, the neat blouse, the pleated skirt and her tie. When I'd first seen her in Sugar Babe's I'd thought she was maybe twenty. In full uniform she'd have had trouble getting served. With her ready I slid forwards on the bed and patted my lap. She hesitated, but came down, laying herself across my knees with her feet and one hand on the floor. I lifted one knee a little, raising her bum.

'What are you going to do?' she asked. 'Tell me I'm naughty and stuff while you do it?'

'If you'd like that.'

'Maybe. Talk to me anyway.'

'Okay.' I said, trying to think of all the things girls had said to me while I was being punished, and the spankers in Uncle Rupert's magazines. There was one thing they all did, just about.

'First then,' I went on, 'I'm going to tell you why your knickers have to come down.'

'Do they?'

'Of course they do. It's so you're showing everything. The first rule, when spanking a girl, is to open her clothes, especially to pull down her pants, so that her bottom is quite bare. That way, she will understand that by being naughty she has forfeited her right to modesty.'

I might have been quoting straight out of one of the magazines, or from Rupert. Zoe giggled.

'Do it, then,' she said.

She wiggled her bum, looking back at me. I shook my finger at her, took her firmly around the waist and began to pull up her school skirt. I was genuinely hoping she'd like it, but that didn't stop me indulging myself. I did it really slowly, easing the hem of the green tartan skirt up over her thighs, to reveal the pale, rounded flesh inch by inch. She hung her head, maybe enjoying having me perving over her bottom, maybe not. She let me anyway, her skirt coming up, to show the curve of her little white panties where they disappeared between her thighs. Next came the tuck of her bottom, more panty material, and at last the full, sweet glory of her seventeen-year-old bum, encased in tight white cotton. It would have given Uncle Rupert a heart attack. Zoe gave a little purr, and I knew I'd won.

'Next,' I said, 'I'm going to have a good feel, just to bring home the position you're in to you, that I can do what I like, and you've got to take it. If you struggle I'll just have to tie your arms behind your back.'

She wriggled immediately, making me clutch at her to keep her on my lap. I smacked her across her panties and she stopped, to look back with a pleading expression on her face.

'Who wants to be tied, then?' I asked. 'Naughty little girl.'

I took her by the tie, tugging the knot loose as she obligingly put her arms up behind her back, crossed. The tie came away and I twisted it around her wrists, into a figure eight, which I tied off at the middle, leaving it so that the school crest showed clearly. Taking her skirt and the tail of her blouse, I ticked them up under her wrists.

'Now you really are going to get it!' I said. 'Imagine that, tied up for your first spanking! Not yet though, I want to feel you up.'

I began to fondle her bottom, gently, stroking her cheeks through her panties and tracing my fingers across her skin where the flesh stuck out at either side. She was slim, but not so skinny that her bum-cheeks didn't bulge out a little at the leg holes, while her panties were at least a size too small. Her crease showed as a gentle valley in the white material. I ran a finger down it, then up, and hooked it into the waistband of her panties.

'Here goes,' I said, 'knickers down, and we'll have it all bare!'

She gave a little sob, and I began to pull. The school knickers came down, tugged slowly off her bottom, to reveal her neat, firm cheeks and her deep bum-crease. She sighed again at the feeling of exposure, much as I would have done in her place. As her bum came bare as I cocked my knee up a little more, making her bum-cheeks come apart to show off the little rosy dimple between and a little of her pussy. Again she sighed as I turned the panties down around her thighs.

'There we are,' I said, 'knickers down ready, but not for a cock, oh no, for a spanking. A spanking, Zoe, with your bottom bare and your pussy on show. I can see your bumhole too, darling, all pink and wrinkly. I'm going to touch you up, Zoe, like this, bare-bottomed over my knee.'

It was good, and she was beautiful, but it was hard not to think of how much I'd have liked to lick the little pink bumhole I could now see, and kiss the tight cheeks I was about to smack. That's just me, though, and it wasn't going to stop Zoe getting it. She was ready too, held still, but with her bottom quivering ever so slightly and her anus twitching as if it was trying to wink at me.

I put my hand on her bottom again, feeling the soft, girly meat, scraping gently across the twin mounds with my fingernails. She was so lovely, smooth and pink, ever so neat, with just a little puff of hair on her pussy visible between her legs. Her lips were cute too, two little plump ridges of girl's flesh, ever so rude, and ever so kissable. Even her bumhole was pretty, a tight knot of baby-pink flesh, perfectly regular, with a spray of tiny pink lines disappearing into the firmly closed hole.

My hand went down between her cheeks, tickling in her crease, lingering on her sweet little bottom hole, and onto her pussy, rubbing in her wet until she began to sigh and lift her bottom. I stopped abruptly.

'Uh, uh, we'll have none of that,' I chided. 'Not yet. First you've got to be spanked. Then you can come.'

Zoe let a out a soft, frustrated sob. I lifted my hand, biting my lip in sheer delight at the sight of her bottom.

'Right, young lady, spankies time,' I announced.

There was a meaty smack as I brought my hand down on Zoe's bum. She squealed, the sound turning immediately into a giggle. I went to work, gently, little more than pats, applied with just the tips of my fingers to make her skin sting and tingle. She purred, wriggling her bottom for more, and I started to get harder, bringing the pink flush slowly to the tops of her cheeks.

'Good?' I demanded, pausing.

'Yes,' she answered. 'My bum feels all warm. Carry on.'

'Sure,' I answered, slapping her.

I did it harder, and she squeaked again, but stuck her bum up high. I gave another, harder still, and she gasped and moaned. It was getting loud, and the noise of a girl being spanked is fairly distinctive. I stopped.

'Carry on!' she protested. 'I was getting into that!'

'It's getting noisy,' I told her and so are you. 'Put your stereo on.'

'How? I'm tied up!'

She made to get up, but I pushed her down, tucking her skirt up properly before letting go. That left her lovely pink bum bare as she stood, wobbling uncertainly on her feet. She went over to her system, trying to turn it on with her bound hands and look over her shoulder at the same time. Music blared out, and she struggled to turn it down, almost falling over.

I was in fits of giggles, and caught the most wonderful look of consternation from her as she finally managed to get it right. She made a face at me, dipping lower to put the CD on repeat. As she did so, she jogged the table, and her mouse, changing her screen from the saver to design of bright pink and yellow stars, which was when I realised that she had a camera on top of her computer.

'Is that a webcam?' I asked.

'It's not linked up,' she said. 'Daddy wouldn't let me. You're so lucky living alone. If I had your flat I'd set a live cam up with a site, so members could watch me in the bath and stuff. It's got to be easy money.'

'Sure. Let's turn it on anyway. You can watch yourself being spanked.'

'No!' she answered, but her tone was a dead give-away.

'Show me how,' I ordered, rising.

It took a while, but I did it, setting it up to focus on the chair in front of the computer. Ready, I sat down, patting my lap. This time she came over with a lot more enthusiasm, sticking her bum right up and giggling at the picture on the computer screen. It was good, but mainly her bum, framed in green tartan and white cotton, with just a little of her blouse tail showing. I adjusted it, until I had a picture that would have gone well in any of Rupert's books. Zoe was head down, her small breasts hanging in her blouse, her hair trailing to the floor. The highest part of her body was her bottom, with the cheeks well raised and flushed pink above the lower panties and long, schoolgirl legs.

'Time we had your boobies out, I think,' I told her, and reached down to pull her blouse free, then her bra, leaving her little round tits hanging bare under her chest.

Her nipples were hard, and as she turned to see herself on the screen I quickly took a video capture.

'That's for your album,' I told her. 'Now, where was I? Ah yes, spanking your naughty bottom, how could I forget.'

I set to work on her, smacking away happily to make her bum bounce and quiver. I knew I might spoil it if I was too rough, but her cheeks were getting red anyway, her breathing deeper and less controlled, and her squeals louder. I kept right on, hoping that the music would cover what was being done to their daughter from her parents. She was getting hot too, her pussy swelling and moistening, while she kept looking back to enjoy the rude view from the camera.

A quick adjustment made it ruder still, pulling my leg between hers to spread them and turning a little. The picture then showed the full glory of her rear view, complete with her open, moist pussy and the dimple of her bumhole. She gave a little moan at the sight, looking back, just as I took a second video capture.

'Oh, you bitch!' she sighed.

'Shut up!' I answered her. 'I want you to remember this.'

I set the camera to take a picture every five seconds and went back to her bum, giving her another, harder smack. She really yelped, worse with the next two, squealing like anything. I gave three more, then stopped.

'You're a big baby!' I told her. 'Come on, get these in your mouth. I want you good and warm.'

I'd already put my hands on her panties, and she watched as I drew them down and off her legs.

'Not too hard, Jade,' she said.

'You need it quite hard,' I told her, 'but don't worry. It'll be good. Trust me, you don't know the meaning of hot until you've been given a proper spanking. I'm going to warm you, and make you come, and when I've finished I'm going to make you get down on your knees and lick my pussy. While you're licking you can think about how bad you've been, and how hot your bum is as a result.'

'I haven't been bad!' she wailed.

'No?' I demanded. 'Wanking off cab drivers to get out of paying your fare? Letting other girls pick you up in bars? You're a dirty, smutty little bitch, aren't you, Zoe?'

'Yes,' she sobbed.

'And you deserve to be punished?'

'I'm not –'

'Yes, you do, and you know it, so if you can't take your spanking like a big girl you've got to have the gag. Now open up!'

Her mouth came open, reluctantly, but at least as willingly as mine would have done if someone was going to stuff my panties in it. I made her take the lot, leaving just a little tag of white cotton sticking out from between her lips, and went back to spanking her.

She was already warm, her skin a rich pink and hot to the touch, her pussy moist and puffy around the hole. I laid in, harder, and harder, until the slaps were making my hand sting and her bottom-cheeks were bouncing and quivering. She responded too, kicking and bucking over my lap, with odd, muffled little noises coming through her panty gag, which I ignored.

Not that she tried to get off my lap, but I could sense her arousal in the way she moved, rising through her pain, until what I hoped was the right moment. I cocked my leg up hard between hers, hard, spreading the wet flesh of her pussy over my leg. It was a trick I'd had used on me before, and sure enough, Zoe began to rub herself on my thigh with just the same show of wanton excitement I'd have given if it had been me taking the spanking.

She just went crazy, squirming herself on my leg, her bottom bucking up and down with frantic speed, her smacked cheeks wobbling crazily, just lost to anything except her pleasure and the spanking she was getting. I kept on smacking her, as hard as I could, jamming her hot wet pussy onto my thigh with each slap, until my palm was stinging furiously and my arm was starting to ache. At last she started to come. I saw her pussy and bumhole clench, her thighs and bottom too, her whole body shaking with the force of her climax as I beat her furiously down onto my knee.

She was gasping by the end, with the soggy panties on the floor under her head where they'd dropped out of her mouth. Her bum was as red as a cherry, and bruised. I was pleased with that because, although I'd dished it out to a few girls before, I'd made such a mess of a bum with my bare hand. Unfortunately my palm was just as bruised as her bum.

Zoe got up, slowly. Her face was as red as her bum, her mouth open, looking as if she'd just had the shock of her life, which maybe she had.

'Good?' I asked.

'Great!' she answered.

'I'm glad, because you've really slimed my combats. Look!'

'Whoops,' she answered, looking down at the dirty white smear on the leg of my trousers. 'Sorry. Could you untie my hands?'

She turned her back, her hot bottom just inches from my face. I set to work on the tie, which she'd tugged really tight when she lost control of herself.

'You didn't mind, did you?' she asked. 'I mean . . . on your leg?'

'No, silly, that's what you were supposed to do. Best way for a girl to come, OTK, rubbing on her spanker's leg.'

'OTK?'

'Over the knee, the way I spanked you.'

'You know a lot about it.'

'I've had a lot of it, and read a lot.'

The knot came loose and she slid her hands free, rubbing them as she went on talking. She sat down, on my lap, and I gave her a gentle kiss, taking her hot bottom in one hand.

'I used to get it at Whispers,' I went on, 'in the back room, just about every weekend.'

'Whispers?' she responded. 'That's scary! I've heard they do stuff with hot wax and whips and chains and all sorts . . .'

'I got thrown out.'

'What for?'

'Peeing on the floor . . .'

Zoe's hand had gone to her mouth, her eyes wide in astonishment.

'It was an accident!' I blurted out. 'It wasn't fair, either. This girl had me on a cross, tied up. Instead of punishing me she tickled me! I'm so ticklish, I couldn't stand it, and when she did under my bum I just wet myself, all over the floor, and her.'

'No!' Zoe exclaimed. 'And you got thrown out?'

'Yeah, and it wasn't my fault. It was Sam's, the girl who had me tied up. She's supposed to be this big, hard leather dyke. She should have known better, or at least taken the blame.'

'You are into some heavy stuff, Jade! Doesn't it scare you?'

'Not really. I'm used to it, I suppose. Sometimes the girls get a bit too rough with me, but I can look after myself.'

'I'd never have the guts!'

'You went with me.'

'Yeah, and I didn't expect to end up with a smacked bottom!'

'Nice, though, isn't it?'

'Yeah, warm and glowing.'

She put her hands back, rubbing her sore bottom. I put mine on top of her, and kissed her again. Her mouth opened under mine, and her arms went around my neck. We snogged, our mouths open, tongues just touching, both of us stroking and soothing her smacked cheeks. She was pushing it out, and her kisses were getting more passionate. I hadn't come, and I was just about ready.

'Stand up,' I told her, 'turn your bum to me and put your hands on your head.'

She giggled, but she did as she was told, standing and sticking her bum right out, tucking the skirt up into its waistband before she put her hands up. I leaned forwards, to kiss the hot flesh of her cheeks. Her pussy-lips were showing between her thighs, and I could smell her, while her crease was quite well parted, the flesh pale in contrast to her reddened cheeks. I ran my tongue up the groove, tasting her skin.

'You are way into my bum, aren't you?' she said.

'It's lovely,' I told her, letting my tongue push in between the soft cheeks.

I'd spanked her, but I was rapidly losing my sense of dominance. With that hot little bottom in my face it was impossible to hold back. I found myself burrowing my tongue in deeper, to find her bumhole, licking at the little dimple with my tongue tip. She bent forwards, putting her hands on the desk. I took her hips, pulling my face into her, and licking at her bottom. She sighed, and wiggled it. I went lower, to lap at her pussy, and to run my tongue right up, from the swell of her pubic mound to the top of her bottom crease, again and again, until it was wet with saliva.

'You were going to make me lick you, Jade,' she reminded me. 'You said you'd spank me and make me lick your pussy. I want to.'

'All right,' I answered, 'get busy, then.'

She turned, sinking quickly to her knees. I stood, briefly, pushing my trousers and panties down to the floor. With my thighs well spread I sat back, watching the view from the camera as Zoe began to nuzzle my pussy. It showed her in all her glory, the school skirt tucked high, her naked bottom pushed out, the cheeks red, the crease wet with my saliva. She began to lick, urgently, lapping at the whole of my pussy, touching my clitty each time.

I focussed my eyes on her bottom, thinking of how I'd punished her, making her dress up in her school uniform and spanking her, until she'd come on my leg. It had been lovely, and I wanted more, but most of all I wanted it to be me, laid bare over the knee of the beautiful girl who was licking my pussy so sweetly.

'Come on the bed,' I said, pulling at her arm.

She came, rising with a sticky smile and took my hand. I lay down on the bed, opening my arms for her as she climbed on top, head to toe, and settled her bottom into my face as her own found my pussy. We started to lick, feeding on each other's pussies, lapping and probing as I felt the hot cheeks of her bottom. Her hands curved under my bum, squeezing my cheeks.

'Touch my hole,' I begged. 'Do anything you like.'

Her fingers found my pussy, two slipping inside.

'My bumhole too,' I urged, 'please, Zoe, darling.'

'Dirty bitch,' she said and a third finger touched me, tickling the little damp crevice of my anus.

I moaned, licking hard at her, my ecstasy rising. She responded, her fingers pushing well up my pussy and just a tiny bit deeper into my anus. I clutched her bottom, pulling her cheeks wide, lapping at her, revelling in her taste, my fingers probing at her. I touched her bumhole, and she tensed, briefly, but went loose.

'Do it, then,' she gasped, pulling up from my pussy. 'You want to, don't you?'

My finger went into her pussy, pulling out wet with juice. Again I touched her bumhole, watching entranced as the little ring slowly gave, opening to the pressure. I was sure she would be a virgin, and pushed gently, in, and out again, opening her. She began to sigh, then to

113

make her little purring noises again. I probed deeper, past her ring, into the hot, slimy cavity of her rectum.

'Dirty bitch,' she repeated, 'dirty, dirty bitch.'

'I'm going to lick it,' I moaned. 'I'm going to stick my finger right up, then put it in my mouth and lick it. I want to taste you, Zoe, while I make you come . . .'

I'd pushed my finger right up her bottom as I spoke, as far as it would go, pushing the little hole in. It was so hot up her, and so tight, and as I fingered her bum she tightened the hole, squeezing her ring.

'Do it,' she moaned, 'just do it, you dirty little bitch, Jade, you dirty, bum-licking bitch . . . Ah!'

She had gasped as my finger popped out of her bumhole. I put it in my mouth, straight in, sucking on it, tasting the rich, dirty flavour as my eyes feasted on the little hole I'd just been up. Only when my finger was thoroughly clean did I pull it out of my mouth and take hold of her bottom.

'I've done it, Zoe,' I panted. 'I've sucked my dirty finger. Now sit up, in my face, and let me do you.'

She went, riding my face, her beautiful bottom settling onto my head, my mouth wide on her pussy, my nose pressed to her wet hole. I began to lick and she giggled, squirming herself onto me to make my nose move in her anus.

'Now I know what they mean by brown nosing!' she giggled. 'Go on, then, make me come, Jade, in your face! This'll teach you to smack my bottom!'

She wiggled again, laughing as she spread her buttocks across my face, to get my nose just that little bit further up her bum. It was well up too, so far that I could feel the little ring splayed out on my nose tip, tightening as the first twinges of her climax began. She gasped, aloud.

'I'm nearly there,' she sighed, 'just lick, yes, like that. Come on, bitch, lick me, lick me out with your nose up my bumhole, oh, you dirty, little fucking bitch!'

She really screamed out the last word, coming full in my face, her bottom squirming, her anus tightening, her pussy too, her buttocks locking on my head, in one long, drawn-out climax. Her bum was pressed hard to my face, and for a moment I couldn't breathe, until she went suddenly forwards, burying her face in my pussy. Her school skirt fell down at that instant, covering my face in green tartan, with that and the pert curve of her bottom all I could see.

I lay back, my eyes fixed on the wet, juicy pussy I'd just licked, and on her open bumhole. She was licking me, right on my clitty, and I was going to come, at any second. My hands went to my boobs, feeling them through the cotton of my top, their plump curves pressed out under her tummy. They felt huge, as always when I'm really aroused, and as I started to come, the most wonderful fantasy hit me.

I'd be at Zoe's school, a girl with ridiculously large boobs, a girl who got picked on, teased, bullied. They'd have set on me, her and her friends, teased me until I'd lost my temper. I'd have tried to smack her, but they'd just have laughed. They'd grab me, tugging at my clothes, my hair. I'd fight, pathetically badly, and they'd grow bolder, throwing me on the ground, pulling down my big white knickers. Soon I'd be lying shivering on the ground, held down, with my fat boobs out and my legs held up to show off my equally fat bottom and pussy. Zoe would come to me, to squat over my head, so that I could see up her little tartan skirt. She'd pull off her panties, under her skirt, and toss them aside. She'd squat down, slowly, to the sound of the others' laughter as she lowered her pert, perfect bottom into my face. She'd reach back, spreading her bottom-cheeks, in front of all of them, showing off her bumhole, wrinkly and brown between her sweet cheeks, and I'd be forced to kiss it . . .

I did, pulling my head up at the exact moment I came, to plant a firm, wet kiss on Zoe's anus, before slumping back, writhing in the ecstasy of my orgasm, with the filthy, humiliating fantasy through my head, over and over. I screamed too, really loud, never for a moment thinking where I was.

We clung together for a moment, content, Zoe making her odd little purring noise, me with my head thrown back. I kissed her bottom one last time, to say thank you, and she rolled off, giggling. The computer was suddenly visible, and it was only then that I realised our entire dirty little sixty-nine had been captured on video. We played it back, giggling together at what we'd done, with our arms around each others backs.

'I was right,' she said emphatically as the last shot appeared, 'you really are a dirty bitch!'

'Do you always get so rude when you're coming?' I demanded.

'Too many dirty stories off the net, I'm afraid,' she laughed. 'I love all that. It scares the boys too.'

'I'll bet it does.'

She began to undress, casually, peeling off her clothes. I watched, until she was nude, with the precious uniform a pile of cotton on the floor.

'Could I borrow that?' I asked.

'My uniform?'

'Yeah. The girl I was telling you about, Sam, would just love to have me in it.'

'Is she your girlfriend?'

'Not really, no, but I've got a date with her next week.'

'Go ahead, just stick it in a plastic bag so Mum and Dad don't see it.'

'Thanks, Zoe.'

After that it was simple, laughably simple. Zoe changed into casual clothes, sticking her bra and panties into the laundry basket. I asked if she'd mind making a coffee. As soon as she was out of the door I was at the computer. It took moments to send myself and Uncle

Rupert the images of me spanking her, and as the message disappeared into cyberspace I had a wonderful vision of him downloading them in front of Sarah. That done, I retrieved Zoe's bra and panties and stuck them in with the uniform. When she came back with the coffee I was sitting innocently at her computer.

Six

Zoe and I had swapped numbers, and I'd been fighting down my guilt as I kissed her goodbye. Not that it was too hard, because I was well pleased with myself. On the way back to my flat I retrieved my mail, with the gorgeous pictures and no less than five replies to my ads. Three were from men, including some foreign guy who wanted to keep me in a cell and feed me on his spunk. The fourth was just meaningless drivel, and the fifth from Andrea, hoping I'd recovered and that I'd like to play again soon. I replied to Andrea and deleted the rest.

What I wanted to do most of all was go and show Zoe's school uniform off to Uncle Rupert. I couldn't, not with Sarah there, which made for a very frustrating Saturday night. I did at least wash and iron the uniform, ready for its place in the collection. It was a good one, maybe the best. After all, Zoe's sixth-form college was small, so it was rare, even if schoolgirls as such aren't. It was traditional too, and formal, although it didn't score too highly on the risk front. More importantly, when it comes to spanking fantasies, there is no image so popular as the British schoolgirl. In fact, Rupert's collection of spanking literature probably contained more images and stories with schoolgirls in them than all the others put together. The collection would simply not have been complete without a schoolgirl's uniform, and I had got it. Even more importantly, Rupert was very unlikely to have succeeded himself.

I waited until after ten on the Sunday night before phoning him, certain that by then he would have put Sarah on her train. Sure enough, he was there, alone, and full of questions about the mysterious picture that had arrived showing me with a genuine schoolgirl across my knee. I explained, listening to his little exclamations of pleasure and envy with growing delight. In the end he said he would come over and collect me, unable to wait to see the uniform and get it onto his mannequin.

An hour later I was there, admiring the finished product, complete with photograph. He was jealous, but pleased too, while I was thoroughly happy. Despite that, there was a change in the atmosphere between us, which I was painfully aware of. He seemed a tiny bit reserved, or at least uncertain, and as we swapped stories he kept his hand firmly away from his crotch. That wasn't good enough, not when the description of me spanking Zoe should have been enough to have him wrestling with his fly. He knew he could take it out in front of me, and I wanted him to do it, Sarah or no Sarah.

'Are you going to wank, or not?' I demanded, breaking off.

'I . . . I'm not –' he began.

'Don't spoil it, Rupert,' I broke in. 'I know you and Sarah are in love, but don't spoil it for me.'

'I wouldn't, Jade,' he said quickly. 'You know that.'

'Prove it to me, then; get your cock out. I'll wank it for you. No, I'll suck you, willingly. I'll do it properly, on my knees in front of you, with everything showing. I remember you saying that's how a girl ought to suck a man's cock, bare and kneeling.'

He swallowed, looking ashamed for one moment before nodding acquiescence. I stood, my hands going to the button of my jeans, looking into his eyes for the slightest spark of doubt. All I got was lust, his eyes glued to my body. I popped the button, pushed them down, knickers too, baring myself to him. My top followed, pulled high over my boobs, and my bra, so that I was showing, from chest to knees, without a stitch.

His cock was out, lying pale and flaccid on his lap, ready for my mouth. I came close, feeling a strong sense of reconciliation as I got down on my knees, as if by the act of sucking his cock I was reaffirming the strength of our relationship. He might be in love with Sarah, but that didn't mean he was going to reject our friendship. He was letting me perform a truly intimate act with him, so I could be sure of that.

The time before I'd just let him stick it in, fucking my head more than having his cock sucked. This time was different, very much me attending to his cock, and for me a very submissive act. After all, I was near nude, and on my knees, while he was fully dressed save for his cock and balls.

I suppose Sarah had drained him, because it took ages to get him erect, sucking and licking at his cock, his balls too, and using my hands as well to tickle his sack and masturbate him into my mouth. He did respond, in the end, but only after taking a break so that he could move a squat mirror into a position that let him admire my bare bum as I sucked him.

That worked, with his eyes glued to the rude reflection in the mirror as I sucked on him, his cock now growing, and quickly reaching full erection. Soon he was stroking my hair, his breathing getting faster, until at last he came, full in my mouth. I swallowed it, gagging on the disgusting, slimy taste, but knowing it was what girls were expected to do, what Sarah did, and so what I ought to do to.

The first thing I got at work on Monday morning was Sam demanding that we fix a date, on the Friday. I agreed, a little awed by her urgency to have me, but flattered too. She also demanded to know if I'd been spanked over the weekend, and to inspect my bottom. I was due on, and a bit tense, so I tried to refuse, but she made me anyway. Fortunately Zoe hadn't marked me, while the older bruising was fading fast. Sam had a quick feel and told me to put it away, declaring that I'd be ready for Friday.

So I knew I was going to get a whacking, all week. I love that, the awful sense of apprehension when I know I'm going to be punished. The best is when I know exactly when and exactly what, so that I can work myself up into a real state. This was nearly as bad because, although there was no formal punishment scheduled for me, I knew Sam would be hard.

I could expect the tawse or perhaps a whip, probably while in bondage and probably with an audience to gloat over my exposure and pain. After the last occasion it was possible that she would tickle me, maybe even make me wet myself again, which was enough to set my jaw shaking every time I thought about it. What I was sure of was that she'd want me naked, or near naked, easily available and submissive.

So I took an extended lunch on the Thursday, shopping in Camden. I managed to get hold of a second-hand waspie corset in black leather, complete with D-rings. Having got that, it was impossible to resist some heavy-duty wrist cuffs, which more or less matched my doggie collar. Both were perfect, and on the Friday I hurried home to change in an absolute lather of expectation.

Bathed, powdered and scented, I put myself into my choice of gear. The corset was wonderful, taking my waist down to twenty inches, which I can only ever do just after my period. It made my boobs and bum look simply huge, exaggerated, with all of the helpless femininity I knew Sam liked. Thigh boots added to it, along with the wrist cuffs, collar and lead, leaving me covered in shiny black leather except for the bits she would want to get at. I felt vulnerable, female and above all sexual, which is me all through, so much so that I couldn't bear to spoil the effect with a bra. I even thought twice about panties, but there's feeling vulnerable and there's feeling unsafe, so I put on a tiny pair of black ones, telling myself I could take them off if I needed to.

I went out like that, in fetish gear, and topless under my coat, which added a delicious touch of naughtiness. When I met Sam I gave her a flash, in the street, and was pleased to see her eyebrows go up in surprise. Not that she'd exactly underdone it herself, what with black leather trousers and bra, brilliantly polished boots, shades, a black leather cap, even a whip at her belt. I was impressed, and when she took me by my lead I just melted.

She led me down Old Compton Street, where we'd met on the corner, to a gay men's pub, where she seemed to know half the people and got a really friendly reception. Like Whispers, it had a back room where the harder people could play, and at every moment I was expecting to be dragged in and thoroughly humiliated in front of an audience of gay men. I was sure they'd have found it funny, even if not sexy. That would have made it worse for me, and I thought it was what Sam intended, only for her to leave after our third drink, pulling me behind her.

Three bottles of Bud on top of the sandwich I'd snatched for tea already had me tipsy. I was enjoying being led through the streets on a lead immensely, with plenty of looks coming our way; shock, envy, disapproval, but mainly desire. Soho was busy, the streets crowded as the last of daylight gave over to the yellow glare of the lamps, with every type of person thronging the streets, and yet it was me who drew the attention.

Sam seemed not to notice, as cool as ever, no more concerned than if she'd been walking a dog.

We were going towards Whispers, and for a moment I thought she might have managed to get me back in, only for her to stride past, turning up into Wardour Street. There was a crowd of girls outside Sugar Babe's, and as we passed I caught my name, shouted out in excitement. I turned, finding Zoe hurrying across the road. Sam stopped, her dark eyes travelling slowly down Zoe's body. Zoe kissed me, and threw Sam a nervous, admiring glance.

'Jade, hi,' she said. 'You look . . . wow! Better than in my uniform, any day! This is . . .'

'Sam,' I supplied. 'Sam, this is Zoe.'

'Baby dyke?' Sam asked casually.

'Baby baby,' I said. 'She's seventeen.'

'Shh!' Zoe hissed. 'We're having enough trouble as it is. The girls on the door don't reckon my friend looks eighteen. I told her to lose the Telly Tubby top!'

'Does she lick cunt?' Sam asked.

'Does she . . . does . . .?' Zoe stammered. 'Yeah, she does . . . she has.'

'Yours?'

'Yes,' Zoe managed, her face flushing crimson in the light.

Sam pulled at my lead, twisting it around a lamppost and clipping it off on my collar. Four quick paces took her across the road, to where a huge woman with a shaved head was standing foursquare in front of the door to Sugar Babe's. Sam pushed through the crowd, spoke a quick word to the woman and came back.

'You're in,' she told Zoe, 'but if Angie wants to take you in the loos, don't turn her down.'

'Er . . . thanks,' Zoe managed, throwing a seriously worried look at the massive Angie. 'You coming?'

'No,' Sam answered. 'Another time, babe.'

She had unclipped my lead, and tugged on it, pulling me away to leave Zoe looking after us.

'Couldn't we go?' I asked. 'Zoe's cool. You could have us both. Maybe her friends too.'

'Another time,' Sam answered me.

'Oh, come on, Sam –'

'Shut up,' she interrupted, 'unless you want a whipping in front of your little baby dyke friends.'

'In Sugar Babe's? Great, let's do it!'

'In the street, you slut. With men watching, and I'll make sure your cunt gets a good airing.'

'You wouldn't dare, not even you!'

'Want to try me?'

'No, Sam . . . I'm sorry. Where are you taking me, then?'

'You'll see,' she answered.

She had me puzzled. After getting Zoe and her friends into Sugar Babe's she could have been on a roll. Zoe would have been up for it, quite likely her friends, and I'd have helped. Sam could have ended up with three girls to take back to her flat, maybe four, as I wasn't sure how many friends Zoe had been with. Just the thought of it should have been irresistible – I mean, she could have had us bent over in a line, bare bottomed, hands tied behind our backs, or anything. I was amazed she'd turned down the chance.

Not only that, but we were getting out of Soho. We crossed Oxford Street, moving on into the quieter roads beyond, with only a few late workers about and clusters of drinkers outside the pubs. I began to feel more conspicuous, with fewer people around who were cool about the way we were dressed. People had started to laugh, the women sniggering, the men cracking coarse comments. I started to wonder if Sam had some really appalling humiliation planned for me, perhaps sending me on as a stripper in some sleazy bar, or even carrying out her threat to whip me in public. She walked on, indifferent to other people, angling through the streets until she came into a cobbled alley, where she stopped.

'What's here?' I asked, wondering, and hoping, that one of the rear basements of the buildings beside us would prove to be some leather dyke drinking dive.

'This,' she said, patting the boot of the old blue BMW she was sitting against, even as its door opened.

Naomi got out, grinning at me. She had something in her hand, and it took me a moment to realise what it was, a sack. An instant later Sam had wrenched my coat down, exposing my bare boobs to the street. I squealed in shock but shut up as Naomi pushed a ball gag into my mouth, Sam quickly fastening it tight behind my neck. My coat was pulled off, panic rising up as I found myself showing just about everything. I struggled, trying to make them stop before someone came. They didn't care. Sam caught my arms, twisting them hard behind my back, to clip my lead catch onto one D-ring, then the other.

Then it was the sack, tugged down over my head, right down. Naomi tripped me, and I went down hard on my bum, my breath knocked out through my nose. Sam caught hold of my legs, Naomi holding the sack wide, and they were stuffed up into it. For one awful moment my bum was stuck out to the street, with nothing but the tiny thong of my panties to cover me. Sam slapped it, laughing, and I heard the click of the car boot as the neck of the sack was pulled tight around my feet.

I was lifted, and dumped in the boot, hard. The sack was lashed off around my ankles, tight, to leave me trussed up, like a chicken, with my legs up to my chest and my arms behind my back, utterly helpless. I tried to mumble through the gag, babbling questions. They ignored me, slamming the boot to turn partial darkness into absolute black. I lay panting, in shock, wondering what was in store for me.

'Neat,' Sam commented, her voice faint but clear enough. 'I said no one would see us if we did it here.'

'Good place,' Naomi agreed. 'What are you going to do now?'

'Go to Sugar Babe's,' Sam replied. 'Dumplings just introduced me to the sweetest little thing, real kitten. Seventeen but licks cunt, her friends too. Big Angie and I are going to see if we can't share a couple. Join us, there's enough to go around.'

'I will if I can. Better go, then.'

I heard them kiss, and the click of Sam's boots on the cobbles. The car door opened, slammed, and the engine started. I lay trembling, wild thoughts running through my head, of being made a permanent slave. I'd be chained up in a cellar somewhere, and abused by Sam and her friends, or sold to some horrible man, maybe like the one who'd replied to my ad, to be kept in a cell and fed on spunk. Silly, maybe, but not so silly when you're tied up in the boot of a car with a ball gag in your mouth and no way of even talking to anybody.

Naomi drove slowly through the London traffic, turning repeatedly, until I had no idea where we were or even how far we'd gone. I couldn't see, I couldn't speak, I could barely move, and I could hear only the rumble of engines and occasional voices. It was too much. Soon I was near panic, the tears welling in my eyes as I tried to fight down the urge to struggle. It nearly got me, and I was wriggling stupidly in the sack and panting hard through my nose, before I managed to calm down, telling myself that it was just a game, that they wouldn't really hurt me, that I'd taken what they liked to dish out before, and that I could do it again.

I was sure it was true, but a nasty little voice in the back of my head kept telling me otherwise, and it wouldn't go away. Sam thought nothing of ruining my clothes. They stripped me with men looking on. They'd pushed my head down a toilet and made me lick bum, again with a mixed audience. That had been in a club. This was going to be private.

All that ran through my head, telling myself I'd be okay, and wondering if I really would, round and round. So many times I'd fantasised about being in the same situation, or one like it, bound helpless at the mercy of some really cruel girl gang. Now I was, and I didn't know if I was excited or terrified, whether I wanted to burst into frightened tears or masturbate myself dizzy.

Not that I could masturbate anyway, with my body strapped up the way it was. I couldn't even move inside the sack, because it was tied around my ankles. My bum was pushed out against it, so that the coarse material was pulled tight over my pussy-lips, with just the flimsy panties to protect me. My boobs were against it too, scraping on my nipples every time I moved, to keep them in a state of furious, agonising erection. It was turning me on, but it hurt too, and that wasn't all. My bladder was beginning to feel tight.

That was really going to be the last straw, if I wet myself. It was going to happen too, if Naomi didn't stop soon, and then when she opened the boot she'd find me lying in a pool of pee. It couldn't happen, it really couldn't. My corset would be ruined, my boots too, never mind the way they'd laugh at me and the awful shame of peeing in my panties. It would look awful, and I could just see the wet bum shape I'd make against the sack when I'd done it.

I hung on, telling myself that it couldn't be far, that wherever I was going had to be in London. I hoped it was anyway, because otherwise it didn't bear thinking about. I did anyway, imagining myself delivered to some lonely house in the country, or a Parisian brothel, to be made into a pony-girl, or used as a speciality for perverts into rubbing themselves off between girls' boobs.

It had to be wrong. Naomi had said she might make it back to Sugar Babe's before closing time, which gave her . . . six hours odd, enough to get to Birmingham and back, and would leave me in pissy panties for certain, maybe worse. That really was too much, imagining her undoing the sack to find me with a disgusting lumpy bulge in the back of my panties, and the tears began to squeeze from my eyes.

We took a bump, unexpectedly, and it nearly did happen. My bladder stabbed with pain as I forced myself not to let go, and again as we took another bump. I shut my eyes, starting to blubber as I realised I was going to have to let go, and then we were slowing, turning, and the car had come to a halt. I was panting with relief, immediately, breathing hard through my nose, in pain, but sure I could hold on. Naomi would be sweet and let me do it before subjecting me to whatever they had planned – even if it was just on the ground with my knickers held aside, she had to.

I heard the car door again, and Naomi's footsteps. The boot came open, and immediately I was mumbling through the gag, trying to push it up with my tongue and speak at the same time.

'You what? You've peed your panties?' she asked. 'You're going to? Not in my car, you don't, girl!'

She bent, grunting as she lifted me, and catching my hip on the boot. I gulped in pain, and so nearly let go, but held on, my toes wiggling in desperation and my tummy muscles clenching and unclenching.

'Hold it in, Jade,' Naomi instructed. 'Don't your dare piss down me!'

I tried to speak, to tell her to put me down, to undo the sack, to just let me squat for a moment.

'Shh!' she urged. 'You'll spoil the surprise! Hold it, and I'll put you over a drain.'

I tried to thank her, muttering gratefully through the gag, over and over, keeping my muscles tight, the pain growing, but now sure I could make it. She put me down, on something, the bonnet of the car, I think. I heard a metallic groan, a clang. I was lifted again, a little way, and put down, with the welcome shape of a metal drain grid pressed to my thighs. Naomi's fingers went to the ropes around my ankles and the sack, pulling at them, only to let go, with me still tied.

She had stepped back, away from me. I felt a new pang of fear and frustration, scared she'd been teasing me and was going to leave me to wet on the floor. I tried to speak again, pleading, but stopped in surprise as my ankles started to lift. My legs went up, with me wriggling in confusion, lifted, my shoulders and head dragging along the ground, then clear. I was hanging, upside down, by my bound ankles, on the end of a rope, pulled higher, and higher still. I started to panic, wriggling in my bag, thrashing my body from side to side.

'Hey, hey, calm down, Jade,' Naomi chided. 'We're just having a bit of fun with you, that's all. There's no need to get in a state.'

It was easy for her to say. She wasn't hung upside down in a bag, about to piss herself. It calmed me down though, a little, enough to stop struggling anyway.

'Done,' she said. 'See you later, Dumplings.'

She gave my bottom a smack and a moment later I heard the same metallic noise as before. Then there was nothing, just darkness and my fear, building very quickly back towards panic.

A bell rang. I heard footsteps, voices, too faint to make out, more footsteps. Someone was coming, and I was so grateful. I didn't care what they did to me, just so long as I had company, anything other than hanging upside down in the darkness, alone, with my ankles burning and my bladder a hard ball of pain in my belly. Again there was silence.

I hung, listening, fighting down my pain and desperation, biting my lip. The car's engine sounded, starting with a cough, then fading. Naomi had left, maybe with whoever else was there with her. Blood was going to my head, making me dizzy and faint. Much longer, and I'd pass out. The panic started again, worse, my teeth chattering, my mouth coming open and shut in little spasms, my bladder twitching, the first drops of pee spurting into my panties as the tears burst from my eyes . . .

A door opened, close to me, and shut. I heard footsteps, different, the sharp click of high heels on stone. It was a woman, and the relief that flooded through me at that pushed everything else to the side. I hung still, waiting. She spoke.

'A present? How sweet. And wrapped too.'

I recognised the voice immediately. It was AJ, the woman who'd made me show my smacked bottom to a crowded bar, the woman who'd made me lick her anus in public. New feelings started, fear, but very different from before, focussed, on my body. I mumbled out a plea to untie me.

'It talks,' she said. 'A girl, I hope. Just what I wanted. Now, where's that knife?'

I heard clicks, a metallic grating. She took hold of the sack. Bright light appeared, and a knife blade, cutting at the rough material. I stayed still, trying to calm my shivering, the blade inches from my boots, then from my bare skin as she cut round. The slash widened, showing more light as my body slowly uncurled, as if I was a butterfly squeezing out of a chrysalis. The sack fell away, to leaving me hanging, head down, my face a few inches above a concrete floor and the grate of a drain. Above me a bare light bulb glared into my eyes, showing the concrete floor, a workbench, bits of motorbike, greasy cloths, a garage. AJ stood over me, the knife in her hand, in boots, knickers and bra, all black leather.

'Well, if it isn't Dumplings!' she said. 'And in such a state. There's no need to cry, little one; your make-up will run.'

Again I tried to speak, to tell her how urgent I was, to beg to be let down. She smiled down at me, pretending to cock her ear so that she could hear my desperate mutterings.

'Let you down? But sure I'll let you down. Soon enough.'

She stepped away, ignoring my choking pleas, my frantic wriggling. My belly was twitching, the corset crushing my flesh, and suddenly I just couldn't hold it any more. My bladder gave, my panties flooded, soaking, until they could hold no more, and pee began to bubble out of the front. AJ laughed, her eyes glittering in pleasure to see my wetting. I couldn't stop it, or my tears, which were running down from my eyes as my pee bubbled up through my panties, to run down over my belly and between the cheeks of my bum.

It was spurting through the material of my panties, little jets bursting out in time to my frantic breathing. It was in my bumhole, soaking the back of my knickers, running down my crease and into my corset. From the front my knickers were running with it, the stream parting across the low bulge of my belly, to drip down, onto my overturned boobs and into my face.

AJ watched as I urinated over myself, her face set in a truly demented glee. Still it came, rising out of my panty crotch in a little fountain, to run down, front and back. My knickers were sodden, my corset ruined, my boobs wet, with drips hanging from my upside down nipples. Some had even gone in my mouth, around the gag, up my nose too, and my hair was hanging in a slowly expanding puddle, half blocking the drain as my piddle dripped off me.

At last it stopped. Or it stopped coming out anyway. My body was soaked, the soggy panties clinging to my flesh, my belly and boobs dripping, my hair utterly soiled. As for my face, my make-up had run, with tears and trickles of pee, and I knew I would look a real state.

The pain was gone, though, and amid the chaos of shame and dizziness and misery in my head was a relief so strong. I'd given in. I'd surrendered, piddling myself, and it was impossible not to feel better.

'Pretty,' AJ said. 'Do you have any more?'

I shook my head frantically.

'Pity,' she went on. 'Still, I could make you drink a little water, say a gallon, and watch the show again in an hour or so.'

Again I shook my head, harder, sending a spray of pee droplets out around myself in a halo.

'No?' she queried. 'Perhaps not. After all, what would I do while I waited? How about an enema, then? Into your panties. Now that would be messy.'

She laughed, because I was thrashing crazily on the hook, pleading with my eyes and struggling to get the words out through my gag.

'What if I touched you up while I did it?' she said, her hand reaching out to squeeze the soggy material over my pussy and the plump mound beneath.

My muscles twitched, my pussy responding despite myself. Her finger pressed into the groove between my sex-lips, rubbed. I twitched again. She tugged my panty crotch aside, her finger moving to the wet mush of my pussy, and up into my vagina. For a moment she fingered me, stopped, pulled it out with a wet sound, and squatted down. The finger went to my nose. I smelt my pussy, my pee too, and saw the glistening wet on her skin. She smiled, and casually wiped it in my face.

She rose. My soggy knickers were twitched up to my thighs and knotted off, tight, to hang dripping down onto my flesh. She stepped away, walking to the workbench, her long legs elegant, her pace unhurried, her slim bottom moving in the leather knickers, taunting me with her freedom. At the bench she reached up to a shelf, taking down a grease gun. She came back, holding it, here eyes fixed on mine. I was shaking, my head swimming and light.

Her fingers came down, pushing in between my bottom-cheeks, parting them, until my anus was showing. She flicked at the little hole, splashing away the pee which had collected in it. The nozzle touched me, the hard metal pushed against my sensitive flesh. Cold grease squirted out, up my bumhole, filling the dimple, coiled on top. She let go, withdrawing the nozzle. My cheeks closed, the grease squashing out between them, leaving my hole lubricated and ready.

Again AJ went to the bench. She took a tube, an old fuel line, cutting each end. Three quick paces took her back to me. Once more my bum-cheeks came apart. Up went the tube, into my greasy anus, slid deep. She nodded, thoughtfully, and left the garage.

My head was swimming, the blood singing in my ears. I could feel it, all of it, the cool air on my bare skin, the pee still dripping from my body, the tube up my bum. It didn't matter. It seemed distant, unimportant. I was going to faint, I was sure of it, at any moment.

AJ came back, almost skipping, grinning like a schoolgirl. There was a bottle in her hand, transparent plastic, showing water and bubbles within. She stopped, legs wide, looking down into my face as she took the tube, put the bottle to it, forcing the nozzle into the end. She licked her lips, grinning maniacally, and squeezed the bottle.

I felt it spurt cold in my rectum, bubbling into me, air and water. She turned the bottle up, squeezing harder. More went up. I felt myself start to bloat, my belly swelling, uncomfortable, pressing to my tight corset. Her mouth was open in sheer joy, her eyes on my face, my sex, and back. Again she squeezed, the last of the water gurgle into my bottom.

She dropped the bottle, snatching at my panties to pull the knot loose, settling them over my bum and pussy, cold and wet. Her hands went to my sex, one pulling my panty crotch aside, the other tugging the tube from my anus. As it popped out an awful, frantic desperation hit, me, my anus clenching to keep the fluid in. I was wriggling, struggling on my hook, my muscles jerking and twitching, my head back, her boots faint though a film of red.

Her fingers found my pussy, dabbing, full on my clitty. I felt my vagina close and heard her laughter. A finger went up my pussy, a second. The feel on my clitty changed, her firm tongue tip applied right to the bud. I was going to come, I couldn't stop it, or anything else. She had me, my body totally beyond my control. My sex was going into spasm, my back arching, my bumhole opening. My enema erupted into my panties, and I was coming, writhing and thrashing on my hook. My boobs were slapping together, pee spraying everywhere, hot dirty water running down my bum-crease and up my pussy, bubbling in the hole, spurting out as I contracted again, my brain ready to burst ...

It went, everything, my senses failing, my body unable to cope with what was being done to me. The next thing I felt was a shock of cold on my face. I couldn't see, and could feel only the concrete beneath me, on which I was lying, no longer on the hook. I came round, gagging and coughing, only slowly becoming aware of what was going on. I no longer had the ball gag in, my hands were free and my boots were off.

The shock of cold came again, and my eyes came open. I was on the garage floor, over the drain, with AJ standing over me, her thumb on the end of a hose. She smiled as I looked up, and let the hose go, full against my leg.

'Better get those knickers off,' she said, flicking the hose down to spray my bum.

I nodded, suddenly aware of the heavy, soggy feeling in the seat of my panties. Pulling myself painfully up onto my knees, I lifted my bum towards AJ. It didn't matter what she saw, what I did in front of her. I was too far gone to care. Reaching back, I peeled down my panties. The hose caught me immediately, full between my buttocks, then lower, into my panty pouch. I let her do it, washing my bum-crease and pussy with it all spread in front of her, sharing an intimacy I only find possible under another woman's command.

Even when she put the hose to my bumhole I didn't flinch, letting her fill my rectum with water and expelling it down the drain. Even that didn't get to me, with my bumhole spurting water right in front of her. I just felt too detached, too dependent on her.

With my bum washed, she did the rest of my body, finishing with me in a squat as she ran the hose over my hair. By then I was utterly bedraggled, like a drowned rat, with my hair plastered over my face and down my back, my elaborate make-up gone, and my insides feeling strangely empty. I was shivering too, and hugging my body as the cold water cascaded over my limbs.

AJ stopped, twisting the hose off at the tap. Without a word she came to take my lead. I followed, padding barefoot after her, out of the garage, into her house and upstairs. In the bathroom, she stood watching as I peeled off my corset and cuffs to go nude, towelled myself down and took a badly need drink of water.

'Better?' she asked.

I nodded, still a little faint, and stiff, but nothing worse. She settled herself against the door post, a coquettish pose, easier than when she'd been with her friends. So was her outfit, sexier, more vamp and less diesel. I wondered if she'd changed for me, or if she just wore leather to bed.

'Good,' she went on, 'then you can make me come.'

Again I nodded. She lifted a finger, beckoning me. I went down, to my knees, my eyes fixing on the tight V of her crotch, where the soft leather had pulled into the groove of her pussy. She stepped forwards, and I opened my mouth, wondering if she'd pull down her short pants, or make me do it through the leather. She walked past me, patting my head, to the loo.

I watched, my heartbeat once more starting to pick up, as she casually pushed down the leather panties, her bum almost in my face. Lifting the seat, she sat down, knees cocked apart, panties in a tangle around her ankles. I crawled forwards, my mouth coming wide.

'Not that. Not yet,' she ordered. 'Lick my boots.'

I went down, catching the scent of her pussy, from her, then from her panties as I put my face down at her feet. There was a soft plop from above me as my lips puckered out, kissing one shiny toe cap.

'Remember Betty's?' she asked as I began to lick. 'How I made you lick my bum in the toilet? Didn't the men just hate it? Every one of them had a hard on, I'll bet, and I bet they thought they were going to get them up you too, maybe even up me. We didn't let them, though, did we, darling?'

I shook my head, busy with her boots. She reached down, to gently stroke my hair. There was another plop, and the tinkle of pee in the bowl.

'They saw, though, didn't they?' she went on. 'Your pussy, everything. Have you been fucked? By a man, I mean?'

I nodded, thinking of kneeling in mingled disgust and rapture as my last boyfriend had jammed his cock clumsily in and out of my pussy from the rear, one hand on my bottom, the other clutching a can of lager. My top had been off, my jeans and panties around my knees, in a railway siding, somewhere near the Arsenal football ground. It had been the last time.

'Slut,' AJ said. 'That's enough. Now polish, with your hair.'

She lifted a foot. I bent down, taking a hank of hair in my hands to rub it over the moist black surface. My mouth was full of the taste of boot polish and leather, my tongue sticky and sour.

'You called me a bitch, too, didn't you?' she asked.

'Sorry, Miss AJ,' I managed.

'I should punish you, really,' she went on.

'I'm ready for whipping,' I said softly. 'Sam made sure.'

'I'll bet you are. I'll bet you'd love it too. Right, I'm ready. Stop.'

I sat back, my hair sticky with saliva and polish, my lower lip trembling. She stood, closing the seat beneath her, turning, bending down to lean on the lavatory bowl, her bottom pushed out, looking back. Her cheeks were wide, her tiny brown bumhole moist and slimy, her pussy on plain show, with the little silver rings hanging down, each with its drip of milky pee. I swallowed, hard, poked out my tongue, shut my eyes and pushed my face into her bottom crease.

'Good girl,' she sighed as my tongue found her bottom hole. 'That's right. Clean it up, properly.'

I was already licking, my mouth full of her earthy musk, the taste of female bottom filling my senses. She pushed it out, firm against my face, moaning. I took her by the thighs, licking hard, burrowing my tongue right up her bottom, until the root hurt. It had been good in the toilets at Betty's. Now it was better, more intimate, ruder, with me cleaning her bum for her, on my knees, with what she'd done still in the loo beneath us.

Nor were there any men watching. I reached up, took her bra and flipped it up over her titties, still licking. My thighs came apart, wide, my hand going to my pussy. I began to rub, slowly, taking myself, my aches fading as my pleasure rose. AJ had one hand on her boobs, the other supporting herself, her bottom pushed well back.

I went lower, kissing the drops of pee away from her sex-lips and her rings, sucking at her clit. She cried out, softly, and I pressed my face in, licking her, with my nose in her bumhole, just as I had to little Zoe. There had been others too, many others, only not as a toilet

137

slave, not after being so cruelly treated, brought down to my knees, nude and abused, brown-nosing my mistress in utter, grovelling submission.

Her fingers came back, pushing at my face. I obeyed, going higher, my mouth wide over her sloppy bumhole, licking, probing, sucking. She was coming, her breathing rising, deep and strong, moaning, gasping as I licked at her. I was rubbing hard too, clutching at my sex as the orgasm tore through her, her bottom hole tightening on my tongue, going slack once more, and I was coming too.

It was beautiful, wonderful, utterly and totally submissive. As I came the whole evening ran through my head, kidnap, the sack, being hung upside down from that awful hook, peeing all over myself, the enema in my panties, spurting out as I was brought to orgasm. It really hit me, so hard my vision went red again and I felt my senses starting to slip, so dirty that at the very highest peak I was wishing she'd just let go, and fill my mouth.

I slept with AJ, cuddled up to her in her bed. It had been good, wonderful, and I was still on my submissive high in the morning, for all my aches and pains. My corset wasn't ruined after all, which made me happier still, and I found my coat, hung up in the garage.

Not that I was entirely happy, because while I didn't mind being put in a sack and given to AJ as her birthday present, which was what I was, I did resent being kidnapped. It had really scared me, and it hadn't been necessary, when I'd have happily gone along with it anyway. It wasn't really AJ's fault, and I was more than happy to spend the Saturday as her slave, and the Sunday too if she wanted.

The morning was lazy, with me padding about in the nude, making her breakfast and kissing her pussy after she'd been for her morning pee. I did get a spanking, across her knee in the kitchen, but only enough to leave my bum glowing warmly, and in the mood for more.

She seemed indecisive, not sure what to do with me, until noon, when she suddenly ordered me to dress. I put on what I'd had before, with no choice, except for a pair of her panties in place of mine, which really were beyond hope. She, meanwhile, got into full leathers, and when she passed me a crash helmet from a peg by the door I realised why.

Her motorbike was outside, a big, black shiny thing, which looked huge and powerful, although I wouldn't know one from another. It was actually a bit scary, but I got on it anyway, behind her, clinging on for dear life and hoping that my coat wouldn't blow up to show off my panty-clad bum.

We'd been in north-west London, Kingsbury, although for all I knew it might have been Kingston, or anywhere else for that matter. I needed to change, so I asked if we could drop in at my flat. By the time we got there I was feeling more resentful than ever. One thing was clear, which was that Naomi had taken an unreasonably long time to get there, even allowing for the Friday evening traffic, and I began to wonder if they hadn't planned to have me wet myself all along. After all, Sam had bought three beers in Soho, which hadn't really been necessary if they'd just wanted to kidnap me, and Naomi had refused to hold me in a squat when she could perfectly well have done so.

There were other things, too – my spoiled bra, getting thrown out of Whispers, having my bum inspected in front of a load of leering men. I am submissive, and I like to be bullied by stronger, bigger girls, but within my own boundaries, and they were really pushing it, especially Sam.

Not that I wanted to miss out on my fun, and AJ seemed content with me as hers alone. I made her a coffee and changed, with her choosing what I was going to wear. Knowing her, I expected something revealing, certainly submissive, and was surprised when she went for a pair of perfectly ordinary white panties, a plain bra, my combats and a green top. It was more or less what I'd been wearing when I first met her, and nothing to raise an eyebrow anywhere. I did as I was told anyway, and was soon back on her bike, feeling a lot less conspicuous and not nearly as sexy.

We drove back towards the west, stopping in Southend Green, where AJ made me pay for beers and some ready-cooked chicken, which we carried with us up to Hampstead Heath. As I'd guessed, Sam and Naomi were already there, and so was Zoe. They already had everything spread out, both food and booze, on a patch of grass well sheltered by bushes and a little rise of ground.

Zoe was in great spirits, chattering eagerly to me as the others crowded round AJ. Sam had picked her up, one of her friends as well. They'd gone back, with Naomi too, and got what I'd suggested myself, their hands tied behind their backs with their trousers and panties down while they were beaten. Her friend had taken it, but not too well, and had ended up being put in a cab to her parents' house. Zoe had stayed, calling home to say she was with friends, which she thought was immensely funny.

I told her my own story, which she listened too with increasing wonder, gasping at all the right moments, and her face screwing up in disgust when I told her I'd licked AJ's bum clean.

'Too dirty for me,' she said. 'I'll kiss it, yeah, but not like that!'

'Kiss what?' Naomi demanded, as she approached.

'Another girl's bottom hole,' I told her.

'Sometimes you've just got to do what you're told,' Naomi said. 'Like now. Strip, both of you, down to your panties.'

'Here?' Zoe demanded.

'Yeah, here,' Naomi said. 'Nobody's going to see. Not many anyway, and plenty of girls go topless on the Heath.'

'To sunbathe, in bikini bottoms, yes –' I began, Zoe glancing at me uncertainly.

'If you want to be with us, you do as you're told,' Naomi answered her. 'If you're going to be babies, fuck off home. What's it to be?'

I hesitated. Zoe and I shared another glance, and suddenly she had taken hold of her top and was peeling it off, revealing her little braless boobs beneath. I followed suit, not at all sure of myself, but not wanting to leave her to do it alone.

'Good girls,' Naomi said, 'and don't pout, Zoe. Count yourself lucky you'll still have your knicks on.'

I stripped quickly, still sitting, so that the long grass hid me. My feelings of resentment were boiling up again, but excitement too. Three dominant women, and we'd be serving them, topless in the open air. They'd be able to have us, too, taking turns in the bushes while the others kept watch, or making us do dirty things together in front of them.

Zoe was bare first, stripped to nothing but a tiny pair of bright pink panties, her socks and trainers. Her eyes were bright, moist too, and she was biting her finger nails as she glanced over to me. I reached out and squeezed her hand before pushing my combats down over my ankles.

'Very cute,' Sam remarked as I struggled a boot back on. 'Here we are, AJ, a pair of baby dykes in panties and boots. Don't they look sweet?'

There was a chorus of agreement, which brought the blood to my cheeks, Zoe's too. She stepped forwards though, really game, and made a curtsey to AJ. I followed suit, and we began to serve, opening beers and piling food onto plates, most of the time crawling or on our knees, while the girls sprawled in the grass.

It was impossible not to get horny, just because I was crawling around in nothing but my panties. Not just that, but as we served I was forever being presented with Zoe's beautiful little bottom, with just the pink panties to cover her cheeks. The material was caught up in the groove of her pussy too, which did look good. I was getting plenty of attention as well, and so was she. Again and again our bums would be slapped or pinched, or we'd be made to kneel up with our hands on our heads while our boobs were fondled, until both of us had damp patches between our legs.

Not surprisingly that got noticed, and commented on. Zoe got held down, her knickers pulled off and Sam's fingers pushed up her vagina. I was made to lick them, tasting her juices as she quickly scrambled back into her panties. The girls were drunk by then, and so were we, having sneaked at least our share of booze and food as we served. Even being topless didn't seem to matter much, and the only people we'd seen had been gay couples, who'd given us a wide berth.

It got ruder too, and drunker. Sam was getting really horny with Zoe, feeling her at every opportunity, kissing her too. Soon they were rolling together in the grass, mouths open with Sam's hands down Zoe's knickers, frigging her front and back. She made Zoe come, masturbating her, with a hand down the front of the little pink panties and two fingers up her pussy.

Zoe was so full of energy after that, completely drunk and really manic, crawling around with a big damp patch showing on the seat of her panties. She just didn't seem to care any more, and nor did I, really, not even bothering to resist as Naomi pulled me down into her arms.

She held me by the hair, fiddling with her trousers, and pushing them down one-handed. Her knickers came with them, baring her pussy, and as she rolled up her legs my face was pulled into her. I licked, urgently, eager, yet scared of getting caught. It didn't happen. She came in my face, a really strong orgasm, her teeth gritted in reaction as it hit her. That left me as wet as Zoe, and badly in need of an orgasm, if not quite such a public one. I was going to ask, only for AJ to get there first, declaring that it was her turn.

'Over here, both of you,' she ordered.

We went, crawling. Sam stood, to glance out from our hiding place, nodding the all clear as she came back. Immediately AJ undid her trouser button, scrambling over as she did it. The trousers came down, her knickers with them, and her bare bum was showing, ready for our tongues. We crawled closer, our flesh touching. I could feel Zoe's shivering and my own as we went down on AJ, kissing her bottom and thighs. She sighed with pleasure, and I kissed her bumhole, pushing Zoe's head lower.

The others watched as we licked and kissed at AJ's rear, Zoe on her pussy, me seeing to her bum. It didn't take long, with both of us rapt in our job; before I'd even really got the taste of it AJ was moaning, with her hole starting to pulse on my tongue. A moment later she came in our faces, immediately slumping down to pull up her trousers. I was wetter than ever, and desperately wanted to come, so I took Zoe in my arms, our bottoms still stuck out towards Sam and Naomi. She responded, kissing me, and we began to snog, her hands going to my boobs, mine to her bum.

'It looks like they've wet themselves!' Naomi laughed. 'Talk about sopping.'

'We should make them do it,' Sam laughed.

'No, we shouldn't,' Naomi crowed. 'I've got a better idea.'

I broke away from Zoe, suddenly nervous as Naomi rolled over towards what was left of the food. Taking some French bread, she pulled out the centre, piling it on a plate. I watched, still holding Zoe, in growing apprehension as she added tomatoes, paté and guacamole, mushing it up to make a revolting straw-coloured paste.

'You going to make them eat it?' AJ laughed.

'No,' Naomi answered.

'Do it!' Sam urged. 'Off each other's tits!'

'I've got a better idea,' Naomi said. 'Zoe, hold out the back of Jade's panties.'

I hesitated, realising what she was going to do, although my hands had gone instinctively to my bottom. Zoe didn't care, or she was too drunk to know what was going on. Giggling, she put her hands around my back, holding out the pouch of my knickers.

'Hands on head, Jade,' AJ ordered, 'or we'll just hold you down and do it anyway.'

Reluctantly, I obeyed, slowly lifting my hands as Naomi waded the disgusting-looking sludge into a rough ball. She picked it up, shuffling closer. I shut my eyes, my face screwed up. Her arm touched my side, and the wet, squashy ball of spoiled food was dropped down my panties.

'Let go, Zoe,' Sam ordered.

Zoe obeyed, my knicker elastic snapping back against my skin. Naomi pinched the seat of my knickers, pulling out the pouch to let the ball roll a little further down, right under the tuck of my bum, below the hole. I could feel it, hanging heavy in my panties, and I was imaging exactly how I'd look, and what people would think if they saw. Again Naomi's hand touched me, cupping the bulge in my panties and pressing, to squeeze the mess up between my cheeks and over my pussy. They were laughing, all of them, even Zoe, picking on me, and I could feel a great bubble of humiliation welling up inside myself.

Zoe came into my arms again, hugging me. I kissed her, just giving in, and stuck my bottom out, horribly aware of the weight in my panties and the laughter of the girls. They wanted to watch, to make me show off as if I'd loaded my panties, and I just couldn't stop myself. Zoe's mouth opened under mine. I held her to me, close, feeling our breasts press together. She responded, cuddling tighter, pulling me into her. I went, climbing on top of her, my bum stuck up high. Her arms were around my back, our mouths together. She broke away, suddenly.

'Spank her!' she giggled. 'Spank her hard!'

I squealed in protest, but Zoe's grip tightened, holding me into her. Sam laughed, smacking out at my bum, to catch one cheek. I gave a yelp of shock and pain, even as Naomi caught me around my waist. A hand caught in the back of my panties, pulling them hard up into my crease, the mess in them squelching out to the sides and over my pussy, even up the hole.

They just set on me, all four of them, Zoe holding me, still snogging me as the others beat me. It was hands first, smacking hard where my buttocks bulged out at either side of my filthy panties. I struggled and squealed, writhing in their grip, but to no avail, smack after smack landing on my defenceless bum until both cheeks were hot and smarting.

Zoe's leg had come up between mine, pushing to my sex. I remembered how I'd done her, spanking until she lost control and rubbed herself off on my leg in wanton lust. She was going to make me do the same, only with the three of them to punish me and a load in my panties, which I knew full well I'd be made to eat afterwards.

It hurt, a crazy stinging, with no respite, hands smacking hard at my bum, my thighs too. At some point they pulled off Zoe's trainers, using both of them on my poor bum and making the pain worse, far worse, until I was kicking my legs and yelling my head off. That was when my panties came off, tugged hard down my legs to leave the sticky mess plastered up my crease. They were forced into my mouth, mess and all. After that I couldn't squeal, but only make a pathetic mewling noise as they beat me to the sound of their drunken laughter and Zoe's shrieks of encouragement.

My pussy was now bare on Zoe's leg, her warm skin slimy with the food that had been smeared over my pussy. I was rubbing, not really knowing I was doing it, but jammed my sex onto her each time a new slap caught my burning bottom. They saw, and the smacks got harder, more rhythmic, Naomi holding me down, one other to each bum-cheek. The pain was driving me mad, out of control, the spanking coming in hard, heavy smacks to jolt my whole body and smack my pussy into Zoe's leg. I was shaking my head, writhing my bottom, then bucking it as my climax started and I could no longer stop myself, frigging with desperate energy on Zoe's thigh until it hit me. I screamed, the soggy panties erupting from my mouth, the smacks reaching a furious crescendo as I stopped, holding my pussy hard to Zoe's thigh, my mouth open, the red pain gone, in utter ecstasy, stripped, beaten and used, high on the sheer rapture of it.

That was it. As I collapsed they stopped, falling away, still laughing drunkenly. I was spent, utterly, indifferent to the mess of food smeared over my bottom, my mind dizzy, but held to the irony that only by my own utter degradation could I achieve such ecstasy. They'd made me strip to my knickers, made me serve them, had me lick them to order, made me pose as if I had a load of poo in my panties, and laughed at the sight. They'd beaten me, all four of them, even Zoe, younger and smaller than I was, choosing to torment me. What had I done in response? I'd come on Zoe's leg.

Still, it was me, and I do know myself, I like to think.

I just lay there, exhausted, my mind numb, until finally the bark of a dog nearby pulled me back to where I was. Rolling over to sit up, I quickly pulled my coat over my breasts.

'Relax,' Sam chided. 'Even if someone does come they'll have seen a pair of tits before.'

'Not mine,' I answered. 'It might be a man.'

'Who gives a fuck?' AJ put in. 'I used to strip, all the way. I'm a virgin, the way straights look at it. Did I care when I had my arse on show at Betty's?'

'You've got to get used to the way men look at you,' Naomi added. 'You mustn't let it get to you.'

'Easy for you to say!' I answered. 'You're really strong! Who's going to mess with you?'

'It's confidence, mainly,' Sam retorted. 'You've got to break out of your own fear. Drive a lorry through it.'

'How?' I demanded.

'Make yourself,' Naomi said.

'Walk back to the bike, with your top off,' Sam suggested.

'No way!'

'Just do it,' Sam urged.

They were teasing me – they had to be, I could tell by the tone of their voices. They were just trying to talk me into doing something stupid, to get a laugh out of me.

'I'm not going to do it,' I said.

'Yeah?' Sam queried. 'What if we take your top?'

She snatched out for it, pulling it in to her chest, my bra and trousers with it.

'Neat!' Naomi crowed. 'Make her do it in her boots and dirty panties!'

'That's not fair!' I wailed, snatching for my clothes.

Sam jerked them away, holding up a warning finger to my face. I drew back, biting my lip in frustration, with the tears already threatening to start in my eyes. Being toyed with sexually was one thing. Now they just wanted to make an idiot out of me.

'Bare tits in the street!' Sam taunted. 'Won't the boys love that!'

'And the dirty panties!' Naomi laughed. 'They'll think she's shit herself. Oh, that is good!'

'Please, Sam!' I begged. 'Please!'

'Be fair on her,' Zoe said. 'You can still get arrested for that stuff. In the street anyway.'

'No way!' Sam said, 'Not with just her tits out. A warning, tops.'

'Leave it,' AJ said. 'Too much chance of shit from the police.'

Sam went quiet, taking a pull from her bottle. I'd really thought they'd do it, and felt relief and gratitude well up inside me. AJ had real strength, and they followed her lead without question, making me wonder what else they did for her. For a moment there was quiet.

'I've got it,' Naomi said suddenly. 'Stuff her trousers like we did with her panties, and send her home like that, all the fucking way!'

My face must have gone red immediately, betraying my emotions. I looked round wildly for support. Naomi was grinning, Sam no better, Zoe looking worried, but more for herself than me. AJ had her bottle tilted up to her mouth, and her eyes gave nothing away behind her shades.

'AJ?' I asked.

'Yeah, let's do it,' AJ answered. 'What the fuck.'

I would have run, if I hadn't been stark naked. I'd have been caught anyway, but as it was they were on me in seconds, dragging me down. I struggled, furiously, but they were too strong, far too strong. They pinned me down in the grass, bum up, AJ holding my arms, Naomi on my legs. Laughing and shouting instructions to one another, they pulled off my boots. My panties were put back on, tugged up over my bum, the material cold and slimy. Sam got my combats, forcing one foot into them despite my desperate kicking, then the other. They were pulled up, all the way. They didn't bother with my top or bra, AJ and Sam just holding me as I writhed and thrashed in their grip.

148

It didn't stop them. My trousers and panties were held open at the back, and every single bit of food from the picnic stuffed down them, bread, tomatoes, paté, guacamole, olives, salad, cream cheese, margarine, bit by bit, to make a great lumpy, sodden mass. Before they'd finished I had stopped struggling. There was no point. It was down my panties. I was soiled.

Sam and AJ relaxed a little, but I didn't even try to get up. Naomi laughed as she put her hand down my trousers, and all I could do was screw my eyes up in defeat as she began to pulp it up into a thick paste. That done, she pushed it right down, under my bum, and between my cheeks, as if it had all come out of my hole. It felt awful, a huge bulge in the back of my trousers, straining against my dirty knickers. It was up my crease, and over my pussy, even in my vagina. They pulled me up, and I stood, unsteadily, grimacing, my eyes screwed up against the tears, feeling the awful, obscene weight in my trousers.

Zoe had run for it, probably scared that she'd get the same treatment, and I didn't blame her. Not that there would have been anything to stuff her panties with. It was down mine, all of it. They let go of me, and I reached back, touching it, finding a huge bulge in my trousers, ridiculously large. It felt realistic, squashy and warm against my skin. I was sure it looked realistic, except for the sheer volume of it. Nobody was going to question that, I was sure. It just made it horribly obvious, and they'd just assume I ate far too much and had had the most appalling accident as a result. Some of them would probably even think it served me right.

The girls had stood back, watching me and sniggering. Sam passed me my top and bra, which I put on, with my face set in what I knew had to be the most pathetic look of consternation ever. I couldn't help it though, with my tears beginning to well up in my eyes.

'You do look a sight!' Naomi chuckled, breaking the silence. 'That is so funny!'

'It's not,' I answered, trying to fight back the catch in my voice.

'Sure,' Sam answered, 'don't think we don't know your sort, Dumplings? We know you better than you know yourself. You'll be masturbating in it the moment you're home!'

I couldn't say anything, because I knew it was true. That didn't make it any better though, which is something dominants never ever seem to understand. Just because it arouses me doesn't make it any less humiliating for me. Worse, I knew I'd be back for more.

Not then, though. It was too much. At the realisation that Sam knew exactly what I was like I just burst into tears. She had my coat. I snatched it and ran, to the sound of their drunken laughter.

Seven

I couldn't face the journey home after being bullied on the Heath. With my coat on it didn't actually show, but the thought of sitting in the mess on the bus was unbearable. I needed some sympathy too, and the company of someone who didn't see me as an over-endowed sex toy. Fortunately I was in walking distance of Uncle Rupert's.

I'd been in such a panic that I'd run a good hundred yards before it dawned on me what I looked like. Having the huge bulge in the back of my combats looked awful, but running, with tears streaming down my face made it worse. There's not much dignity for a girl who's pooed in her panties, but throwing a tantrum over it loses the final shred.

Two people had seen me, and both were staring, so I was absolutely crimson in the face as I pulled my coat on. Like that it didn't show at all, and if I smelt like a delicatessen, it was better than if I'd really done it. I could feel it though, squashing and squelching in my panties as I walked, and it was hard to keep the contrite, miserable look off my face.

It can't have been more than half a mile to Rupert's in a straight line, but the Heath is confusing, with all those little tracks and ponds and paths that come out where you don't expect them to. I'd walked a good mile by the time I got to Rupert's door, and by then the mess was smeared right up the back of my panties and all over my pussy, while it was running down my legs. I was sore, hot and miserable, while all the way I'd been telling myself that I'd prove Sam wrong and not masturbate over what they'd done to me.

I didn't even know if Rupert would be in, and I didn't bother to knock, using my key and walking straight into the kitchen. I stopped dead. I'd forgotten about Sarah. She was there, and how!

She was on the kitchen table, rolled up, with my Uncle Rupert holding her by the legs. Her boobs were out, her skirt turned up, her panties twisted into my uncle's hand. She was getting a spanking, and I could see the lot, every wet tuck and fold of her pussy, her wide red bottom, and everything between. She was masturbating, but the real shock was that I could see what he had done to her. Her bumhole was stretched out, a little rosy star between her spread cheeks. Well, quite a big, rosy star really, sloppy too, with sperm dribbling out of the hole. Rupert had buggered her, and now he was spanking her as she took her own orgasm.

We froze, Rupert and I, for about five seconds before Sarah realised that something was wrong and opened her eyes. I heard her scream of shock even as I ran for the stairs.

It took an awful lot of talking, hours in fact, before Rupert finally managed to smooth things over. For all her exhibitionist streak, Sarah was horribly embarrassed, and angry. That put my back up, because she was being really proprietorial, not just over Rupert, but the house too, and she'd only known him a few weeks.

She resented me coming down in his bathrobe too, and in the end I had no choice but to explain what had happened, more or less, as I needed to get rid of the messy stuff and put my clothes in the washing machine. That left us both red-faced and silent, each thinking about her own humiliation, while Rupert struggled to make things better.

It was long after dark by the time my clothes were dry, and even then the atmosphere hadn't really thawed out. I went, feeling thoroughly fed-up, and unbearably horny at the same time. I hadn't fulfilled Sam's prediction, but only because of what had happened with Sarah. That was bad enough, and I knew full well I wouldn't be able to hold out once I was alone, but to make things worse I kept getting images of Sarah's spanked bottom with the hole dribbling sperm.

I've watched plenty of girls take spankings, in clubs, even in bars where it's not really supposed to happen. This was different, intimate, intrusive. In a sense it was far more normal, with none of the leather, rubber and general kinkyness that I'm used to. That made it stronger, more domestic maybe, as if I'd walked in on a genuine punishment spanking. Not only that, but she'd been buggered, and freshly buggered. Minutes earlier and I'd have caught him with his cock up her bum, the cock I'd twice sucked, up another woman's bottom hole. The thought made my own ring twitch.

By the time I got back to my flat I had abandoned my efforts to preserve my self-respect. My trousers came straight off, my top up and my boobs into my hands. For a moment I played with them, telling myself I'd come over the memory of having sex with Zoe. It wasn't going to work. I threw myself down on the bed, closing my eyes as my hand slid down the front of my panties. I thought of Sarah, buggered and then spanked while the sperm dribbled out of her bottom hole. On face value it was an appalling way to treat a woman, utterly humiliating, even if that was what she wanted. Rupert was a dirty bastard, no question of it, and I just wished I could have sucked his cock after it had been up Sarah's bum . . .

I was masturbating, hard, sure I would come over the image of her violated anus and spanked buttocks, only for my mind to slip to my own degradation. With a

153

groan of anguish at my own inability to control my feelings, I thought of the way the girls had held me down, of how they'd spanked my bottom, in a public place, in nothing but panties, and panties I appeared to have just done my toilet in. It had been truly awful, but maybe no worse than running across the Heath with that huge load swinging in my trousers, blind with tears.

Even then I'd wanted to masturbate, and it was impossible not to think of what might have happened if I had. I'd have gone into a kneeling position, among some bushes, pushing my trousers down in my urgency. I'd have stuck my bum in the air, showing off my squashy load to the sky, my fingers would have gone back and I'd have started to masturbate in it. Only I wouldn't have been alone. Some dirty old man would have been watching me. No, watching us, all afternoon, getting a good eyeful of parts of me I never, ever wanted a man to see.

He'd have caught me, taken me by surprise, whipped out his cock, wrenched my panties aside before I could react and stuffed it into the mess, and up my well-lubricated bumhole. He'd have buggered me, right there, his dirty big cock squelching about up my bottom as I knelt there, my mouth wide in horror, my hand still down my panties. I wouldn't have complained, though, not a bit of it. I'd have let him spunk up my dirt box and then masturbated myself dizzy as I sucked on his filthy penis and his sperm dribbled out of my open bottom hole . . .

I came, screaming the house down as it hit me, bouncing on the bed and babbling over and over that I needed to be buggered and buggered hard. It took ages, and it was only when my senses of shame and neighbourly concern caught up with my obscene head trip that I stopped. I didn't get up, though, or take my hand out of my panties. With the humiliation of what I'd come over had come the memory of who had taken me there, and how they had been exactly right about my reaction. I'd done it, I couldn't deny that, and my fantasy had probably been dirtier than even they would have guessed. That didn't stop me thinking about what I'd have liked to put them through in return.

So I lay there with my hand down my panties, idly toying with myself and thinking thoughts of revenge. A hundred schemes went through my head, all impractical, or unsatisfying, or just plain silly. I didn't want to hurt them, as such, or mess up their lives or anything. What I wanted was to have them feel the same helpless sexual humiliation they had put me through. Just to have given the three of them good, firm, panties down spankings would have been marvellous. Better still would have been to make them suck cock, in front of each other, one at a time.

Unfortunately it just wasn't possible. The idea of forcing them was ridiculous, and I'd have felt far too bad about it anyway. Well, bad about some things. If I'd had the strength to do it I'd have given them their spankings, like it or not. Not that it mattered. Any one of them could handle me with ease.

Then there was the question of what they'd do to me afterwards. That ruled out possibilities such as sucking up to a really powerful girl, like Big Angie the bouncer, until she was friendly enough to do my dirty work for me. It might have worked, and physically she would have had no trouble at all, spanking them like the bullying brats they were. Unfortunately I wouldn't be able to rely on her protection all the time, and in due course they'd get their revenge, and it would be truly awful.

Another irritation was the nagging voice at the back of my head, which kept telling me that they'd actually been rather good to me, and that I should be grateful. They knew I liked to be dominated, and they'd obliged. True, they wouldn't always accept my limits, but in a

155

sense that was just because they set the limits just that little bit further than I did. After all, why should they accept my choices?

They hadn't done anything really awful either, like giving me to a man for a fucking, or taking me into a park and making me suck off drunks. I'd heard of submissive girls being made to do both those things, and the thought put a cold knot of fear in my stomach.

I still wanted revenge, and I spent hours thinking about it, on my bed, and afterwards, wandering around the flat in just a top, with my poor smacked bottom well covered in cream. My cheeks were very red, and quite bruised, from Zoe's trainers, which made it impossible to forget how it had been done.

When I eventually went to bed I was still thinking about it. Not coherently though, but merely pouting and resentful, powerless to act effectively, but fantasising about how they'd look taken one by one across some really big woman's knee. Mo came to my mind, but then I'd pinched her dress uniform, and it was far more likely to be me who ended up getting the spanking, so that was out.

In any case, unless I managed to establish some sort of authority over the girls it would be next to impossible to get them to submit, short of brute force. I doubted Mo would have done it. Then it hit me. Andrea. She was perfect, less solid than Mo, but six foot tall, which gave her two inches even on AJ. She'd be game too, I was sure of it. She liked dressing up and she liked spanking girls. Better yet, she was bisexual, but had nothing to do with the London lesbian scene. We'd talked at length, and she didn't know anybody.

I thought it through in the morning, so that by the time the cyber café opened I had it all worked out. I was going to get the girls one at a time, three at once being just too much to ask. Naomi would be first, then Sam,

AJ last, in the order I resented the way they'd treated me. That way, if they got wise to the scheme I'd at least have got some satisfaction. Not that I expected them to tell each other. What I had in mind would be far too humiliating.

I emailed Andrea, packing all my enthusiasm into the message and more or less promising myself as her sex slave for life if she'd help. I even told the truth, except for the minor lie of saying that what happened would be the favourite fantasy of her victims. I sent it off with a prayer, then checked my inbox, which contained more rubbish, including another from the mad spunk-feeder.

The rest of the day was spent in serious frustration and endless cups of coffee at the café. Again and again there were no messages, until just before it closed, when there were two. One was from Andrea and Mark, eager to meet, the other from Uncle Rupert, asking me to call him as soon as I could. That meant he had rung my flat in the last few minutes, so I replied to Andrea, suggesting she come down on Saturday, and hurried back.

Rupert was seriously excited, thoroughly pleased too, and talking so fast that it took me a moment to catch on to what he was saying. The Saturday wasn't even mentioned, and Sarah only to say that he'd just put her on a train. What had happened was that he had another good response to his dodgy lonely hearts ads, and that it was from a nurse. Not only that, but it had come through an SM site and she was up for spanking and role play. The problem was that she was only willing to meet couples, and that was where I came in. I accepted, more than happy to take on something that wasn't going to end up with me at the bottom of the heap.

The date was already arranged, for the Wednesday, when we'd be picking her up directly from the care home in Romford where she worked. Rupert was sure she'd be in uniform, and that it would just be a matter of teasing her into a few rude photos, perhaps with me. We'd then spoil her uniform, pay for it along with profuse apologies and that would be that, our nurse.

She was called Heather, and she was everything we could have wanted, about five foot six, dark-haired, as wholesome as Sarah, but with a gentleness about her face that seemed at odds with her desire to indulge in dirty role-playing games. We met as agreed, outside the block of flats she worked in, where we waited in the car, with Rupert holding the little photo of her he had downloaded from the net.

We recognised her at once, and sure enough, she was in uniform, a uniform that had Rupert drooling. It was pale blue gingham, knee length, with a white belt and collar, very smart and formal, complete with a little white cap and shoulder tabs with the name of the company she worked for. That made Rupert tut, saying he would have preferred NHS, but I told him not to be so pedantic, opening the car door as she approached.

'Heather?' I queried, just in case there were two girls who looked the same working there. 'Hi, I'm Jade.'

'Rupert,' Rupert put in as he climbed out from his side. 'How are you?'

'In need of a drink,' she answered, her accent soft, with a hint of Irish mixed with the London.

'A drink it is,' Rupert said.

He took over from there, beautifully, setting her completely at her ease while I chatted merrily and filled in the gaps. We had it all worked out, with military precision, the result of a busy Tuesday night over a bottle of wine and an *A to Z*, ending as usual with his cock in my mouth.

She had a bag with her, and wanted to change in the car, but I put a stop to that by snogging her, quickly making her lose interest. She responded well too, and from then on I knew we were going to work sexually, whatever else happened.

We drove out to Epping Forest, for our drink, which in her case was Irish whiskey, drunk straight and in doubles. After three we could probably have had her in the bar, and her hands were all over Rupert, and me too. When we eventually left she and I were giggling together, our arms around each other's waists, ready for play. Rupert was stone cold sober, having wisely stuck to orange juice, but high on what we were doing.

It was up to me to suggest the naughty photo session in the woods, which I did. Heather accepted with enthusiasm. So it was deep into the Forest for a thoroughly rude photoset, with Rupert on camera and Heather and I provid the smut. I was in a dress, which we'd felt would be right for Rupert's supposed young girlfriend, so first it was skirts up, flashing our panties with out bottoms stuck out to the camera. Bare bums followed, panties down, then off, before her boobs came out, with her uniform open at the front and her bra pulled off down one sleeve. They were lovely, round and firm, maybe half the size of mine but hardly small, with lovely big nipples, just right to suck. I did, Rupert snapping away as I took them in my mouth, one by one.

That really had her going, and nothing would do but to get mine out too, which meant unzipping my dress and letting it down to my waist. My bra seemed pointless like that, so off it came and I was topless, for her to suckle. I got my bottom spanked after that, bent over a low branch with my boobs swinging, giggling crazily as my cheeks bounced to her slaps. She got the same, then both of us, side my side, snogging as Rupert fondled and smacked at our bottoms.

It was only when it was actually happening that I realised I was getting my first ever spanking from him, something I hadn't meant to give. It was too late though, as I could hardly back out in front of her, and he was obviously oblivious to anything but having two plump female bottoms to chastise. We got it too, quite hard, with my cheeks rosy and warm before he'd finished, while my pussy was very wet indeed.

Spanked and hornier than ever, we started to pose again, showing everything. Rupert continued to photograph us, in one lewd pose after another, then natural as our passion got the better of us. We came together, kissing and fondling each other's bodies, until I got completely carried away and pushed my face into her pussy. She let me lick, climaxing with a lovely soft sigh and a boob in either hand.

By then Rupert's cock was in his hand, rock hard as he took pictures one handed. What I wasn't going to do was end up with it up my pussy, so I suggested he fuck her while I took the pictures. She went willingly, leaning on the low branch she'd just been spanked across, with her uniform skirt turned up over her bum and her big boobs bulging out at the front, a truly excellent nurse shot, quickly made better still as Rupert entered her from the rear. It didn't take him long, and he came over her bottom, so I took a last photo, the same rude pose, only with her pussy fully on show between her thighs and a spatter of white come across her buttocks. She was looking back too, her pretty face loose with her pleasure. I could already see the picture on its little stand in front of the mannequin.

I might not have wanted to be fucked, but that didn't mean I couldn't come. I had Heather do it, squatting to lick me with my pussy pushed out in her face, much as I'd done her, on which dirty show Rupert finished the third roll of film. Rupert was ready for more, but the light was starting to fade and I suggested we head back into London and get down to fully indulging our fantasies. Heather agreed, and we dressed with nervous haste, giggling as we made each other decent.

The drive to Highgate was hectic, with Heather and I cuddling in the back and Rupert doing his best to concentrate on the road. We still had no idea what she wanted us to do, but there was no question of not playing together, and I was sure we'd be able to accommodate her.

At Rupert's the first thing she did was change out of her uniform and into casual clothes, a baggy jumper and tight blue jeans that made the best of her full bottom. The uniform went into her bag, which was pushed casually into a corner. Rupert had been busy with a bottle while she changed, aside from an occasional pause to ogle her body, and put three glasses down beside it as she took a seat.

'So what are you into?' I asked. 'Medical fetishism?'

'Anything but!' she answered. 'I couldn't possibly do anything that reminded me of work. All the time I have to be responsible. I like to lose that, completely, just for a few hours.'

'How so?' Rupert asked.

Heather had gone pink, which was quite something for a girl who'd just giggled as a photo of her smacked bottom was taken from about a foot away. She took a gulp of wine, swallowing before her mouth curled up into a nervous smile.

'Pigs,' she said softly.

'Pigs?' I echoed.

'Not real pigs,' she said quickly. 'Being a pig, a piggy-girl. That's why I asked about the mud in my email. Look.'

She reached back for her bag, pulling it close and burrowing inside. I caught a glimpse of black leather, which she pulled out, then a pink object, and a second. The leather I recognised, a head harness, if not quite like the ones I'd seen worn in clubs. For the other two things it took my mind a moment to register before I realised that one was a tail, the other a snout, both cleverly made in flesh-tone rubber. I'd never heard of it before, but I could imagine it, and I could imagine it being done to me, and how utterly humiliating it would be. Heather

161

was looking shy and I gave her a big smile in an effort to reassure her, determined not to behave like AJ and company.

'That is terribly sweet,' Rupert said. 'We'd love to play with you, wouldn't we, Jade?'

'Sure,' I answered. 'So, you stick the snout and tail on, and wear the harness. Anything else?'

'No,' she said. 'A piggy-girl should be completely nude except for her harness.'

'This is fancy,' I said, picking it up. 'Where did you get it?'

'It's custom made,' she answered, 'by a woman in Hertfordshire, Amber Oakley. She made the snout and tail too.'

'Cool! I want her address.'

'Fine, I'll give it to you.'

She wrote it down on the spot and I pocketed it, already picturing how Sam or Naomi would look as a piggy-girl in a club, preferably with an audience composed of all their friends and a few dozen dirty old men. Not that I could think how to make it happen, but it was nice to dream.

We finished the wine and got down to it. Rupert, now in gumboots, took us into the garden, carrying Heather's bag for her in a show of supposed gallantry, and showed her the area that was invisible from the other houses. He had the security lights on, and it was brightly lit. I got into the hammock, watching as she quite calmly stripped off, stark naked, while Rupert used the hose to turn the area under his big poplar into a sea of sandy mud.

She had explained that she liked to be beaten with a switch, and he made one from three long suckers as she glued on her snout and tail. The tail was cute, and rude, accentuating her bottom in the most wonderful way, so that her cheeks seemed plumper, and basically, more piggy. The same was true of the snout, making her face seem rounder and altering the lines so much I wasn't sure if I'd have recognised her. Rupert had reloaded the camera, and I took a few more photos of her standing, then crawling.

I could sense her feelings as she went down, the release, the gloriously irresponsibility of a sexually submissive role. It was rude too, very rude, with her big boobs hanging down like a pair of udders and the little tail waving above her nude bum, with her pussy and anus on show and just begging to be filled. She had told us we could do anything we liked, subject to her stop word, and I intended to make the best of it.

For the time being I was content to watch and take photos. Rupert had finished his switch, and gave her a couple of flicks across the breadth of her bottom to test it. Both left long red lines, drawing little high-pitched squeals from her, which left me grinning in sadistic delight. She stuck her bottom up, wiggling it to make her tail move, a sight that had me wishing I had something to fill her with.

Rupert gave her another stroke, harder, and stood back, calling her a bad pig and telling her to come to him. She crawled away, further into the mud, ducking down to rub her boobs in it, with her snout twitching up and a big smile on her face. Rupert came closer, flicking the switch out to catch her bottom again.

'Bad girl! Not in the mud!' he ordered, but Heather only sank herself deeper in, rubbing her boobs in the mess and wiggling her bottom right at him.

He smacked her again and she rose, her breasts pulling out of the ooze with a sucking sound, to leave twin marks in the soil and drops of muddy water hanging from her erect nipples. Again she went down, rubbing herself in the mud, rolling, legs wide to show off her pussy, right over, before sitting up to wiggle her cheeky bottom into the cool, wet earth. She was covered in it, from the neck down, slimy and brown, with clots

163

of earth stuck to her skin and her thick black pubic hair caked with dirt.

She was enjoying it so much, nude and free and filthy, without a trace of the humiliation I'd have felt in her position. I felt a trace of envy, and found I wanted to get in with her, to be twin pigs in the mud pool, but without a snout or tail I wasn't sure if I could.

Rupert had stopped trying to control her, and was watching her wallow. She was rolling, her whole body brown and filthy except for the pink opening of her pussy, even her face, which she'd pushed into the mud, and her hair, which was thick with in. I swallowed the lump that had been rising in my throat, again thinking of how I'd feel in her place, or with her. It meant stripping in front of Rupert, which I wasn't sure about, but I wasn't sure if I could hold off either.

He had begun to squeeze his crotch, and it was easy to imagine him getting carried away and fucking us both, or porking us, which seemed to be the right term if we were piggy-girls. I didn't want that, I was sure of it. Sucking him was one thing, just a friendly duty – fucking another, while there was also the uncomfortable knowledge that my bumhole would be available and slimy with mud. I was under no illusions about what he liked to do to girls' bumholes, and I wasn't certain if he'd hold back from mine, or if I'd stop him when I was close to orgasm.

To delay my decision I took some more pictures of Heather wallowing in the mud. She was thick with it and kept dipping her boobs and bum in, to pull them out with a rude sucking noise. I could see it felt good, and was determined to have a go myself, eventually, when I wasn't going to end up with Rupert's cock up my pussy or bumhole.

We watched her wallow, both of us entranced, just enjoying the show, until she turned with her muddy bottom lifted towards us, the pink mouth of her pussy showing in open invitation. That was too much for Rupert. He reached down to open his fly, pulling out a half-stiff cock. He stepped close and I took it in my hand, tugging at the shaft.

'Fuck her,' I suggested. 'How can you resist that pussy?'

'I'm not going to resist it,' he answered. 'Help me, wash her down.'

I rolled out of the hammock, suddenly urgent. Snatching up the hose, I twisted the nozzle, sending a gush of water out, full across Heather's spread cheeks. She squealed in surprise, turning. I moved the stream, playing it on her tits, exposing the pale pink skin as the water spattered off her body.

Rupert had taken the harness, and was undoing the buckles, his fingers fumbling in his urgency, with his cock and balls still sticking out of his fly. I moved closer, to take him in my hand again, wincing at the obscene rubbery feeling of male genitals, but stroking anyway, like a good girl should. For a moment I was distracted, and the hose caught Heather in the face, leaving her spluttering.

There were no complaints, and I continued to play the water over her body, wanking Rupert at the same time, until she was pink and clean and he was hard in my hand. She turned her back to us, sticking out her broad bottom, the big white cheeks splayed to show herself off, blatantly on offer, with the little tail bobbing over her crease. I twisted the nozzle shut and picked up the switch, eager to give her what I hoped she wanted. Rupert stepped in with the harness as I put a cut across Heather's piggy buttocks. She squealed, wriggling her bottom. I gave her another cut as Rupert took her by the hair, and paused, waiting as he began to buckled her into the harness. It certainly held her, with two straps behind her head and another over the top, linking to a cleverly made cage of straps and brass fittings that closed her mouth and covered her nose. He fixed each buckle into place, leaving only one, her chin strap, which allowed him to briefly stuff his erect cock into her mouth before completing her bondage.

Taking the lead which hung from the rear of the harness, he pulled her out of the thick mud, to the patch of muddy paving beside it. Her bottom came up, the plump white buttocks wiggling. I put a cut across them, and another, making her squeal and drawing thin red lines across her soft flesh. It had to hurt, but there was no doubting her eagerness, so I laid in, whipping her as Rupert held her lead twisted in her hand, her head pressed low to the ground.

It was so horny, just beating her as she was held for my attention. I could see her pussy juicing, the chubby lips slowly growing puffy and the hole moist. My own wasn't far behind, with a wet patch in my panties, and I put aside thoughts of my own submission as I laid in, harder and harder.

She was really squealing, exactly like a pig, and loud enough to have Rupert glancing uneasily towards the houses. I didn't care, it was just to good to spoil. Her whole bottom was criss-crossed with thin, scarlet lines, the skin inflamed where the crooked bits of the twigs had caught her. I knew the pain she would be feeling, and the helplessness, a whipped, punished pig, held tight as she was punished.

I could see why she had insisted on no clothes. It would have been totally inappropriate. She needed to be nude, totally bare, totally vulnerable. I hadn't been sure about the fantasy at first, but I could see it now, with her moaning at my feet, in grovelling, ecstatic submission.

It would have been nice to frig myself off as I whipped her, but some of the cuts were bad and I didn't want to make her bleed, while Rupert was going to burst if he didn't get up her soon. Giving her one last, vicious cut, I dropped the switch, taking her lead from Rupert.

He didn't hesitate, but got down behind her and plunged his cock up her sopping pussy. It went straight up, Heather taking it as only a truly aroused girl can. He began to fuck her, holding her hips and pushing against her, to make her whipped bottom quiver and the pig's tail wobble. I grabbed for the camera, knowing I just had to have the shot, a fucked piggy-girl, red buttocks squashed out against her master's front, eyes wide, nose turned up to me in its little leather cage.

I need my clitty rubbed to come, always. Heather didn't, climaxing just on the feel of Rupert's cock in her pussy, her whipped flesh and the whole piggy-girl head-trip. I watched it, such a beautiful sight, a woman at orgasm, and in such a condition. Her bottom and thighs tightened, her head went down and she moaned, long and low, coming even as Rupert's eyes went wide to the feel of the contraction of her hole.

There was no more holding back for me, not after that. A moment later I had my panties down under my dress and was frigging myself, with my hem held up and my tummy pushed out to show them what I was doing.

Heather was still trembling, her bottom quivering with the aftershock of climax. I set my eyes on her, feasting on the big, hanging breasts, the big, pale buttocks, so womanly, and in beautiful, filthy, rude contrast to the curly pig's tail and upturned snout on her face.

I came, crying out as it hit me, my knees going weak and my head dizzy. Rupert gasped, and at the very peak of my orgasm I saw him snatch his cock from Heather's hole, push it fast up into the wet crease of her ample bottom and come, over her back and in her hair, finishing himself by milking his cock into her bum-crease and over her anus.

Heather's knees had already begun to slide apart, and her hand went back to her bum as she sank down. I watched as she smeared the sperm over her whipped buttocks and into her crease, briefly dabbing some into her bumhole, only to stop as she slumped into the muddy puddle beneath her. Rupert rose, still holding his cock.

'Good, thank you, my dear,' he said, and blew out his breath.

Heather gave a faint oink and rolled over onto one elbow, smiling happily up at us.

'No, I should be thanking you,' she said. 'You treated me so well.'

'Any time,' I offered.

'Again, soon,' she said. 'What time is it?'

'Nearly ten,' Rupert answered.

'I'd better get back,' she sighed. 'Six-thirty I've got to be up. Thanks again, though, really. That will keep me happy for a long time. Could I use a towel, please?'

'Come in, I'll get you one,' I offered. 'Rupert can clean up.'

I took her by her lead, pulling her behind me before she could think to retrieve her bag. She followed, and I took her up to the bathroom, where I helped her out of the harness and peeled the nose and tail off. They'd been stuck on with spirit gum, which was quite hard to get off, and left red marks on her skin. I watched her dry her body too, and creamed her smacked bottom for her. That would undoubtedly have turned into something more, with her leaning on the bath, bum stuck out as I rubbed the soothing lotion into her skin. I would have happily licked her from behind, or taken a punishment myself to even things up a bit, but she seemed content with what she'd had and genuinely hurried.

We talked though, openly, all the time with my guilt for what Rupert and I were about to do building up. When we came downstairs, her uniform was going to have been discovered to be wet and muddy. It would already be in the washing machine. She was so nice, and it just wasn't fair, while I was feeling like a real bitch.

By the time we came downstairs to the kitchen I'd decided on a different plan.

'May I ask a favour?' I said, slipping an arm around her waist.

'Of course,' she answered.

'When we play with people,' I started, 'we like to take a trophy, the girl's panties usually.'

'They're yours,' she said immediately.

'Thanks,' I went on, 'but in your case I like a little more, because you were, well, special, and it'll remind me of the fun we had in the woods.'

'What then?' she asked.

'Your uniform,' I said, 'undies too.'

Rupert had been listening, his face horrorstruck, and trying to make frantic signs at me behind Heather's back. She was looking doubtful, but he rallied, laughing.

'What she's trying to say,' he told her, 'is that she wants to wear it herself, preferably for a good spanking. She's always been into playing at being a nurse. Her favourite is to pretend to be a junior being punished by a sister.'

'Well, I'm not sure,' Heather replied. 'You can borrow one, of course. I've got three. They come from the company though, and they're not really mine. For now I've really got to get back, or I'll miss the last tube.'

'Tube?' Rupert queried. 'Nonsense. We'll drive you back.'

'I couldn't possibly expect you to drive all the way to Romford and back!'

'Not at all. I insist. Besides, some of your things were muddy, and I put them in the washing machine. I didn't realise you were in such a rush.'

'What?'

'Your uniform and the bra you were wearing. I put your panties in too.'

'Well . . . Okay. Look, borrow the uniform for now, and I'll pick it up next week, if you don't mind me

169

coming around? I could spank you in uniform, Jade, nurse to nurse.'

'Yes, please,' I answered automatically.

'How about you as well?' Rupert asked her. 'Side by side. I'd adore that.'

I opened my mouth to protest, but shut it quickly, remembering who I was supposed be. He seemed to have forgotten how much of a game we were playing. Heather shrugged.

'If you like,' she said, 'although being done in my uniform isn't really my thing.'

'Not even being spanked in it?' I asked.

'Well, no,' she answered. 'Getting spanked does, sure, and I know lots of men get off on the idea of punishing a nurse, women too, but not me.'

'That's only natural, I suppose,' he agreed. 'After all, much of the fun of role play is to be something you're not. Still, a nurse is a very sexualised image, however far from reality the fantasy may be. You must get plenty of offers.'

'A few. Mostly from men who want to be mothered rather than spankers. One guy even wanted me to treat him like a baby, changing his nappy and so on. As if I don't get enough of that sort of thing at work!'

'Oh, right,' I put in. 'I'd have thought it would be more from men who wanted to dominate you?'

'Not really, no. I don't let my submissive side show normally, either. I have to be really tough at work, sometimes. My life would be a misery otherwise.'

'Hard work, I imagine.'

'Not that so much. It's being between our managers and the clients' children. The children are hardest, the girls especially. The women can be awful, real bitches. Whatever I do it's not right. Now there are a few there I would like to spank, for real!'

'That I would like to see,' Rupert sighed. 'There are so many women in this world who would benefit from a good spanking now and then. If only . . .'

'Ignore him,' I laughed. 'He thinks feminism means being into lacy undies and print frocks.'

'No, he's right,' she said. 'It's true. There's nothing like a spanking to stop someone getting above themselves, or to put them in their place if they do.'

'Well spoken,' Rupert put in.

'In a fantasy, sure,' I said, 'or if a girl wants it. Not for real, though!'

'Why not?' she went on. 'In the right circumstances.'

'You'd spank a girl, say, if she . . . say, tried to snatch your bag and you caught her?'

'No, of course not,' Rupert cut in, 'because society would deem her as much the criminal as the bag-snatcher. What Heather is saying is that she ought to be able to do it.'

'That's what I meant, more or less,' I answered him.

'Imagine,' he said dreamily, 'a girl out bag-snatching, down at the Archway, on those rollerblades, maybe. She snatches a woman's bag, and off she goes, laughing, and expecting everyone to just let her get away with it. Instead some passing gentleman sticks out a foot. Over she goes, flat on her face, and before she knows it a whole ring of angry people are standing around her. They pull her up, throw her over the back of a bench. Men hold her, two on each limb. Up goes her little skirt. Down come her panties. There's her round little teenage bum, well parted, with everything showing, and she's struggling and using every bit of filthy language she knows. They ignore her, and the woman she tried to rob dishes out a damn good spanking. How the girl would howl!'

'And she'd think twice about doing it again,' Heather added. 'Don't you agree, Jade?'

'Well, I . . .' I started, and stopped. 'No, it's too open to abuse. Who's to say when the girl's been naughty enough to deserve it? Or what she should get? You'd have businessmen spanking their secretaries for spilling the coffee, and doubtless demanding blow-jobs after-wards. You'd end up with girls getting put in the stocks and raped for wearing too much make-up or short skirts. It would never work.'

'You're right, of course,' Rupert sighed. 'Pity, though.'

'That's true,' Heather agreed, but it doesn't alter the fact that a good spanking can put someone in their place, woman or man.'

'I always see it as being a woman's natural place,' Rupert remarked. 'Why else did nature provide you with such wonderfully padded bottoms?'

'Not so you could smack them!' I retorted. 'Isn't he rotten, Heather? You should see his collection of dirty magazines. Every one of them full of girls getting spanked.'

'How about ones of you getting spanked?' she asked me. 'I'd rather see those.'

'There are some, yes,' I lied hastily. 'Not that many.'

'We've only been together a year,' Rupert added.

'I'd love to see them,' she said, 'and the ones you took of me.'

'You will,' I promised, 'next week. For now, we'd better get a move on.'

'You're right,' she agreed. 'I'd better get dressed.'

We left, Rupert driving as before, with Heather and I in the back. I meant to keep my hands to myself, more or less, but we were both still pretty drunk, and high on what we'd done. Before we got to Finchley we were snogging, and only holding back from more because people could see in at the windows.

It got better once we'd reached the North Circular, which was pretty well empty. In no time Heather had her top up and her boobs out of her bra, while my dress was around my waist. I suckled her, which always makes me want to be spanked, and before long I'd crawled across her knee, with my bottom pushed up for her attention.

172

She was gentle, stroking my bum and my hair too, giving me little pats, but nothing hard. After a while my panties came down, and she got more intimate, stroking my bottom crease, the insides of my thighs, and at last my pussy, from behind, with her hand pushed down between my legs. It tickled crazily, and had me writhing, but I took it, getting more and more turned on. I had my dress right up, boobs out, and was feeling them, sure that she was going to bring me to the most beautiful orgasm, but just in her own time.

It didn't happen. We came off the main road, and over a roundabout, where there was a police car waiting for drunks. Rupert asked us to cover up, and we obeyed, which was just as well, because a few minutes later we were on a busy, well-lit road, with plenty of pedestrians able to peer in at the windows. Not that I was prepared to let it go. I was far too horny.

'You're going to have to find somewhere to stop,' I told Rupert. 'I need my panties pulling down. I need spanking and I need to come.'

'I know a place,' Heather said. 'Turn left at the next lights.'

Rupert turned, and before long we had reached a road that stopped at a great heap of rubble. By then I was back across Heather's knee, bum up as she fondled me. She'd been getting harder too, and my cheeks were pleasantly warm.

'Rupert can watch,' I sighed. 'Come on, Heather, make me come.'

'Rupert can help,' she said decisively. 'Come on, young lady, so far I've been getting much too much of the attention. It's your turn.'

She took me by the ear, pulling me up. I went, allowing her to turn me over on the back seat, with my bottom stuck out towards Rupert. I knew he could see everything, or would be able to once my panties came down, but I wasn't sure if I wanted him to or not.

I didn't get much option. First they turned the light on so that they could see properly, and then Heather pulled down my panties. I moaned at that, imagining the view from behind, with my big pink bum stuck out and my cheeks open. He could see my pussy and bumhole, and I was going to be spanked, and frigged off, right in front of him. Well, he'd done me earlier, and we were supposed to be together, so I shut my eyes and tried not to think of prying male eyes on the most intimate parts of my body.

Heather's arm came around my waist, tucking under my tummy to hold me firmly in place. Her hand came onto my bottom, stroking the seat of my panties, patting me, moving to make my cheeks wobble, stroking again, higher, one finger tracing a slow line up the shallow groove of cotton that hid my crease . . .

Suddenly my panties were down, whipped off my bum without the slightest preamble and I was bare, showing, with the air suddenly cool on the moist flesh of my pussy and up between my open cheeks. I'd squeaked, loudly, and braced myself, expecting a torrent of hard spanks. None came, Heather's hand returning to the gentle fondling of my bum.

She was patting, too, using her finger tips to smack playfully at the crests of my cheeks, not hard, but hard enough to tingle and make me want more. I stuck it up, swallowing my angst at making a yet ruder show for Rupert, and she began to get harder, smacking, breaking off to stroke and tickle, smacking again.

I'd began to wiggle my toes in my shoes, having trouble handling the tickling in my bum-crease despite being so turned on. I'd peed before we'd left, for which I was deeply thankful. I could still feel the muscles of my pussy twitching in response, my bladder too, which I knew would be filling from all the wine I'd drunk. I was trying to stop myself from giggling as well, and was making odd little noises in my throat, with my control slipping quickly away under Heather's hands.

Fortunately she got rougher before there could be a disaster, her arm tightening around my waist and her pats changing to proper spanks. I could hear a slapping noise too, which I knew was Rupert tugging at his cock, and realised that she was purposefully making a show of me, turning play to punishment to turn him on. My response was a whimper, thinking of his big ugly cock hard in his hand and my pussy gaping and bare between smacked cheeks. She stopped, abruptly, both hands going to my bum.

'Oh she does have a lovely bottom,' she said, smoothing her hands across my hot cheeks. 'Couldn't you just eat her? You'll fuck her for me, won't you, Rupert?'

I managed a mew of protest, nothing more. Heather carried, on, oblivious to my feelings, doubtless thinking that there would be nothing I'd like more than my boyfriend's cock up my pussy once I'd been properly spanked. I wasn't sure I could stop myself either, if he did try it, because my feelings were getting quickly stronger, my desire to surrender myself growing.

It happens to me, always, but not usually with the one man I could actually bear to have sexual contact with tugging at his cock behind me. It was going to go up, I was sure it was, and I couldn't stop myself from wanting it, any more than I could stop my pussy juicing over Heather's attention to my bottom. Faintly I was hoping that Rupert would have the decency to hold back, but even that wasn't so strong.

My bum was glowing, the smacks, making my cheeks wobble and bounce, each one sending a little jolt right through me. She was getting lower too, onto my sweet spot, making my pussy react, bringing me towards that most special orgasm.

'Like that, harder,' I panted. 'Much harder, hurt me.'

Her grip tightened. She laid in, hard, just in the right place. I let my mouth come open, closing my eyes, feeling the slow rise to orgasm begin as smack after smack landed on my burning bottom . . .

It stopped, abruptly, Heather letting go of me.

'I can't!' she said. 'Ow! My hand! She can take some, can't she!'

'Please, Heather, you nearly had me there!' I wailed, turning back.

'I really can't, my palm's already bruised,' she said. 'You'd better take over, Rupert. She'll be used to a man's strength.'

It was true. I was sure he would be able to do it, and my feelings were warring in my head as he quickly climbed into the back and settled himself beside me. Like Heather, he took me around the waist and set to work, his first smack making me cry out.

'That's more like it!' Heather said. 'Let me keep you ready!'

I felt her arm touch me and knew she'd taken his cock in her hand. It was rock hard, I'd seen as he moved back, ready for pussy, ready for my pussy. I was ready too, physically, my vaginal mouth wet and vulnerable, open behind me. I couldn't stop it, I was just too horny, and I wasn't at all sure he could.

He smacked me again, catching my sweet spot, a touch high, then perfectly. I cried out in ecstasy, a choking, high-pitched squeal that rang in my own ears as the next slap caught me, harder still. It was enough, I was going to get there, and suddenly nothing else mattered, just the stinging pain and my approaching orgasm.

'Harder, beat me, hurt me!' I screamed and I was coming, Rupert smacking his hand into my bottom as hard as he could, over and over.

It hit me, every muscle in my body tightening, my whole being focussed on my sex, dizzy with pleasure, screaming out as my back arched, my bottom fat, throbbing, smacked . . .

He was on me, mounting my back, his fat knob round and firm against my flesh, my pussy-flesh, and up, in my hole, pumping into me with desperate energy, his body on mine, humping me, the way dogs do it. I had a cock up me, and all I could do as my orgasm slowly faded was lie inert beneath him, letting him have his way, until at last he pulled it free, jerked hard and came all over my bottom.

Eight

I'd been fucked, something I'd told myself I'd never do again. Not that I said anything. After all, what was there to say? He'd fucked me and that was that. I could hardly claim it had been against my will, and making a big deal out of it wasn't going to turn the clock back. I could sympathise with him, too, because I'd lost control no less than he had.

He did at least have the decency to be sheepish about it, instead of gloating, the way most men would have done. That made it a little better, but we were still silent most of the way back from Heather's house, both feeling rather guilty. The only thing we did talk about was Heather's uniform. We'd got it, but we had a problem. Two problems in fact. She wanted the uniform back, and she expected to be shown some juicy spanking photos of me, with Rupert doing the punishing.

We didn't even discuss the possibility of just cutting her completely. She was too nice, and too much fun. With someone like Naomi I could have done it and not felt even a twinge of guilt. Not with Heather.

So we were going to have to run with it, which meant either pretending the uniform had been ruined in the wash or replacing it. It also meant two or three photo shoots to provide a convincing number of pictures of me getting my bum warmed. I didn't have enough dignity left to object to that, accepting it with both resignation and expectancy, ambivalent as always.

We didn't have much time either. Rupert was off to Sarah's in Cornwall on the Friday night and wouldn't be back until late on Sunday. That gave us two days, on both of which I was supposed to be working. That left Thursday evening, and I agreed to come straight to his house after work, for spanking, dinner and more spanking, in a variety of styles and outfits.

He was also feeling a touch of guilt about Sarah, who was apparently getting seriously keen on him. Nothing had been said as such, but he was pretty sure that she would have been less than happy to learn that he had had sex with two other women, especially when one of them was me. She was apparently jealous of my intimacy with Rupert, which was annoying, but at least made me feel a little better about my fucking.

I was half asleep on Thursday, Rupert having dropped me off at my flat at nearly one in the morning, and having had considerable trouble getting to sleep even then. Work was at Sam's office again, and she was her old self, bossy and cruel, making me show her my boobs and bum in the store room just to humiliate me. Alert and in a naughty mood, I would have enjoyed it. Sleepy, I didn't, but I did it anyway, and was rewarded with Naomi's address when I asked for it, saying I fancied a date. That really made Sam laugh, and she gave me the line about knowing me better than I knew myself again. I said nothing, thinking of Andrea with my determination growing inside me.

Rupert met me at my flat, which we'd decided would provide a useful alternative background for the spanking photos. We got down to it without preamble, with me across his knee in my office clothes and the camera stood on the mantelpiece and set to automatic. It was a good set, with me looking very prim and also very sorry for myself with my grey woollen skirt turned up, first to show my big white panties, then my bare bum.

I was still bruised, especially under my cheeks, where both he and Heather had done me pretty hard, AJ and Sam too, so we were careful not to take any real close-ups, or to let too much light to my bum. The flat shots done, we gathered up a selection of my clothes and made for Highgate, stopping in Queen's Wood on the way for a few of me flashing my panties and bum, also getting it across the seat of my jeans with a stick while the camera was balanced precariously in the fork of a tree. I put my hair in bunches for those, which drew Rupert several dirty looks from people who guessed that he was up to no good with a woman half his age, if not exactly what.

At Rupert's house the bunches came out and it was into combats and skinny top for a session in the garden, with what was left of Wednesday evening's mud pool kept carefully out of shot. He had fetched a tripod, which made it easier. It was trousers, then panties, then bare, with a few rude poses to add variety, and my boobs out at the end. By then my bum was too red to start a new session, so we broke for dinner, Rupert cooking while I made adjustments to my make-up and once again restyled my hair.

I was beginning to realise how the models in his dirty magazines must have felt during their photoshoots. There really is nothing like a good spanking, but I'd had three in a row and there were more to come. My bum was sore and I was tired, and while my pussy felt wet and urgent I knew that if I let my feelings go we'd very likely never get it done. So we ate quickly and he took a set of me washing up in just a pinny, with my smacked bottom showing behind. He seemed to have a thing about the kitchen table, and finished the roll off with me rolled up on it, the same way he'd been spanking Sarah when I'd caught them. Rolled up is very rude, with the cheeks wide and not the slightest concealment. That got to me.

180

The next session was in his living room, spanking and corner time, very carefully posed. By then I was nude, and the shots were getting ruder, with more and more pussy and bumhole on show. His cock was getting seriously hard too, and I could feel it through his trousers as he did me across his lap. I knew where it would be going, and was simply too far gone to feel more than a little contrite.

Sure enough, after a few pictures on the stairs it was up to his bedroom. His cock came out, and into my mouth, as I lay sideways on the bed, red bum turned up for the attention of his belt. That got photographed, and I got my mouth filled, although I wouldn't have stopped him if he'd wanted to fuck me. I did come though, on my knees with one hand on my pussy and the other stroking my hot, sore bum-cheeks, an exhibition which got photographed as well.

By then I was truly exhausted, and I ended up going to sleep in his bed. Slightly to my surprise, he didn't take advantage of me, although it would have been so easy to just slip his cock up my wet pussy. There was a touch of regret too, in the morning, which brought more awareness of my feelings than I really wanted.

I was late for work, but not by enough to warrant more than a mild rebuke. That didn't bother me, but what Sam had to say did. She had been to Whispers, and apparently a big woman had been asking about a small, curvy girl, and in less than friendly terms. From the description it could only be Mo.

Sam hadn't let on, which left me seriously grateful, almost grateful enough to strike her off my revenge list. Unfortunately, too many other people knew who I was for me to feel secure. I was nervous all day, and in the evening, imagining what Mo would do to me if she found me. It was scary, but it was impossible not to find it sexy too, and I ended up masturbating over the thought of how severely she might punish me.

Andrea arrived late on the Saturday morning, alone, as I'd requested. I explained what I wanted her to do, painting it as a fantasy treat for a friend. She was delighted by the idea, and agreed, which just left the problem of getting Naomi into the right place at the right time. That proved easiest of all, as she rang me, having been tipped off by Sam that I was after a date. What was less easy to plan for was that she wanted it that evening. Fortunately Andrea was up for it, and after a frantic afternoon's shopping, we were ready.

I had told Naomi how much what they had done to me on the Heath had turned me on, and asked if our date could start with an outdoor punishment for me. She had agreed with enthusiasm, and we'd settled on the loneliest part of the Heath, where hardly anyone but cruising gay guys go, and there's enough dense foliage to get away with some bare flesh and a few pained squeals.

Andrea and I drove up in her car and parked behind Jack Straw's Castle. I left her there, walking slowly down the hill until I found my place. Five minutes later Naomi's old blue BMW appeared, pulling up beside me. Even before she'd stopped I had realised that she wasn't alone, with Sam in the passenger seat beside her. That was not how I had planned it, but it was too late to back out.

'Dressed the slut, I see,' Naomi greeted me as she stepped out of the car, her eyes flicking quickly down over my straining top to where my little floaty skirt ended more than halfway up my thighs.

I just shrugged. She was dressed for it, no doubt, in tight leather trousers and bra, all black. Sam was the same, like to like, from her brightly polished boots upwards. Both showed plenty, nipples, bums and pussies clearly outlined, revealing, yet as strong as ever.

Naomi took me around my shoulders and kissed me, hard on my mouth. It was so forceful, too much for me to stop, and my mouth came open under hers, despite the disapproving glance of an elderly woman walking her dog. My eyes had closed in pleasure, which made it an even bigger shock when Sam's hand settled on my leg, casually slipping it up my skirt to take a handful of my bottom. They would have had me so easily, just from the rough, uncompromising way they were treating me, except for Andrea.

She appeared around the corner, right on schedule, over six foot tall in her thick-heeled shoes and as stern as anything. The uniform suited her to the ground, and she wore it with absolute conviction, from the plain stockings, through the neat navy-blue suit, to the little hat with it's tell-tale yellow band. I'd have been fooled, and Naomi never questioned it for an instant.

'Shit, a warden!' she swore.

'Aren't we safe, after one o'clock?' Sam queried.

'I don't know,' Naomi answered. 'Excuse me –'

'Is this your vehicle?' Andrea interrupted her, speaking in a voice that just oozed officiousness.

'Yes,' Naomi answered. 'I –'

'You are parked illegally,' Andrea went on brusquely, 'on a yellow line and too close to a corner, also –'

'We'll move,' Sam said hastily.

'No,' Andrea answered. 'In accordance with our new zero tolerance policy you are subject to a one hundred pound on-the-spot fine.'

'One hundred pounds!' Naomi gasped. 'You've got to be joking!'

'Come on!' Sam put in. 'Be reasonable. We'll go, now.'

'Let them off, be fair!' I put in.

'That's out of the question,' Andrea retorted. 'The zero tolerance policy means all illegally parked cars are subject to on-the-spot fines. If you leave your car here it will be towed away, at much greater expense.'

'What about these other cars?' Naomi demanded, waving her hand at the long line of other parked cars behind hers.

'They're all due to be towed,' Andrea told her. 'Now, your ticket . . .'

A convincing ticket was one of the things we hadn't been able to get. I acted.

'Hang on,' I said, addressing Andrea. 'I recognise you, I'm sure I do. You appeared in *Slap!*'

'I did no such thing!' Andrea answered angrily.

'It is you!' I accused. 'You know what it is, don't you? Why else get cross?'

'I . . .' Andrea began, only to stop abruptly and begin again. 'My private life is not at issue, here, especially as those photos were taken before I joined the service. Now, our zero tolerance . . .'

'What the fuck are you talking about?' Sam broke in. 'What, Jade, has she been in a dirty magazine?'

'Not just any dirty magazine,' I crowed. 'A spanking magazine, aimed at dirty old men in macs. She was a school teacher, caning a pupil, then getting it from the headmaster for abusing her power.'

'That's not going to stop you getting a ticket,' Andrea said coolly.

'Isn't it?' I said. 'From the look of those pictures I'll swear you loved it. How about the three of us, in the bushes for a few strokes and a lick, and you let us off?'

'No fucking way!' Naomi exclaimed, Sam echoing her angry answer immediately. 'What the fuck are you talking about, Jade!?'

I'd hoped she'd go for it. Alone, maybe she would have done. Not with Sam there, and of course Andrea had expected her to catch on at that point and go for it. The whole thing was going to fall apart, but I got an inspiration at the exact moment I needed it.

'It's from AJ, a set-up,' I hissed, leaning in behind Sam and Naomi.

'It's what?' Sam demanded.

'A set-up,' I said. 'AJ set it up for you. She's not a real traffic warden.'

'Why?' Naomi demanded.

I just shrugged, my inspiration having run out as suddenly as it had arrived. Naomi and Sam exchanged glances, puzzled and a little worried. As we'd spoken Andrea had held her poise, despite having no idea what was going on.

'Hang on,' Sam said, and pulled Naomi by the arm.

They stepped aside, conferring in insistent whispers. I was dreading them deciding to phone AJ, but I was hopeful. They always deferred to her, and I was praying that went as far as taking the occasional punishment. I was right.

'Okay,' Sam said as she came back to Andrea and I. 'Sorry if we spoiled the surprise. It was just such a shock. You're so convincing!'

The last comment was to Andrea, who smiled and nodded. Sam was nervous, and so was Naomi, but they were going to go for it. My heart was absolutely hammering as I introduced them, the girls responding to Andrea's cheerful greeting with sulky looks.

'I bet you'll find a tawse in the boot,' I told Andrea, 'that or something as good.'

'Open the boot,' she ordered, nodding to Naomi.

Naomi went, with such a gorgeous look of consternation on her face that it was a real struggle for me not to laugh out loud. She was going to take her punishment, but that didn't mean she had to be enthusiastic about it, which was just the way I liked it. She opened the boot, and sure enough, they'd packed some kit, kit which had been intended for me, and was now going to be used on them. There was no tawse, but there was a vicious-looking black riding whip, and rope, along with a gag, some real mean-looking nipple clamps and two strap-ons. It made me swallow hard, just to see what I would have been in for – punished, tortured and fucked, probably up my bum.

'That will do nicely,' Andrea declared. 'Take it all.'

They obeyed her, concealing what they could and passing Andrea the whip. She took it, and gave Sam a cut across the seat of her leathers, which brought out a little hot sob. Naomi scurried across the road before she could be given the same treatment. We followed, down one of the little sandy tracks and across an area of grass, into woodland, scrubby gorse and rhododendrons. Andrea chose her place without much fuss. It was risky, a little area of grass shut off by gorse bushes on three sides and a big holly tree. We weren't the first to use it for sex either.

'Here?' Sam queried.

'It's as private as the place you made me serve topless,' I pointed out.

'Well, okay, but I'm not stripping,' she said, Naomi nodding hasty agreement.

'You won't need to,' Andrea told her. 'Right, first, I'm not having any screaming. Samantha, open wide.'

Sam was going to protest at the use of her girly name, but thought better of it, quickly cutting off her words and meekly opening her mouth. I gave Andrea the ball gag, and she put it in Sam's mouth, strapping it tight behind her head. It was wonderful. Just having that big red plastic ball in her open mouth changed her completely, from a hard leather dyke to a frightened girl about to be punished.

'Only one proper gag, I'm afraid,' Andrea addressed Naomi. 'Let's see . . .'

'Panty-gag her!' I cut in immediately. 'Go on, Andrea, do it!'

'Don't forget you're getting it too!' Naomi answered me.

'It's a good idea anyway,' Andrea said. 'Come on, Naomi, let's have those knickers off!'

'I have to take my trousers off, everything!' Naomi protested.

'No problem,' Andrea answered.

She was so cool. She just reached up under her skirt, right in front of the horrified Naomi. I caught a glimpse of flesh and the straining hem of one stocking under her uniform skirt, then the white of her panties as she took hold of them. They came down, and off, to be waded into a tight ball of cotton and presented to the hapless Naomi's mouth.

'Come on!' Andrea urged. 'Open wide.'

Naomi's mouth came open, slowly, reluctantly, but she did it. Immediately Andrea wadded the panties in, all of them, to leave Naomi with her mouth slightly open to show a little piece of white material. I was giggling, unable to hold back my amusement, and both of them gave me dirty looks as Andrea began to uncoil one of the hanks of rope.

'Hands behind your back,' she ordered Naomi. 'Stand straight.'

I could see Naomi shivering, and she was seriously reluctant, but she did it, turning, to cross her wrists in the small of her back. Andrea twisted the rope around them in a tight figure of eight, tying the centre off. More followed, the rope wound around her waist to fix her wrists in place, then up, to her head, and around her mouth, holding the panties firmly in.

'There we are, I bet that feels better already,' Andrea teased as she lashed off the knot behind Naomi's head. 'Now you, Samantha. Hands behind your back.'

Sam obeyed, and was given the same treatment, tied up so that she would be unable to protect herself during the coming punishment, except by running, and with her trousers down that was just going to look comic. It would also mean they got seen.

'Good girls,' Andrea stated, patting Sam's bottom. 'Now, Jade, if you could find me a nice strong piece of wood, we'll see about punishing these two, shall we?'

'Just twigs, or shall I make a birch?' I asked, catching Naomi's look of surprise and worry as she realised I was not to be punished at the same time.

187

'Neither,' Andrea answered. 'A stick, say six foot, and thick. Nothing rotten.'

I found what she wanted, which took a few minutes. By the time I got back, she had the girls kneeling, side by side, with their bottoms pushed out into twin balls of glossy black leather. I was sorry she hadn't stripped them, but they hadn't been so lucky with their boobs. Both had had their bras pulled up, and the round, girlish globes of flesh hung bare from their chests, swinging slightly to their breathing, the nipples erect. Their heads were hung too, but as I approached Sam turned to give me a look of reproach and a quick nod, indicating that I should get down beside her.

'Samantha thinks I ought to be getting it too,' I told Andrea as I passed her the stick. 'Isn't that right, Sammy?'

Sam nodded furiously, Naomi joining in.

'I would punish Jade,' Andrea said as she laid the stick across the girls' backs. 'In fact I might do, later. For now I choose not to. Besides, I need her to help me fuck you.'

That got a reaction out of them, both turning their heads in protest and mumbling through their gags. I couldn't help laughing, but Andrea took no notice, calmly lashing the stick across first Naomi's wrists, then Sam's, fixing them together and leaving them more helpless still.

'All yours,' she announced, standing. 'Sorry about taking their tits out, but I just couldn't resist it. You can do their bums anyway. I'll hold them down if they need it.'

'Thanks, Andrea!' I answered.

I knelt, grinning like an idiot. Both Sam and Naomi were looking back, their eyes filled with impotent rage at the realisation that they weren't going to be punished by the stern, powerful Andrea, but by me. Not that they could do a thing about it, bound and helpless, with her easily able to keep them under control if they tried to get up.

Their bottoms were just so tempting, stuck out in their trousers, round and girlish, with the shapes of their pussies encased in black leather. I could so easily have kissed them, and rubbed my face into their bottoms, but held myself back, determined to stay dominant. I had a grope anyway, stroking them and smoothing my hands over their cheeks, to feel the roundness and the soft texture of their flesh.

Being felt up made them squirm, but with Andrea stood over them neither tried to rise. I took my time, and even began to smack, letting them think they might get away with bare boobs and a spanking on leather. There was no chance of that.

'You have lovely bottoms,' I declared, patting both at once. 'Yours is meatier, Sammy, a little, but Naomi's is wonderfully round. Which is the most spankable? I'm not sure. Perhaps I can decide once I've pulled down your trousers.

That set them off again, mumbling through their gags and wriggling their bottoms about, until Andrea had to slap Sam's face. That shut her up, and she was as good as gold as my fingers found the button of her jeans and popped it open. Her zip came down, and I did it, easing her trousers off her hips and bum, slowly, letting her feel it as she was exposed, inch by inch, of flesh, then the tight black panties she had on, and more flesh, the chubby tuck of her bottom, most of which was spilling out of the sides.

With her trousers down and her panties on show I could hear her breathing, urgent, almost in panic. There was no doubting her arousal though, with a big damp patch making a harp shape over her pussy.

'You're wet, Samantha,' I told her. 'Come and look at the little tart's pussy, Andrea.'

Andrea came round, and together we inspected Sam's pussy. She held still, to my surprise, even when Andrea used the handle of the whip to poke a fold of panty material up the wet hole.

'Hot little bitch, isn't she?' Andrea said, watching it go in.

'Who'd have thought it?' I agreed. 'So much to only getting off when she's on top.'

I moved to Naomi, leaving Andrea to explore Sam's rear. She fought a little, but it was hopeless, and I soon had her trousers loose, then down, to discover bright red panties underneath. Just like Sam's, they were wet at the crotch. I stood, licking my lips at the sight, with my fingers shaking at the thought of what I was about to do.

'Right,' I said, 'panties down and it's time you had your bums whipped.'

Bending, I put a hand into the waistband of each pair of panties. Sam's bottom twitched, Naomi gave a muffled protest, and I began to pull. Out they came, two round, naked bottoms, flared to show bumholes and pussies as the panties came down, and off, settled down into their leathers to leave absolutely everything showing. Again, I just wanted to lick their rears for them, but again I resisted my natural inclinations. Instead I took the whip from Andrea and walked around in front of the girls, showing it to them. Sam gave a little broken moan. Naomi shut her eyes, unable to look.

I've been punished side by side with another girl often enough to know how it feels, sharing your shame, but each knowing how the other looks and feels, and that they in turn know. In some ways it's comforting, in others worse than being done alone. Hearing them cry as they're beaten, for instance, and knowing it's my turn soon, or watching as they crawl to lick at their persecutors while I'm still in the throws of punishment.

It's bad enough in a lesbian club, where I want everyone to see what I've got. Outdoors it's worse, far worse, and I was sure the girls felt the same, for all their confidence. Nude is one thing; tied up with your panties around your knees is quite another. It was revenge, it was perfect, and I was going to take my time.

I began to flick the whip at their bottoms, gently, barely hard enough to leave marks. They reacted though, wincing and making the funniest little sounds through their noses. I made the smacks harder, aiming some at their pussy-lips, and they started to squeak and whimper, shaking their heads and looking back to beg my mercy with their eyes.

That's the thing with whipping a dominant. They're not used to it. Smacks which would have had me giggling and sticking up my bum for more obviously hurt. It just made me worse, laying the whip in harder, until they were really gasping, both of them, making the most pathetic sobbing noises. Their skin was starting to redden, and they were well on heat, with both their pussies swollen and wet with juice. I began to tease them, telling them it was time for their fucking, but going back to beating them.

Andrea watched it all, smiling in delight and occasionally reaching down to stroke one of the girls' heads, or to pet her boobs or bum. She was sweet about it, soothing, but I knew that for them her sympathy would only add to their humiliation. She was getting horny too, I could tell, and I wasn't at all surprised when at last she gave in. Her uniform skirt came up, her panties were pulled to one side as she sank into a squat. The gag was pulled free, and Andrea's pussy shoved firmly into Sam's face. Sam began to lick, straight away, and I just laughed.

'What a little tart!' I crowed. 'Look at your friend, Naomi, your tough, leather dyke friend, licking pussy because she's been given a hot bum! Are you going to be the same, are you?'

I gave Naomi a hard cut across her cheeks, making her kick and blow out the air through her nose in shock.

That looked funny, and I gave her another one even as she frantically shook her head.

'We'll see,' I said, 'maybe you need fucking first, up your bum.'

That really had her squirming, kicking and tugging at the stick, until Sam's face was pulled away from Andrea's crotch.

'Stay still, you little bitch!' Andrea ordered, and grabbed Sam by the hair, pulling her hard in.

Sam began to lick again. Andrea's mouth came open in pleasure, and I realised she was going to come. I watched it happen, still smacking the whip against Naomi's bottom as Andrea's face glazed in ecstasy. She came, biting her lip to stop herself crying out, with her hand twisted hard in Sam's hair and the most beautiful expression on her face.

My hand was already up my skirt, pressed to the wet cotton of my panty crotch. I had to come, or I was going to lose control. With a last hard cut for each bottom, I dropped the whip, going to Naomi's head end despite my desire to burrow my tongue up the tight brown bottom hole that tempted me so much. I squatted down, Naomi gasping as I tugged the rope free of her mouth. Andrea's soggy panties came out, my skirt was up and my own panties aside. I pressed my pussy to her mouth, taking her by the hair, only to find her pursing her lips and trying to pull her head aside.

'Lick it!' I ordered.

Naomi did nothing, but Andrea responded, taking hold of the whip. Naomi saw, and before it had even made impact with her bum she was licking, as obedient and servile as Sam, lapping at my pussy with desperate eagerness, just to spare her bottom from Andrea's attention.

She got her whipping anyway, Andrea taking turns with them, smack after smack, and a lot harder than I'd done it. They were soon squealing, Sam especially, but we were too far gone to care, Andrea applying the whip as I rubbed myself into Naomi's face, glorying in my revenge and her submission until my orgasm started and all I could think of was the ecstasy of having her tongue on my clitty.

We'd have fucked them, side by side in their bondage, maybe even up their bums. It never happened though, because Sam's cries got too loud and we attracted attention. It wasn't one of the gay guys either, who wouldn't have mattered. In fact I was sure at least one had had a peep at us through the bushes. Instead, it was some officious-looking bloke in a peaked cap, and it was only Andrea's quick thinking that stopped us getting caught.

She saw him coming, but instead of panicking, she made out that she'd been caught short. He was told in no uncertain terms to keep his distance, and he did. I stayed down, praying he'd go away, and when Andrea called him a dirty Peeping Tom he did.

The moment was gone though, with the girls pleading to be untied. I'd have liked to be as hard to them as they had been to me, but I couldn't find it in myself and obliged, pulling up their panties and helping Andrea to untie them. We made it, but it was a close thing, with the man hanging around on the grassy area we'd crossed to get there, and obviously suspicious. Fortunately he didn't have the guts to face us down. What he thought a traffic warden was doing with two girls in leather and one quite obviously dressed for sex is anybody's guess, but I'll bet it kept him in wanks for months.

If I had any sense at all, I'd have left it there. Both Sam and Naomi were seriously humiliated, and they both had red bums. I'd even come, and it really should have been enough for me.

Unfortunately, as we beat a hasty retreat to our cars, I was thinking of the extent to which they had used me, and I just didn't feel satisfied. Even then, I would probably have left it, but Andrea was up for more and wouldn't let them go. We'd got them high too, for all their chagrin at our close encounter, and they wanted to come.

So we piled into Naomi's car, full of nervous laughter for what had happened, and with Andrea every bit in charge, just as AJ was when she was with them. They were teasing me, and threatening to get even, but it didn't matter, as long as I had Andrea. Besides, there was that ever-present little voice in the back of my head, telling me that the best possible thing to happen was for me to get caught out and comprehensively punished.

I nearly did, because the most sensible place to go to carry on playing was AJ's, and they wanted her to join in. I could do nothing, but continue to lie as they asked why she'd set Andrea up for them, until by the time we reached Kingsbury I'd dug myself into the most enormous hole.

Fortunately AJ was out, and not answering her mobile. That was such a relief, and I'd have quit then and there, only the girls knew where she kept her spare key. So we went in, Sam and Naomi acting as if they owned the place and dishing out beers, also telling Andrea about how I'd been given to AJ as a birthday present.

That really had me blushing, and it got worse. She told them about my session in her cell, including the details of how I'd used the potty. They thought it was hilarious, and countered with the story of putting the mess down my trousers on the Heath. I could feel my control slipping away, sure that at any moment one or other of them would suggest that it was about time I was put in my place. For all my instincts, I had to turn it around.

'Yeah, well you were no better,' I retorted, as Sam described how turned on I'd been by being made to serve topless outdoors. 'You were soaking just now. Which reminds me, Andrea, we never did make them come, did we?'

'No, we didn't,' Andrea agreed.

'How about it?' I demanded of them. 'Believe me, until you've come while you're being punished, you don't know what it's like. That's why AJ set this whole thing up.'

'Eh?' Sam queried. 'What do you mean? She's done that before. Not outside, sure, and always in private. In fact I'm amazed she let you in on it.'

'Outside, that's what I meant,' I said, back pedalling desperately. 'It's stronger.'

'You're not joking,' Naomi answered me, 'but no, not after coming that close to getting caught. I'd rather –'

'I'd like to make you come anyway,' Andrea cut in, saving me from whatever awful suggestion Naomi had been about to make. 'Really, we'd hardly started.'

'Well, maybe . . .' Naomi said uncertainly.

'Come on,' Andrea ordered. 'No nonsense. Strip.'

She was wonderful, so stern. I'd have obeyed immediately, and Sam and Naomi barely hesitated. I scurried back, quickly excluding myself so that I'd be able to enjoy another helping of revenge. Bras were peeled up, boots removed, trousers pushed down, only for Sam to stop.

'One thing,' she said, 'you do it, Andrea, not Jade. She's just too much the sub to take charge.'

'Fair enough,' Andrea answered. 'Jade?'

'I . . .' I managed, stuck, but only for a second. 'Okay, but you can have me as a toy, to use on them.'

'Sorry?' Andrea asked.

'Like, if you want to humiliate them,' I went on, 'to make them kiss my feet or something, but still under your orders.'

'Sounds good,' Andrea answered.

'I'm . . .' Sam began, but trailed off.

She was still on a high, or she'd never have done it. I had no illusions about why either. It wasn't for me, but for Andrea, and by extension for AJ, or so she thought. That was good enough for me.

I watched as they finished stripping, all the way. They were so turned on that I could smell their pussies from across the room. Just seeing them nude was good, a privilege I'd never normally have been permitted. The scene's odd that way, but as a submissive girl I'm much more likely to see my top's pussy or bumhole than her feet.

'On the floor,' Andrea ordered.

They went down, both kneeling, to look up at her with arousal, but fear too, the uncertainty of not knowing what was coming. I did, and they were right to be scared.

'You two, hands behind your backs,' Andrea said. 'Jade, fetch a belt, or a strap.'

'Where are they?' I asked.

'AJ's room,' Sam told me. 'There's a chest of drawers.'

I scampered quickly upstairs, not wanting to miss anything. I thought I knew were AJ kept her gear, but the first drawer I pulled open only had clothes in it, most of them leather. The second was just full of junk. I pushed it to, but it jammed on a book of some kind with a thick cardboard cover. I pulled at the drawer, irritably, only to stop as I realised that the object was a photo album.

It was impossible not to inspect it, and I pulled it out, expecting pictures of AJ in her leathers, maybe rude ones with any luck. What I got was something very different. The inside cover had a sticker on it, and writing, bright pink writing – 'Alice Jemima Croft, aged 12'. It was such a wet name, and I was already grinning as I turned the page, then laughing behind my hand.

There she was, in a big print, unmistakable AJ, but with long blonde curls in place of the cropped stubble, and a pink party dress in place of the leathers. She was obviously well proud of herself as well, with a smug expression on her face. There were more too, all of her, alone or with friends, and every one showing her in little cutesy dresses, some with lace, even frills.

I'd never seen anything so funny. However tough she was now, she had been the wettest, most girly twelve-year-old I've ever come across, and every photo showed it. Not to pinch one would have been a crime. I chose a small one, in the hope she wouldn't notice, slipping it up my top. It was a goodie, small or not, showing her in some sort of fancy dress competition, in a pink and white fairy costume, complete with wings and a little pink wand with a star on the end.

I found her gear the next go, in the drawer below, which really brought home the contrast. To change from wet little girl to hardcore diesel dyke was quite a rebellion, but then it wasn't so very different from what had happened to me, just more extreme. As I selected a huge black tawse from among her selection of punishment implements I was wondering if it wasn't precisely because her parents had made her so girlie that she had ended up so butch.

My mouth was set in a huge grin as I ran back down stairs, and it got bigger as I saw what Andrea had done to Sam and Naomi. They were on the floor, tied up in the nude, their hands lashed behind their backs, their ankles bound together and their legs tucked up to their thighs. Some people make the mistake of tying girls' ankles to their wrists, which obstructs their bums. Not Andrea, she'd put them in loops, from their wrists to the back of their knees, leaving their pussies sticking out, their boobs and bums clear for smacking and just enough slack to thrash a little. Both had their panties stuffed into their mouths, each with a scrap of material hanging out from between her lips.

I snagged myself a beer and curled up on the sofa to watch as Andrea finished tying Naomi's legs into place. Both girls looked seriously worried, their eyes turned up to Andrea as she stood over them, then to the tawse as I passed it over. It was a vicious thing, thick, oiled leather, two foot long and split for the last six inches, guaranteed to leave some serious welts.

'Right, you little bitches,' Andrea said, 'let's make this plain. This goes my way. I'm going to smack you around, quite a bit, your faces as well as your behinds. If you really can't take it, spit your knickers out and call out "clemency". I'll stop, but you'll have to lick my backside if you do.'

'Make it harder,' I suggested. 'AJ probably makes them do that anyway, and not clean.'

Andrea just laughed. From the immediate look of shock on Sam's face I knew I was right. I'd been pretty sure, from the start, that they went down for AJ, but I hadn't known it went that far. I laughed, and stuck my tongue out at them. Both turned me angry looks in response, Naomi especially, only for her expression to turn to shock and pain as Andrea brought the tawse down across her bottom. It had started.

She beat them up, there's no other way to describe it. Sure, she was careful not to risk really hurting them, and they got off on it, but that doesn't alter what she did. Most of it was by hand, smacks and pinches to their bottoms, their faces, their boobs and their pussy-lips, until it was all flushed pink. The tawse was well used, applied hard to bottoms and thighs and backs, nearly as hard to boobs and bellies. They were soon red with marks, thick double lines of angry scarlet, ending in darker blotches. She put the boot in too, kicking at their bottoms and legs, prodding at their wet pussies, even pushing her heels into their breasts. They took it, mewling through their gags, squirming and kicking their bound legs against the loops of rope, wriggling on the floor, but never trying to cry off.

Andrea was good, reaching down to frig their pussies now and then, just to keep them on heat, high enough to take more, but never high enough to come. They were dripping, both of them, Sam with white pussy juice running down her thighs, Naomi with her hole wide and smeared with dirt from Andrea's shoe.

For me, I had my skirt up and my panties around one ankle, playing with myself and laughing at them. It was just so good, to see Sam with her face slapped red, with spittle running from the corners of her mouth, and Naomi, her skin blotchy with smacks, snivelling and sniffing to try to stop the snot running out of her nose. They were going to be marked, both of them, like I had been, and like I had been, they were just too far gone to care.

So was I, frigging openly as Andrea slapped and kicked and pinched at them, harder and harder, making a real mess of their bums and boobs, a mess that was going to last for weeks. I came like that, watching Naomi's legs kick in her straps as Andrea smacked the tawse down, hard, across the purple flesh of her exposed bottom, with her pussy dirty and swollen and dribbling juice. It lasted so long, on and on, with my eyes fixed on the girl who had tormented me as she was beaten on the floor, ecstasy, but the delight of revenge too, even in the rapture of climax.

I don't think they even noticed, certainly not the girls, with far to much to occupy their minds to worry about what I was doing. Both were in a really sorry state by then, their bottoms and legs dark with bruising, their faces and boobs little better, their skin wet with sweat, flushed and glossy. I kicked my panties off, onto Naomi, but she barely seemed to notice, just jerking to the slaps as Andrea beat her.

She was having her breasts done, her nipples rock hard as the tawse flicked and snapped at her skin. Her eyes were shut, and full of tears, with the snot now running freely out of her nose. The scrap of red material blocking her mouth was wet, soaked, and she was chewing on it, rhythmically, as her boobs jumped and shivered to the tawse smacks. She was ripe, I could tell, beyond caring.

'Frig her off, Andrea,' I urged. 'Go on, make her show what a slut she is!'

Andrea nodded, and spat, full in Naomi's face.

'Time to come, bitch,' she said happily.

She dipped down, sliding two fingers up Naomi's pussy and bringing them out slimy with juice. They were wiped on one smarting bottom-cheek, and pushed back up, to pull out more juice. That went in Naomi's face, smeared across her slapped cheeks and over her nose. More followed, Andrea dipping into the wet honey-pot and slapping the mess onto Naomi's body, face, boobs, belly and bum.

Naomi was moaning, sticking her pussy out for penetration, dirty and wanton as she was soiled. Her pussy was getting looser as she was fingered, until at last Andrea's whole fist went in, engulfed in wet flesh, pushing the sex-lips up and forwards to leaving the clitoris a little hard bud, stuck up at the centre. Dropping the tawse, Andrea touched Naomi's clitty, using one long nail to scrape the tiny bud. At that Naomi's back arched tight, pushing out her breasts, with her legs straining against her bonds. Andrea chuckled, a really cruel sound, and touched the swollen clitoris again. Naomi's mouth came wide, her sodden panties spat free, gasping for air, then screaming as for the third time the nail tip was drawn across her clitoris. She came, just, but was left at the very peak. Andrea stood, grinning, her eyes glittering with pleasure, looking down at Naomi's soiled, beaten body. Naomi looked up, her eyes full of confusion, her mouth wide.

'Finish me,' she begged. 'Please, Andrea.'

'No,' Andrea answered. 'Not yet. Out.'

She gave Naomi a kick on the bottom, making her gasp.

'Into the bathroom, Jade,' she ordered. 'These two need a wash.'

Again she kicked Naomi's bottom, then reached down and took Sam by her hair, twisting her fist hard in the pale locks, and pulling. Sam came, her face twisted in pain as she was dragged by the hair, out of the room. Naomi followed, squirming along the ground like a caterpillar. I picked up the tawse and a couple more beers, standing to watch as Andrea picked Sam up and carried her up the stairs, then Naomi.

The girls were dumped on the bathroom floor, in a pile, with Naomi lying over Sam, bum up. I gave Andrea the tawse, and she applied a couple of hard swats to each bottom, then kicked Naomi so that she rolled off onto the floor. Reaching out to take a beer from me, she upended it over her mouth, not stopping until she had emptied the entire bottle down her throat.

'Good,' she said, 'thirsty work, giving discipline, and they get all the fun!'

She kicked Sam again, and stretched. I sat down on the edge of the bath, taking a pull from my own bottle.

'Right,' Andrea said, 'I think you know what's going to happen. You're going to get pissed on. Now, if you're going to be good girls, and do as you're told, I'll untie your hands. I might even let you frig yourselves. Well?'

Sam nodded, the piece of panty cotton sticking out of her mouth going up and down like a little flag. Andrea turned to Naomi, who did the same, if not so willingly. Andrea nodded to me and I set to work, undoing the loops that held the girls legs up, then their wrists, leaving them with just their ankles bound. Andrea reached down to twitch the soggy black panties out of Sam's mouth.

'I bet you could do with a drink first?' she asked, holding out her empty beer bottle.

'Please,' Sam said, Naomi nodding agreement.

'No problem,' Andrea answered, and immediately began to hitch up the front of her uniform skirt.

Neither girl tried to stop it, but both stared in horror. Andrea was still pantiless under her skirt, and with it up her bare pussy showed. Standing over the girls, she put the bottle between her lips, and just let go. Her pee squirted out, some into the bottle, but more splashing out over the girls and the floor. I laughed, watching the urine fill the bottle until it was bubbling out around the neck. It was quite something, watching an apparently respectable traffic warden piss in a bottle, never mind the two beaten girls on the floor at her feet. When it was full Andrea took it away, but she didn't stop, emptying her bladder over Sam's chest and Naomi's hips and tummy, to leave them lying in a pool of pee.

'Kneel up,' she ordered as the gush finally died. 'Drink it.'

She gave the bottle to Sam, who put it to her mouth, gingerly, tipping it up, to taste the piddle. It touched her lips and her face screwed up in disgust, but then she was drinking, the bottle upended over her mouth, her eyes tight shut as she swallowed down Andrea's urine.

'Enough!' Andrea ordered suddenly, snatching the bottle away and slapping Sam hard across the face. 'Don't be greedy. You friend wants her share.'

Naomi didn't, because she was kneeling there with an expression of absolute misery on her face. She wouldn't take the bottle, and Andrea had to take her by the hair and push it to her mouth.

'Drink!' Andrea ordered. 'That or ten of the tawse across your tits!'

Naomi drank, swallowing the hot piddle down with her eyes screwed up and her body shaking with reaction. She was made to finish it, and by the end she was looking more sorry for herself than ever, with little runnels of pee coming from either side of her mouth and dripping onto her boobs.

'Good girls!' Andrea crowed as she pulled the bottle away. 'Nothing like a good drink of piss, is there? You are a pair of little sluts, aren't you?'

Both nodded, looking up at her, Sam almost worshipful, Naomi still with resentment.

'Ah, didn't I let you come properly?' Andrea said. 'You poor little thing! Never mind, maybe I'll let you masturbate while you lick my pussy. Would you like that?'

'Yes, please,' Naomi answered automatically, Sam echoing her.

'Not yet!' I demanded. 'I want to piss on them, too!'

'Well, girls?' Andrea asked mockingly.

Sam looked at me, doubtful, then just hung her head. Naomi said nothing. I didn't hesitate, standing even as I turned my skirt up. I could feel the pressure in my bladder as I pushed out my pussy, right at them, but I held back, letting them watch, and then suddenly let go.

My pee burst out, full in Naomi's face. Her lips were pursed, her eyes screwed up as I sprayed my piddle over her, then Sam, also in her face, then back. I was laughing, absolutely cackling with joy as I pissed on them, in their faces and over their chests, down their bellies and into their hair, with the yellow fluid cascading down their bodies, dripping from their nipples and soaking their pubic hair, to form a big puddle underneath them.

'Now you can frig,' Andrea told them as my pee finally died to a trickle, 'in Jade's piss, and you can lick us while you do it.'

There was no protest. Their tongues came out even as we pushed our pussies into their faces, Andrea grinning down at me as they started to lick. I had Sam, and it just so good, holding her head as she slurped at my pussy, licking me out while she knelt in my piddle. She was soaking, and Naomi was as bad, their skin wet with piss and sweat, their hair a bedraggled mess, hanging down like rats' tails, and dripping with pee.

They were masturbating though, the pair of them, knees well spread and fingers busy with their pussies.

Sam was truly eager, her bottom pushed out and her face buried in my crotch, lapping up my juice with one hand between her thighs and the other moving over her body, touching the sore, wet skin to get the full thrill of what had been done to her. Naomi was less blatant, masturbating as if it was only because she'd been told to, and crying softly as she licked at Andrea's sex. I didn't believe it, not for a second, and sure enough, she was the first to come, absolutely snivelling, then suddenly going tight, her whole body rigid in ecstasy, only her fingers moving as she brought herself to a climax that just went on and on, and all the while feeding on Andrea's sex.

It was too much for Andrea, who came herself as Naomi was still in climax, hissing between clenched teeth. She'd had Naomi's hair in her hand, twisted, and held it tight until she'd finished, forcing Naomi to lick her to full satisfaction. Only then did she let go. Naomi pulled back, her face plastered in Andrea's juice and her own mucus, a truly filthy mess, and all on the blotchy red skin from her smacking. Her eyes turned up, red with crying, with bubbles of mucus around both nostrils, her mouth wide in the aftermath of her orgasm, and Andrea just spat in her face.

That hit me, such a jolt. I was coming before I knew it, calling out for Andrea as I watched the spittle roll slowly down Naomi's face and over one eye. Andrea's arm came around me, cuddling me as I climaxed in Sam's face, and for the second time I got that beautiful blend of erotic pleasure and sweet revenge. As before, it really lasted, and it wasn't until I'd started to come down that I realised Sam was no longer frigging, but had given her full concentration to licking my pussy. Finished, I sat back on the bath, dizzy with pleasure and effort. Sam looked at me, her face as filthy as Naomi's, her pee soaked hair plastered across her forehead.

'Go on then, finish off, slut, Samantha,' I said.

She turned her eyes to Andrea, then back to me, uncertain, waiting.

'Need to be told, do you?' Andrea asked. 'Right, lick Jade's piss up, then. You too, Naomi.'

Sam got down immediately, Naomi more slowly, both licking at the piss puddle, their pink tongues stuck out. Sam was just gone, wanton and dirty, her bum right up, her knees wide, the wet lips of her pussy spread to us as she lapped up the piddle. Naomi was very different, her face wrinkled up in disgust, sobbing occasionally, but she still did it, sucking and licking at the pee as best she could. She was still crying too, the tears mingling with the pee as they ran down her well-smacked face.

Andrea sat down on the toilet, crossing her legs to leave one shoe stuck out, watching as the girls struggled to clean the mess off the floor. Sam was going strong, and rubbing at her pussy as she did it, while Naomi looked as if she was about to be sick. I didn't know which was better.

'Bring Sammy over,' Andrea ordered. 'I'll do her first. Keep licking, Naomi, you're going to get another one.'

I took Sam by the hair, dragging her over to the toilet. She turned as she got there, sinking quickly into a squat, right on Andrea's shoe, her pussy spread across the smooth toe cap.

'Right, you little bitch,' Andrea spat, 'rub yourself off.'

Sam didn't need telling, but immediately began to rub, squirming her bottom down onto Andrea's shoe in just the most lewd motion. Her buttocks were wobbling as she did it, her boobs swinging in time, a sight both dirty and ridiculous, utterly without dignity. It took her no time at all, coming with her pussy squashed out over Andrea's foot, and a good deal of shoe up the hole. Finished, she slumped down, slowly, right in the piss, her face in a pool of it, just not caring.

'Right, Naomi,' Andrea said, and clicked her fingers at the floor in front of her. 'First, you can lick your friend's mess off my shoe.'

I took Naomi's hair, pulling her up from where she'd been licking at my pee. She came, crawling reluctantly over to Andrea and pressing her lips to the dirty shoe. I watched her lick Sam's cream up, and polish the leather with her hair, just as AJ had made me do. That gave me an idea.

'Do her with her head down the loo,' I suggested. 'That's what they did to me.'

Andrea chuckled, standing. Naomi gave a despairing groan. I lifted the lid, once more twisting my hand into Naomi's hair. She came, grudgingly, her face screwed up in utter shame, but she came, letting me press her face down over the rim of the toilet bowl. Her bum was up, her bound ankles sticking out, her dirty pussy peeping out between her thighs, ready.

'Shame it's clean,' I said, peering at the water below Naomi's head. 'Can you do any more?'

'No,' Andrea answered.

'I could,' Sam said. 'Plenty.'

'Do it, then,' Andrea ordered. 'Over her head.'

Naomi had turned, looking back in utter horror at Sam's treachery. I pushed her head down again, giggling as Sam came to straddle the toilet and Naomi's head. My hand was in the way, but I didn't care, and I was laughing as the hot pee squirted out of Sam's pussy. It splashed on my hand and over Naomi's hair, running down around her head to splash into the bowl and run from her nose and lips. Sam had been right, there was plenty, and it went down Naomi's neck too, running round to wet her boobs and leaving her nipples dripping again. As Sam did it, Andrea had sat down on the bath, pushing her foot out to press the toe of her shoe into Naomi's pussy.

'Wriggle your bum,' Andrea ordered,

Naomi obeyed, squirming her sex onto Andrea's foot as the piss spattered out over her head. I pushed her head further down, right in, forcing her to lift her bum higher. Her wriggling became more urgent, her boobs began to swing, and a sob escaped her. Sam's pee was dying, too weak to squirt out, but running in a trickle down one thigh. I pulled off a piece of loo paper, dabbing at her, and another, a long bit, dropping both into the loo.

'Climb off,' I ordered Sam, 'and get behind me; I want my bum licked.'

There was no hesitation. She obeyed, getting hastily down on the floor as I sank into a squat. Naomi was getting frantic, close to orgasm, as Sam slid herself under me. I sat down, right in her face, wiggling my bottom to spread the cheeks and get my anus over her mouth. She started to lick, right away, probing my bumhole. I could imagine the taste in her mouth, from experience, and it was so good, just knowing, almost as good as the feeling.

My hand went to my pussy, rubbing as I forced Naomi's head still harder into the bowl. She was wriggling her bottom like mad, gasping and panting into the toilet, her boobs quivering, to shake drops of pee from her stiff nipples.

'Flush yourself, you little bitch!' Andrea spat, and lashed out to slap Naomi hard across her bottom.

Naomi's hand came up, slowly, as if she couldn't believe what she was doing. She couldn't stop herself either, and it went to the plunger, and down. Water exploded around her head, gushing out, the level rising, over her face, swirling up until her hair was floating in it. My mouth came open at the sight, my bottom settling harder into Sam's face, her tongue pushing deeper up my hole in response.

My clitty was burning under my finger, my pussy pressed hard to Sam's chin, my bumhole open and sloppy around her tongue. It was perfect, Naomi with her head down a toilet, Sam with her tongue up my bottom, for the third time, ecstasy and revenge, as I came, screaming aloud, clutching at my pussy and jerking at Naomi's hair.

I wasn't the only one. Naomi had climaxed on Andrea's foot as she was flushed, and her muscles were still jerking and twitching as my own orgasm slowly faded. Like mine, it took time to die, and she kept her head down the loo, even though I'd released my grip. When she did come up her eyes were still shut, with yellow water dribbling from her open mouth and her hair full of bits of loo paper.

She spat out a mouthful, leaning forwards over the loo, swallowing, only for her throat to suddenly tighten. Naomi was sick as I was climbing off Sam's face as, emptying her stomach down the loo in tune to some truly awful noises. I was grinning, although I did feel sympathy – some anyway – but I was also thinking of how it had felt to have my panties pulled down in a bar full of men, and of walking across Hampstead Heath with my trousers seat bulging behind me.

It was enough, for me, more than enough. Not Andrea. She waited for Naomi to finish being sick, and calmly ordered them to clean up the mess. They did it, orgasms or no orgasms, crawling nude on the floor, using their panties as rags to mop up the pee and wringing the pathetic little scraps of cotton out over the toilet. I watched, thoroughly pleased with myself, yet still amazed at what a good beating can do to a girl, turning a haughty bitch into a grovelling, servile slut. I mean, I get that way, but then I'm a slut to start with.

In the end I left them to it, feeling thoroughly smug as I went down the stairs to fetch myself another beer. The front room was a mess, with the girls clothes still on the floor and our empty beer bottles on the table. I chuckled at the sight, knowing that it wouldn't be me clearing it up, only to stop short at the sound of an engine from outside.

I ducked down, just in time, as AJ's bike turned in at the drive. Near panic, I ran to the hall, peering out

208

through the spy hole and praying she'd put it in the garage and come in that way. She dismounted, started for the front door, hesitated, and went for the garage. I waited, my heart in my mouth, listening to the grate of the garage door rising. She came out again, straddled the bike, kicking at the ground to roll it under cover. There was a pause, silence, and again the door grated, shut. I opened the front door, and just ran.

Nine

I was in serious trouble, and no mistake. Sure, both girls had come in absolute ecstasy, several times, and it was going to be an experience they'd be masturbating over until their pussies were raw. That didn't make the slightest difference.

If my plan had worked I'd have been fine. Naomi would have been alone, and she'd have fallen for Andrea's lesbian traffic warden act. She would have gone along with my suggestion of taking the cane to be let off her fine, and I'd have had the satisfaction of watching her beaten, and of having tricked her, with no risk to myself. It hadn't worked like that, and if both Naomi and Sam had got far more than I'd ever hoped for, it had been at the expense of my supposed lack of involvement. Then there was AJ, maybe Andrea too, depending on what had happened at the house.

So I didn't go back to my flat, but to Uncle Rupert's house. The first thing I noticed was that the alarm light on his answering machine was on, with ten messages and the memory full. That was odd, and I was about to play them back when the phone rang. It was him.

'Jade?' he demanded as I answered.

'No, it's a burglar,' I quipped.

'Very funny,' he said. 'Look, listen. I'm coming back tomorrow, and Sarah's coming with me, to stay.'

'To stay?'

'Yes, for good. We're engaged . . .'

'Well . . . congrats.'

'Thanks, but never mind that. Look, I don't think she could handle my collection of magazines and stuff, and as for the uniforms . . .'

'She'd freak!'

'You are not joking. So look, I need you to take them down to your flat –'

'How?'

'Not the mannequins, just the uniforms, my collection too, the magazines anyway. She won't mind the books, but above all, you've got to take the photos we took of us . . .'

'They're back?'

'Yes, there's this bloke . . . Look, never mind that. Do it, please. Use cabs, and I'll pay you back.'

'Hang on a minute, I –'

'Just do it, Jade, please! I won't have a chance, and she means so much to me.'

'Well . . .'

'Good girl, I knew I could count on you! Look, we're in a restaurant and she's only gone to the loo, so I'd better go. Bye.'

He put the phone down, leaving me holding the receiver in my hand with my emotions whirling in my head. I was happy for him, of course I was, but this was the man who'd fucked me, only days before, and with who I'd built up one of the most intimate and trusting relationships of my life. It was impossible not to feel jealous, and hurt, but I was still going to help.

Not that I was exactly happy about carting several boxes of spanking magazines across north London, but there was a worse problem than that, the reason I was at his house in the first place. AJ and the girls were sure to come to my flat, and while I was perfectly capable of lying low and pretending not to be there, if I was humping boxes up and down the stairs there was every chance they would catch me.

All I could think of was to get the stuff ready in the hall, and then to go late at night, when hopefully the girls would have given up. If they hadn't, well, that was my bad luck. After all, I was going to get it anyway, or so I kept telling myself.

Actually, it was going to be far worse if they caught me soon. That's just the way it works, and while I was quite happy to take a good beating in some club at a future date, I really didn't want to catch the full force of their vengeance while Sam and Naomi were still smarting from their punishment.

There would be Andrea too, and while I was pretty sure she would be able to stick up for herself, I was equally sure she'd want a word with me for dropping her in it. I knew what she liked to do to girls, and that was in play. I could handle her, maybe. I could handle AJ, just about, or Sam and Naomi. All four together and I'd be in real trouble. I was close to panic, just thinking about it, and I was cursing myself for not just accepting what they'd done to me. Revenge works two ways after all, and I was at one major disadvantage.

Because of that, and trying to sort out Uncle Rupert's huge collection of filth, it was nearly an hour later that I realised that there was a problem. He and I had a date with Heather for the Wednesday, and Sarah was definitely not the sort who would happily join in with her fiancé for a kinky foursome with his niece and a nurse. I was going to have to cancel, which I really didn't want to do. As I lugged the last of the boxes of magazines down the stairs I was really cursing Rupert.

There were twelve boxes, each packed to the top, and I was running sweat. I'd had to stack them too, and my head was swimming with an endless succession of images of girls in various states of undress, most with their bums red or else stuck out for spanking, and with their faces set in expressions of pain, shock, misery or contrition. Normally I wouldn't have minded, anything but, only with my head in a complete whorl already it just made things worse.

So I stopped and ate, helping myself to a steak from Rupert's freezer and an expensive bottle from his cellar, which I felt was the least I deserved. That made things seem clearer, and it made me braver too. By the end of the last glass I had resolved to take control of the situation with AJ and the other girls. They could punish me, yes, but under my own terms. After all, it was my right, or so all the literature always says – the submissive partner has ultimate control.

I still waited until midnight before calling a cab. By then I'd finished a second bottle of wine, and was well pissed. I was wet down my panties too, from the endless succession of punished girls in the magazines, the images rising up in my head, again and again. If Rupert had been there I'd have been begging for a spanking, a hard one, an undignified one, over his knee with my bumhole showing. Then he'd have fucked me, good and hard, with me on all fours, the way he'd done me before, in front of Heather. Better still, he could have done it up my bum, spanked and buggered, the same utter degradation he liked to give Sarah.

If the cabbie hadn't rung the bell I'd have masturbated right there, on the floor of Rupert's hallway. I already had my skirt up, and of course I was still pantiless, which was another thing that turning me on. Unfortunately he did, just as I was getting my boobs out, and I was forced to cover myself up with frantic haste, all the while babbling assurances that I'd open the door in a moment. I was blushing, and I'm sure he noticed, a huge, fat man with a sweaty red face and hands, in jeans that could barely contain his gross belly and a shirt with the buttons straining to reveal slices of pallid, hairy flesh.

'You all right, love?' he asked, smoothing what remained of his hair over the bald dome of his head.

'Fine,' I answered. 'I had to get all these boxes downstairs. I've got to get them to Turnpike Lane. You couldn't give me a hand with them, could you?'

'Yeah, all right,' he answered, eyeing the stack of boxes doubtfully. 'If they'll fit.'

They did, just about, but I ended up sitting in the front with him while both the boot and back seat were crammed with boxes. Some of them hadn't even been shut properly, and although I'd put the top mags in upside down, I wasn't at all sure he hadn't guessed what they were. That really had me blushing, and thinking of the cab driver Zoe had made me jerk off. If he had noticed he didn't say anything, but kept up a steady flow of chatter all the way to my flat. It was well gone midnight, but I had him park a good way up the street first, still feeling uneasy. I was right to be. AJ was there, her motorbike propped up right outside my flat. Parked almost opposite was Naomi's BMW. My heart went into my mouth. I was for it, really for it.

I was going to ask to be driven back to Highgate, only for Naomi's face to appear at the cab window. She was a state, both cheeks blotchy with bruising, but she was grinning.

'Hi, Jade,' she said.

'Er . . . Hi,' I managed.

'Good to see you, doll,' she answered, and pulled open my door.

I just sat there, staring, wondering what I could possibly do. Naomi whistled, and waved. In response Sam climbed out of the BMW, then Andrea. I was starting to panic, terrified at what they'd do, imagining the four of them taking out their anger on my body, all thrashing me at once, probably ruining me for a month. That wouldn't be all. They'd bog-wash me, and it wouldn't just be pee in the toilet. They'd tattoo my pussy as a slut, with a needle and biro ink. They'd make me eat my own dirt. They'd pierce my pussy-lips . . .

214

'I . . . er . . . could you give me a hand with my stuff?'
I asked the driver, really piteously.

'Couldn't your mates help?' he said.

'I'd like you to, please?' I begged. Behind me Naomi
laughed.

He gave me an odd look, questioning, doubtful. I
leaned close, right up to his ear. He smelled of cheap
after-shave and hair gel.

'I want to suck your cock, big boy,' I whispered.

I hoped it was the right thing to say, desperately. Not
that I really wanted his gross cock in my mouth but
sucking him off was a lot better than what the girls
would do to me, and it was the only way out I could see.
He looked at me as I sat back, biting his lip in doubt.

'I mean it,' I assured him. 'I do.'

'Yeah, sure,' he said, 'and as soon as I'm out the car
you friend pulls a knife. I ain't stupid, darling.'

'I mean it! I swear!' I babbled. 'If I was going to do
that, would I have brought all the boxes? Do I look like
a mugger?'

'No,' he answered, 'but they do.'

He nodded his head towards Naomi, who had been
taking the conversation in with interest. She did look
just the sort to mug him, it was true, boots, leathers and
a tatty white tee-shirt with no bra underneath.

'We're no muggers, mate,' she laughed. 'She's just
jerking you around. Come on, Jade, let the guy get on
with his work. We'll help you with your stuff.'

'No . . . really,' I managed, almost in tears as I turned
to the driver. 'Look, help, please. They're going to beat
me up.'

'That I believe,' he said, glancing to where AJ, Sam
and Andrea were walking towards us.

'Help me then, please, please!' I babbled, clutching
onto his arm. 'Just come up with me. I'll suck you,
anything!'

Naomi heard, and laughed, turning to the others.

'Hey, girls,' she called. 'This you ought to hear. Jade says she'll suck this fat bastard if he'll keep us off her!'

'Less of the fat,' he said, and that was it. He was on my side.

He hauled himself out of the car as the three girls approached, leaning one huge arm on the roof. Andrea was actually taller than him, but he probably weighed as much as any two of them together, maybe any three. There was tension though, for a moment, and then AJ laughed.

'Let her,' she said. 'She'll hate it. We'll be back, Jade, be sure of it.'

She turned on her heel, Sam and Naomi following immediately, Andrea after a moment's hesitation. I climbed out of the car as they walked away, praying they'd just go, and leave me to talk my way out of what I'd promised. They didn't, all four of them climbing into Naomi's car, with the windows down, watching me.

My skin was crawling at the thought of sucking his cock, but there was nothing I could do. He drove the car close to the flat, double banked. We unloaded it together, carrying the boxes up the stairs to my flat, and all the while with the four girls looking on and making jokes at my expense. My cheeks were burning, and I was close to tears, in such a state that I didn't even realise how much I'd be showing as I climbed the stairs in front of him until it was too late.

'No panties, nice,' he drawled.

It was stupid, because I was going to suck his cock anyway, and he was bound to make me get my boobs out, so it shouldn't have mattered much if he saw up my skirt. It did, and I reached back instinctively, trying to block his leering view as I clutched onto the box I was carrying one-handed.

That was a mistake, a big mistake, because the moment I took my hand away from under the box the bottom collapsed. About twenty spanking magazines fell out, to cascade down the stairs, *Flushed Cheeks, Slap!*, even *Girls in Shame*, which is the one where they make the girls wet themselves while they're beaten.

Inevitably that was what he picked up. It was open too, at the centre spread, a full colour photo of some poor girl with her red bum bare over some dirty old man's lap and piddle dripping out of her lowered panties. I could think of nothing to say, and he just stood there, drinking the filthy picture in.

'Fuck me!' he said eventually. 'Weird! You into this shit!'

'No!' I answered automatically. 'They're ... they're my uncle's. He's getting married, he ... he wanted me to look after them ...'

'Yeah!' he drawled. 'Sure. I believe you.'

'It's true, honestly!' I babbled. 'They're nothing to do with me!'

'Oh, yeah?' he went on, and picked up something else.

It was one of the packs of photos, and it had spilt. He held one up, a picture of me, quite unmistakably me, naked, my bum as red as a cherry as I sucked on Rupert's cock.

'Your uncle?' he asked.

'Yes ... No ... I mean, not really,' I stammered.

'You dirty bitch!'

'No ... you don't understand ...'

'Oh, I understand all right, love. You're a fucking pervert, that's what I understand. Now get in there.'

I went into my flat to sit shivering on my sofa, my head spinning with emotions; disgust, fear, but above all, the most agonising sexual humiliation I'd ever felt. Before it had been easy. I could suck cock, with my eyes closed, pretending it wasn't happening. I could even have swallowed his stuff, maybe. Now it was different. He knew what I was like, and he was sure to make me put out, really put out. He might even want to fuck me, and I'd have to let him. Even that I could just have tried

217

to blank out. I'd done it before, when a boyfriend had let a mate fuck me. No, it wasn't the thought of a fucking that had me, but of him wanting to spank me, because if he did that it was going to turn me on.

It was risk that, or the girls. I could bargain, yes, but I had a horrible suspicion he wouldn't take any shit. He knew I was a slut, he'd seen, and after the photo of me with Rupert's cock in my mouth, claiming to be a lesbian wasn't going to do any good either. Nor was pointing out that whatever I might have done with Rupert it didn't mean I wanted to do it with him. Men never accept that one.

He came back all too quickly, with the last two boxes, putting them down with the others and picking a magazine off the top. It was an old *Flushed Cheeks*, which he opened as he kicked the door shut. I said nothing, not at all sure what I should do.

'So what's all this?' he demanded. 'Blokes slapping girls around? Not right, I reckon.'

'No, it's not like that,' I answered, instinctively defending myself and just spanking in general. 'It's for play.'

'Yeah, looks it,' he said, and turned the picture he'd been looking at.

I had to admit he had a point, at least to myself. It's one of the harder mags, and designed for guys who would actually have liked to spank girls for real, and have them hate it, if they could have got away with it. Certainly that's the way the fantasies were aimed, but then, so are my own, most of the time.

What the picture showed was a choir girl, very sweet and innocent, with long, thick brown hair and a fringe half covering her eyes. She was kneeling on a chair, with her surplice turned up over a very red bum, while her panties had been turned down around her thighs. A bearded bloke who was presumably supposed to be a vicar stood behind her, slipper in hand. The expression on her face was of absolute misery.

'That's just fantasy,' I told him. 'Pretending to hate it is part of the fun.'

'Yeah?'

'Yes, really.'

'Maybe I ought to do you, then, if it's what you get off on,' he went on.

'Er ... no, no thanks, I'm all right,' I managed, realising how close I'd come to dropping myself right in it.

He just shrugged, turning the page to where the girl was on her knees, her head up under the vicar's cassock, sucking cock with her bare red bum still showing. He nodded, his thick tongue briefly flicking out to moisten his lips, and put the magazine down.

'Better get introduced,' he said. 'You're Jade, yeah. That's what that nasty-looking bird said, wasn't it?'

'Yes, Jade,' I answered.

'I'm Dave,' he said, and to my amazement he stuck out his hand.

I shook it, amazed that he thought it was the right thing to do with a girl he was about to make suck his cock and worse. Only then did it dawn on me that he had no idea whatever that he was doing anything wrong, or that my reluctance was anything other than pretended modesty.

'How d'you want it, then,' he asked If you don't want your arse slapped? D'you like doing striptease, or what?'

'Just don't,' I said. 'Make me do whatever you want, but don't try to make me act like I want it.'

'Kinky bitch, ain't you?' he said. 'Right, Jade, if that's the way you like it. I want my cock sucked, and then some. Tits out for starters, and you can suck while I have a look at your dirty pictures.'

It still hadn't sunk in, but I didn't even try to argue. Instead I pulled up my top, showing him my bra. It was one of my smaller ones, too small really, with flesh bulging out around the top of the lacy cups. He licked his lips at the sight, and nodded for me to go on. I reached up behind my back, my fingers trembling. The catch was tricky, the third hook sticking, and when I finally got it free the elastic snapped back. My boobs just fell out, really awkwardly, the bra snapping up to lie on top of them, but hiding nothing. I pulled it off, all of it, top and bra, leaving myself bare. Again he licked his lips.

'Nice,' he drawled. 'I love 'em fat. You can put those round my cock while you're doing me, all right?'

I gave a resigned nod, adding the thought of a titty fucking to my woes.

'Perk your nips up,' he ordered, nodding at my boobs once more.

I shut my eyes as my hands went to my breasts. They felt heavy, my nipples sensitive as I tweaked them gently. I was hoping they'd stay in, to show him how much I hated what he was making me do. It didn't work. Out they came, as big and stiff as ever, stuck up just as proudly as if it had been some beautiful and dominant girl who'd been giving me the orders.

'Nips like fucking raspberries,' he said. 'I knew you'd have big ones. Feel 'em up then, keep 'em hard for Dave.'

That drew another sob from me, pure humiliation, as I fondled my breasts for his pleasure. It's how I masturbate, usually, my boobs in my hands before I get down to the sticky bit, and it was just awful, doing something so intimate in front of him. That didn't stop my nipples staying up, or the little tingling sensations running through me as I touched myself.

'Open your eyes, love,' he drawled. 'Dave's got a treat for you.'

I did it, although I knew exactly what the so called treat was, his cock and balls. He sat down, making the sofa creak as he lowered his bulk onto it. He really was fat, grossly fat, so fat he had to almost lie back to get his crotch far enough out to stop his belly getting in the way. I could only stare in disgust as he unzipped himself and flopped it all over the top of his underpants. Men's genitals are ugly at the best of times. He was gross, big, and hairy, with a fat, pale cock, the foreskin really fleshy, with the red tip already poking out through the hole at the top. He'd pulled his balls out too, big ones, the size of eggs, in a loose, wrinkly sack covered in goose pimples. A great bulge of fat stuck out above it all, like a hood, with some of his pasty white skin showing through the hair.

If he realised the effect he was having on me, then he hid it well, grinning and sticking it out, as if I could possibly have enjoyed the thought of having such a horrid thing in my mouth. That was where it was going, though, and as I sank slowly to my knees I was wondering if it wouldn't be better to let AJ have me after all.

He bent sideways, reaching out for the packets of photos, grinning as he opened one. He began to look at the pictures, the pictures of me getting my spankings, an act so intrusive that it had the tears starting in my eyes. I shuffled closer, the big lump that had been rising in my throat growing until I felt I would choke, or be sick. He moved a bit further forwards, making himself more comfortable. His cock moved to the motion, rolling down over his balls, which shifted sluggishly in their sack in response.

'You can start by licking,' he said. 'Take your time, and don't forget to use your tits.'

I swallowed the lump, meaning to speak, but finding it impossible. His legs were wide in front of me, and all I had to do was lean forwards, and down, to take the horrid thing in my mouth. It just looked so gross, so ugly, and I could smell it too, pungent and male, stronger than Rupert, and very different from the female smells I'm used to. I knew I had to suck it, but I couldn't do it, not of my own accord.

'Fuck me, tits out in the woods, eh?' he said as he took a new photo. 'Your arse too. You are a dirty bitch, and no mistake. Come on, you can start now.'

'Make me,' I managed.

'Yeah, right,' he answered. 'I forgot you wanted to play like I'm forcing you.'

I was going to say he was, and call him a filthy bastard or something, to try to at least make something of what he was doing sink in. I never got the chance. He had grabbed me by the hair before I could say a word, and all I managed was a squeak of shock, ending in a muffled squeal as my face was pushed to his genitals.

He rubbed my face in them, smearing the oily skin over my lips and nose and cheeks, until I was forced to open my mouth just to breath. It got filled with cock, immediately, fat, bulbous penis flesh, swelling in my throat as he pulled my head hard down. It went right in, choking me, so that I felt my gorge rise and had to pull back to stop myself being sick. He just stuffed it in again, holding the base and my hair, to fuck my head to his own rhythm. It got stiff really quickly, growing in my mouth, the fat foreskin peeling back as the slimy, salty head was pushed deeper and deeper into my mouth.

'Oh, yeah, good,' he sighed. 'Yeah, that's right, suck it like that, deep throat. Fuck, but I could spunk in your mouth so easily.'

It was down my throat, the head anyway, but only because he had put it there. I wanted to speak, to protest, but could only manage a muffled gobbling noise as he fucked my mouth, harder, faster, until I was gagging on his erection, the tears running down my face, my stomach knotting in protest. I was going to throw up, I knew it, and then it stopped, suddenly.

'Nice one,' he said. 'Now lick my balls and stuff.'

He let go, and I pulled off, gasping and wondering if it wouldn't serve him right just to be sick all over his cock. I nearly was, but choked it back, sure that it would either make him angry or that he'd make me lick it up. Resigned, I bent forwards again, holding my breath against the thick smell of male cock. It was hard now, straining up in front of my face, with his fat ball sack hanging below. He was watching me.

'Come on, lick,' he ordered, 'and suck on my balls, I love that. Wank me while you do it.'

I grimaced, thinking how the fat testicles would feel in my mouth, and the hairy, wrinkly skin of his scrotum. My tongue came out, dabbing at the base of his cock. I took it in hand, squeezing the thick, rubbery pillar of flesh. Jerking at his cock, I began to lick, the base of his shaft, then lower, in among the thick black hair that covered his balls.

He went back to looking at the photos, making little sounds of amusement or pleasure as he went through the pictures of me, me spread and punished, every intimate detail of my body on show, me, the girl who was licking on his balls. They'd begun to tighten, the skin growing thicker and more wrinkly as his excitement rose, until my tongue tip was running over meaty wrinkles and crevices. I could feel the balls under the flesh too, fat, egg-shaped masses that squirmed as my tongue touched them. I'd been told to suck them, and I did it, sucking them into my mouth, one by one and rolling them over my tongue, hoping it would make him come and spare me a mouthful of spunk. He just groaned and put the photos down, pushing me off. I sat back, watching as he pushed his trousers down, all the way to his ankles, and once more sat, spreading his great blubbery thighs.

'That feels better,' he said. 'Now you can really get at me, eh? Now how about getting those lovely tits around my prick?'

I nodded, glad to be spared the taste and feel of him in my mouth, if only temporarily. Shuffling forwards, I took my boobs in my hands and folded them around his cock. He began to push himself up and down, fucking the long hole of boob flesh I'd made in my cleavage, with the red tip of his cock emerging between them with each push. It was wet with my saliva, but there were bubbles of another fluid around the little hole in the tip. I knew that meant he was close to orgasm, and began to rub harder.

'That's right, jiggle 'em about,' he moaned. 'Oh, you fucking know how to please a man, don't you? Will you look at your fucking nips!'

I did, and blushed. They were rock hard, poking up from my boobs as if they were trying to take off. Men always think that means a girl's turned on, and I suppose I was, sort of. Physically anyway, because I knew full well that my pussy was wet. What I wasn't going to do was give him the satisfaction of finding out.

'Suck it now, and lick, plenty,' he ordered suddenly.

His voice was now hoarse, and he'd fixed on one photo, with the others spread out so that he could see them. I didn't know which it was, but I could just imagine it, one of those that showed everything, with me flaunting my red bottom, and naked or near naked. His eyes would be feasting on the back view of my pussy, I just knew it, and on my bumhole too, and I was sobbing as I sank back down to take his cock in my mouth once more. He was going to come, he had to, and as he reached down to take me by the hair I knew it couldn't be long.

He pulled me in, not onto his cock, but against his balls, rubbing my face in them until I began to kiss and lick at the wrinkly skin. I took his cock in hand, jerking at it, sure he'd let go at any moment. I sucked his balls into my mouth, both of them, which should have made him spurt on the spot. He just gasped, and as I sucked on the fat, fleshy eggs and the rubbery skin of his scrotum I was cursing him for being so insensitive.

'You fucking love it, don't you, you dirty little whore?' he grated, and turned the photo to me.

There I was, in Uncle Rupert's garden, with my combats and panties down, my huge boobs dangling bare under my chest, my pussy and bumhole on blatant show, spanked and ready for fucking. I gave a choking sob, gagging on my mouthful of ball sack, my head dizzy with the sheer shame of it all.

'Dirty, dirty little whore!' he repeated. 'Lick this.'

He moved, his legs sliding further apart, the fat tuck of his buttocks pressing to my chin. His grip tightened, pulling my head back, and down. I'd thought he meant his cock, and realised to my horror that he wanted his anus licked, even as my face was pressed down, between his great fat cheeks, my eyes on his balls, my lips against the hairy, puckered hole below them.

I struggled, trying to pull away, but he was too strong, holding me in place. I couldn't breathe. I didn't want to breathe. I had to, though, and my mouth came open to the pungent musk of his bottom and balls, only to be pulled in, my open mouth spreading out over his bumhole, my tongue touching it. He just rubbed my face in it, up and down his crease, smearing my face over his anus, just using my nose and lips to get sensation to his skin. It was so dirty, and I was choking on the taste and smell, and all the while wanking on his cock as hard as I possibly could and praying he would come.

It stopped, suddenly, and I thought he'd come. His hand had been twisted so hard in my hair that it hurt, really hurt, and he'd been gasping and groaning like anything. I thought it was over, relief washing over me, along with an utterly humiliating touch of disappointment. Then, as he pulled me up by my hair, I realised it wasn't. He'd just run out of breath, too fat to make it in one.

He was running sweat, his face red and glossy, the skin of his great fat thighs and gross belly damp. Not that I was much better, my whole body prickling with sweat, while I could feel the wet of my juice between my thighs. I looked at him, drawing my breath in.

'Are you going to come?' I asked.

'Yeah,' he puffed. 'I'll be all right. Hang on.'

'You wank,' I told him. 'I'll suck on your balls.'

'In a bit, yeah,' he answered. 'You can have a bit first, just give me a moment.'

He threw his head back, his chins stretching up to expose the sweaty red lines between them, with drops running down his neck. His breathing was deep, his chest rising and falling, and for one horrible moment I thought he was going to pass out on me, or worse. He didn't, and after a moment his hand fixed hard in my hair, pulling me into him, but not towards his cock.

'What are you doing?' I demanded.

'Giving you what you want, your kinky stuff.'

'No . . . really . . . I . . .'

'Come on, you love it! I can do it harder than that poof in the photos and all.'

'No, not that! Not a spanking! No!'

'Yeah, you love it, you kinky bitch!'

'No, please, stop! Not like that!'

He'd pulled me up, not over his legs, but spread across one, with my pussy on his thigh, pressed hard to his leg and my bottom stuck out behind. It was the worst possible thing he could have done, certain to get me horny. Sure enough, the first hard slap pushed my open sex right against his leg, rubbing my clitty on his bare skin. I squealed, cursing him and calling him a bastard, yelling at him to get off, but he took no notice at all, laying in another hard smack, full across my sweet spot, and I was just lost.

He did me hard, so hard, smack after smack of his great heavy arm, each one jamming my pussy onto his leg, until I could do nothing but squeal and babble incoherently. It was right on my sweet spot, and all the

226

while his great hard cock was pressing to my side, rubbing on the soft flesh of my waist, until I thought he'd spunk on me. It was too much, I was going to come, right there on his leg.

I lost it, rubbing myself, bucking up and down, pushing my pussy to his thigh with each awful slap. My mouth went wide, my screams and sobs turning to a gasp of ecstasy . . .

It stopped, his body jerking forwards to shove me off. I collapsed, onto the floor, hard on my bum. I was snivelling, and gasping, tears streaming down my face to splash on my boobs, snot pouring from my nose. I'd been on the edge, too close, and I had to come, and come with my bum up. I rolled, sticking my bottom high, an utterly vulgar display.

He twitched up my skirt as my fingers went to my pussy, showing it all. I didn't stop him, but started to rub at my sopping hole. My mind was fixed on the sensations of my body, my hot bum and wet sex, my straining nipples and the taste of cock in my mouth. I was broken, the last shred of my dignity gone, blown away in that awful, degrading spanking, until all I cared about was getting myself to climax.

I heard him, barely aware of his words, 'What an arse! I've got to fuck it!'

I might have got away with it, maybe, if only I'd had panties on. I didn't, and the next thing I knew the weight of his belly was settling on my bottom and his cock was prodding at my hole. A faint voice in the back of my head screamed at me to stop him. Then he was up me, and it was too late, the full, fat length of his cock filling my pussy as the first glorious twinges of orgasm hit me. I cried out, babbling, calling him a fat bastard, but thanking him too, brokenly, wretchedly, for what he'd done to me.

' . . . yes, please, deeper!' I begged. 'Fuck my pussy, Dave, use me, hurt me, spank me while you do it, you dirty, fat creep ... Fuck my bottom, you dirty, fat bastard!'

'Shut it!' he grated, and the next instant his cock had pulled from my hole.

Immediately I was babbling apologies, begging him to fill me, to beat me, to fuck me as I came. He just grunted, and then his cock touched me again, but not on my pussy, on my bumhole.

'Not there! That's not what I –' I babbled, and shut up, my mouth wide in a wordless gasp of shock and pain as he jabbed the fat head of his cock into my anus.

It just went up. I was slimy, too slimy to stop him, wet with my own juice, and loose too, not as tight as I should be, after all the fingers and dildos and candles I'd had wedged up my bum by my girlfriends.

He didn't stop either, but forced it in, all of it, the full, fat length of his gross cock, shoved mercilessly up my sloppy back passage, inch by painful inch, until at last his balls bumped against my empty pussy and I knew I was well and truly being buggered. I hadn't said a word. I couldn't. I was sobbing though, loudly, and snivelling, with a long strand of snot hanging from my nose, until my face met the floor and it was pushed against my lips. At long last I had a cock up my bottom.

I felt bloated, not just in my rectum, but my tummy too, even my head, as if by the act of sticking his cock up my bum he had taken over my whole body, making me no more than a sex doll to be jerked on his gross penis. As if that wasn't bad enough, his hands had closed on my hips, with his thumbs holding my buttocks wide, so that he could see as his cock moved in my ring. I could just picture it, my little pink hole a straining circle of pink flesh around the fat shaft of his cock, plugging my anus between my round, rosy bum-cheeks.

'Frig your cunt, whore,' he rasped, his filthy, crude language adding just one more awful touch to my degradation.

I did it too. I didn't know why, but I did it. Maybe it was the only way out, maybe I just couldn't help it. As my fingers began to move on my clitty again I slipped back into that dirty, wanton state, when the only thing that matters is my pleasure. Then I knew why, because it was the way out, to admit my own filthy desire to myself, to let it all go, to do what I'd fantasised over so often, and frig with a man's prick in my dirt box.

No sooner had that awful piece of self-awareness hit me than I was coming. I gasped, clutching at my pussy, two fingers flicking on my clitty. My pussy tightened, expelling air in a long farting noise, and so did my bumhole, squeezing hard on the intruding penis. I suppose I screamed; I don't really know, or how long it lasted. All I knew was that I had a man's cock up my bottom and I was masturbating over the sensation of it. I didn't even feel him come, but I heard his grunt, at the very peak on my orgasm, with my ring tight on his shaft, and I knew that I'd just had a load of sperm deposited in my rectum.

I lasted longer than he did, still gasping and clutching at my pussy when he had stopped. Even as he pulled slowly out of me my fingers were still working in my flesh, and they stayed there as I slumped, broken, onto the carpet. He got off me, but I just lay there, with the sperm dribbling out of my bumhole, utterly defeated, spanked and buggered, and as those two words ran over and over through my head I once more began to masturbate.

I spent Sunday out, in Hertfordshire, straight up the railway line from me, but somewhere I was sure I'd be safe. I was feeling sorry for myself at first, sulking really, I suppose.

It was not easy coming to terms with having been buggered. I'd known it might happen, one day, but I'd imagined it would be Rupert who did it, or maybe someone like Mark, a bisexual girl's boyfriend. To have it done by some fat slob of a cabbie was far worse, especially when he'd taken advantage of me so badly. My bumhole ached too, and it was impossible not to play the scene over in my mind. In the end I masturbated over it, I just couldn't stop myself.

I did it in a stand of young pines, kneeling bare-bottomed among the fallen needles. My eyes were closed, and I was imagining how his cock and balls had felt in my mouth, the pain and indignity of my spanking, the weight of his gross belly on my bottom before he entered me, and after, with it slapping on my smacked cheeks. Most of all, though, I imagined how that awful, fat cock had felt up my bumhole, and that was what I came over.

That actually made me feel a lot better. After all, in a sense, I had controlled it. I'd made a sacrifice, yes, my anal virginity, so it was a big one. On the other hand, if I was going to want to come over the experience, then how awful could it have really been? Shameful, yes, degrading, yes, but an orgasm is an orgasm, whatever it takes to get there.

I'd denied the girls their revenge too, or at least, I'd postponed it, because Dave had stayed with me until they'd gone. That mattered, and I knew that every extra day I managed to avoid them would save me a little more suffering. Inevitably there was the nagging voice at the back of my head telling me the exact opposite, that every day I avoided them would reduce my ultimate pleasure. I ignored it. Sadistic sex play is one thing, revenge another.

I'd gone so far in among the trees for my frig that I got a bit lost, but by good luck I came out near a pub. I lunched there, and afterwards visited the place Heather had told me about. To my surprise it was a normal saddler, but I was sure I had the right address, and when the wholesome woman in the shop turned out to be Amber Oakley herself, I managed to find the courage to ask for a piggy nose and tail.

That made me feel a lot better, and I was quickly imagining Heather and I together in the mud, licking and nuzzling at each other's bodies before being whipped and given a good fucking. That assumed Rupert was around, of course, which I knew he might well not be, or at least not to play piggy-girls. For a while that made me feel sad, but I managed to shrug it off.

I came back on the last train, and took great care in getting to my house. Nobody was there, but when I checked with the old lady from the downstairs flat, she told me that my bell had gone several times during the day, and that she'd seen several of what she called 'biker girls' hanging around outside. Late or not, I was extremely thankful once the door was securely locked behind me.

All that evening I was in an odd mood, scared, but rebellious too. I put the photo of AJ as a fairy up on my bedroom wall, which was immensely satisfying. True, I'd rather have had Andrea beat her up and made her lick my bum clean afterwards, but the photo was a lot better than nothing. That done, I settled down to reading some of Rupert's spanking magazines, one-handed, and finally came over a letter from a girl who liked to wear tight leather shorts to take a spanking.

Monday was easier, with filing work in a city office to keep my mind off things. I was still cautious in the evening, but nobody came. The same was true on Tuesday, and while I didn't suppose for a moment that they'd given up on me, I began to suspect that nothing would happen until the weekend. Rupert called in the evening, the first chance he'd had without Sarah being there. He was grateful, and sympathetic when I told him what had happened, although I could tell from his voice that it turned him on, and amused him too. Men!

I also rang Heather, to say that Rupert was ill. We met anyway, on the Wednesday evening, but it wasn't really a success. For one thing the absence of her uniform, supposedly ruined in the wash, didn't go down too well, despite the cheque, which was about three times what it was worth. Also, unlike me, she seemed to need a man to be present in order to let herself go, and while we had a nice evening and finished with a kiss and a cuddle, it was hardly what I'd been hoping for.

By the Thursday evening, nobody had called at my flat for four days. Still, when the bell finally did go I nearly jumped out of my skin. I'd told myself I would hide, but it was impossible not to look. So I got down low and peered carefully around one corner of the curtain, expecting to see the three girls standing waiting in the street.

It wasn't them, only Zoe, looking up at my windows with a puzzled expression on her face. A great wave of relief washed through me, and I immediately decided to let her in. I needed sympathetic company, and maybe a cuddle, but most of all I was hoping she had news of what was going on. I threw the window open and called to her. She responded with a cheerful wave and I tossed down the keys, which she caught, then held them up, as if in triumph, looking directly towards where the little porch hid my front door from view. Something was wrong, and as she skipped happily up the path I turned away, my mouth open in shock at what I was sure was her betrayal.

I was right. Before I could get to my door it was opening, and there was AJ, with others behind her. I was stammering apologies and explanations even as she pushed into my flat, only to shut up as I realised just who was there. AJ was first, but it wasn't Sam behind her, or Naomi. It was Andrea, all six foot of her, with a truly wicked smile on her face. Zoe followed, grinning impishly, then Naomi and Sam. Last was Mo, her shoulders almost touching the sides of the door frame, a vast and terrifying bulk.

I sat down, feeling suddenly too weak to stand. AJ went to sit on the sofa, Sam to one side, Naomi to the other. Zoe joined them, on Sam's lap. Andrea took a place by the window, picking one of Rupert's magazines up and opening it. Mo shut the door behind her.

'This is cosy, isn't it?' AJ remarked, looking around. 'Very femme, except most of my baby dykes don't have quite so many spanking magazines.'

'I . . . They're my uncle's,' I stammered, blushing.

'Fair enough,' she answered, glancing at the cover of a *Slap!* with a look of both amusement and disgust. 'We're not here to discuss your sexuality anyway – well, not entirely. What we do want is a little talk . . .'

'First off,' Mo interrupted. 'Where's my dress uniform?'

'Over there, on the chair,' I said. 'I'm sorry, Mo, I didn't mean anything . . .'

'Shut up,' she spat. 'It had better not be damaged. Let's see.'

She had picked it up, pulling it out from among the others. I couldn't bear to look. Zoe was the first to realise.

'Hey! That's my school uniform!' she protested as the others turned to her. 'Jade!'

'What is this?' Andrea demanded. 'She's got loads! Look, a nurse's uniform, and a Girl Guide! Jesus, Jade!'

'A Girl Guide leader!' I said quickly. 'She's grown up, a teacher. Look, I can explain!'

'You'd better,' AJ said, reaching for the Indian air hostess outfit.

'Out with it!' Mo demanded.

'It . . . it was just for fun,' I stammered. 'Honestly, we didn't mean any harm . . .'

'We?' Mo interrupted. 'Who's we?'

'My Uncle Rupert and I,' I said. 'He had started collecting uniforms, you see, the air hostess one, and an American waitress, and . . . and, well, I just thought it would be fun.'

233

'So you stole my uniform?' she demanded. 'To make a trophy for your uncle?'

'And you weren't going to give mine back?' Zoe demanded. 'You little thief!'

'So that's why you wanted me to be a real warden!' Andrea exclaimed. 'You were out to pinch my kit!'

'No ... yes ... I mean, oh, God!' I babbled. 'I'm sorry!'

I put my head in my hands, almost in tears. They were talking at me, all six of them, three calling me a thief, the others joining in with their own grievances. Finally AJ's voice cut through the others.

'Looks like you're busted, Jade,' she said. 'Well and truly busted.'

'I'm sorry,' I repeated, my voice no more than a feeble whisper. 'Take the uniforms back. I'll make sure the others get returned, I promise.'

'You reckon that's good enough, do you?' Mo demanded.

'No,' I admitted weakly.

'It's not, is it, Jade?' AJ said. 'So where do you reckon you get off?'

'I don't know,' I replied. 'Are you going to punish me?'

'We are,' Sam assured me. 'We owe you from the other night, big time.'

Andrea nodded.

'Is that all right with you, Mo?' AJ asked. 'You get your property back and we all give her a good slapping?'

'Fine by me,' Mo answered. 'That's fair, if she's going to take it. I can hardly have her charged, can I? She'd blab. The army don't approve of pissing on sluts, which is what I did to her.'

'She'll take it,' AJ laughed. 'Won't you, Jade?'

I just hung my head, not willing to give them permission, but unable to refuse it.

'See?' AJ went on. 'She knows she deserves it. Right, Dumplings, strip!'

I stood, my trembling fingers going straight to the buttons of my work blouse. Refusal was pointless, and would mean being stripped by force, my work suit ruined. They sat back, watching, every one of them thoroughly enjoying my fear and misery. My blouse came off, and my skirt, my shoes and tights, to leave me in my underwear. I never even paused, knowing full well that I wasn't going to be allowed a scrap of modesty. My bra came off, my panties last, leaving me stark naked and very vulnerable, standing with one arm over my pussy and the other across my tits.

'You're not hiding much, Jade,' Naomi joked, 'not with those tits.'

'What are you going to do to her?' Zoe asked.

'Whatever takes our fancy,' AJ answered. 'For one I think she ought to lick us, just to get her in her place.'

'Okay,' Zoe answered. 'You . . . you're not really going to hurt her, are you?'

'Oh, she'll recover,' AJ said. 'She's tough. So, Jade, time to lick, all six of us. Get in the bedroom.'

I went, scared and uncertain, but grateful that I'd at least be allowed to get horny before they laid into me. In my room I sat on the bed, wondering if the way I felt was at all like how a prostitute must feel, with a line of men waiting to have her, and no choice over who she takes. Actually it wasn't, because I'd have gladly gone down to any one of the girls outside. I managed a little grin for myself, only for it to fade as I remembered what Andrea liked to do to girls, and Mo, and AJ, and . . .

'Naomi, see what's in her fridge,' AJ called from outside. 'Crack me a beer if she's got one.'

They'd taken over my flat, completely, leaving me as just the sex toy in the bedroom, like a vibrator, to be used as they pleased. I swallowed at the thought, then lifted my eyes as Mo came into the room. I'd thought

AJ would be first, but nobody was going to argue with Mo. She pushed the door to behind her, her hand already at the button of her green fatigues. Outside I heard the pop of bottle tops and Andrea's laughter, as I got down on my knees.

They took turns with me, all six of them, one by one, coming under my tongue, the way they wanted. Mo just sat, spread-legged on my bed as I knelt in front of her. She never said a word, and came really quickly, full in my face. Andrea came next, ordering me to the floor, where I was given a few good kicks before she pulled up her skirt to sit on my face. I was made to do it forwards, looking up at her as I lapped at her pussy, with her grinning cruelly down at me. Sam followed, and gave me the same treatment, only the other way around, with my nose up her bumhole as I licked her pussy.

By the time she'd finished with me my face was smeared with pussy juice and I was dizzy with the smell of sex. Naomi made it worse, making me do it kneeling, with her bottom in my face, so that I had to lick her bumhole before getting down to work on her pussy. It was she who noticed my brand new snout and tail as well, after she'd had me. She made me put them on, turning me into a pig, which made Zoe giggle when she came for her go. Zoe was sweet, and actually spoke nicely to me, but she made me do it anyway, sat on my face as I lay on the bed, and squirming her bum and pussy into my mouth, to make me lick as she brought herself off against my nose.

That left AJ. She gave a snort of laughter as she came in, smiling at the state I was in and at how I looked.

'A pig!' she said. 'Suits you, Jade. Girl, you do look ridiculous!'

I'd forgotten all about the photo, but her remark about looking ridiculous reminded me. Inevitably I glanced at it, which was a really stupid thing to do, as otherwise I'm not sure she'd even have noticed. As it was she did, glancing at it herself, then back, her mouth falling open as she did her double-take.

'You fucking bitch!' she spat, and snatched at it, pulling it from the wall. 'You've fucking had it, you little . . .'

She'd stuck it down her top, and she lashed out, catching me full across the face. I screamed and rolled back on the bed, my hands coming up to protect myself as she scrambled on top of me. She straddled me, her knees planted across my stomach. Her hand grappled for my wrists, catching on, wrenching and twisting to grab the other. My arms were hauled up, above my head, exposing my face. She lashed out again, in my face, scratching me, then across my boobs, and again, backhanded, leaving them stinging hot, with two long red trails across the white flesh where her nails had caught me.

'You fucking . . .' she spat, pulling her fist back, and stopped, turning as the door swung open behind her.

'Hey, leave some for us!' Andrea laughed.

AJ blew her breath out, glaring down at me.

'Hang on,' she said.

Her hands went to her jeans, popping the button. She turned, pushing them down, to take her panties with them, and to leave her naked bottom stuck out, right in my face, her cheeks spread to show the little dirty hole between them. I caught her scent a moment before she settled it in my face, spreading her cheeks over my mouth. I kissed her bumhole, desperate to make up, tasted the bitter tang and started to lick.

She said nothing, waiting until I'd cleaned her thoroughly before easing herself back to press her pussy to my face. Andrea was still watching, and I knew she could see my tongue working in the pink folds of AJ's sex. Not that AJ seemed to mind, hissing between her teeth in anger as she ground her bottom into my face, to push my pig's nose up into the saliva wet cavity of her bumhole. I could barely breathe, smothered in bottom, with the acrid tang thick in my mouth and nose, blending with the girlish, hormonal taste of pussy.

AJ came, or I think she did, with no more than a sharp hiss as her muscles locked in my face. She climbed off, my pig's nose pulling from her anus with a sticky pop, to leave it full of fluid. As her bottom left my face I found not just Andrea but Naomi and Sam watching, delighted at both my appearance and my discomfort. Mo was behind them, and in her hand she held AJ's heavy tawse. I swallowed hard as AJ climbed off the bed.

'Rope,' she spat.

'Under the bed,' I told her, throwing a worried glance at the others as they filed in, Mo smacking the thick leather strap across her hand in satisfaction.

AJ pulled out my toy box, choosing two hanks of black rope. I lay submissively on the bed, in utter surrender, and she and Sam tied my wrists, well apart on the bars at the top of my bed. The others stood watching, smiling, their eyes glittering at the thought of what they were about to do to me. I was shivering, with a big knot in my stomach and my breathing hard to control, my jaw shaking uncontrollably.

'Roll her up, someone,' AJ said, tying the rope off. 'Right up, so her little pig's tail shows.'

Andrea pulled my bed out from the wall and took hold of an ankle, pulling my leg up as Naomi took the other. They held me like that, hard, with my bum stuck out and my pussy-lips vulnerable between my spread thighs. Mo raised the tawse, hefting it in one massive hand and nodding in satisfaction. I moaned, fear and despair rising, near to panic, and screamed as she brought the horrible thing down across my bum cheeks with all her force.

It hurt so much, flaming agony, the blow jamming my insides up and laying a burning, sting line across my bottom. She laughed, and lifted it, bringing it down again onto my thighs, leaving me shaking my head and thrashing my body in my pain. A third hit home, and a fourth, Mo warming to her task as my flesh jumped and quivered. One caught my pussy and I screamed again, then farted loudly as the next came low. It stopped leaving me panting and shaking, to look up and find Mo holding the tawse over me, but not sideways, not to be laid across my bum, but lengthways, for my pussy.

'No!' I screamed, even as her forearm slammed down, the tawse lashed out, onto my pussy and my whole being exploded in furious pain, my body jerking against their grip, my back arched, my teeth gritting.

She didn't do it again, and I was left shivering on the bed, my teeth chattering and my breath coming in short, hard pants. My pussy was throbbing, my bum too, feeling fat and swollen and puffy. It hurt crazily, but I could feel the warmth building up, and the wet trickle of my juice as it ran down between my bum-cheeks. My nipples were hard too, and quivering as I shook.

'Just look at those titties wobble!' Sam remarked. 'We've got to do them.'

'No, please, not my boobs,' I panted, but she took no notice, bending down to rummage in my toy box.

'Titty-whip you? I wouldn't dream of it,' she said. 'I was –'

'I would,' AJ put in. 'Come on girls, pick a toy, she's got plenty. Tie her legs, you two.'

Sam stood as AJ finished speaking. She was holding one of my candles, a thick red one. I swallowed, wondering if it was going up me. She sniffed it.

'She's a candle wanker,' she said. 'Surprise, surprise. Do you like them lit while you do it, Jade?'

I shook my head frantically, but she just laughed. It had been up my pussy more than once, but never lit. I'd been waxed, though, and I knew how much it hurt. My muscles twitched at the thought, making my boobs shiver.

AJ had tossed a second hank of rope to Andrea, who was twisting it around my ankle as Naomi worked another loose. I thought they'd spread me, but they pulled my ankles high, the same way they held me to be spanked, tying them and running the rope back around the top of my bed. It left me exposed utterly, my boobs, my pussy, my poor aching bum, with the pig's tail hanging obscenely below my crease, all on show, all completely vulnerable. Both my holes were stuck out too, utterly blatant, and I knew the state I was in, because I could feel my wet running down from my pussy into my bumhole.

By the time Naomi had tied off the second rope I was completely helpless. My legs were rolled so high that they could get at the whole of my bum, and even if I closed them it meant rolling up even more, to leave my pussy-lips and boobs sticking up in the air, just as vulnerable as ever. It didn't stop them getting at me with whips either, not from the sides, and certainly not with wax.

That was what Sam was going to do to me, and Andrea too. Both had candles, and they'd fetched matches from the kitchen. Andrea had lit hers, and just to look at the flame was making my heart jump. That wasn't all either. Mo still had her tawse, and AJ had taken a thong whip from my toy box, small, but meant for delicate bums, not boobs. Naomi was armed too, with the little spiky roller I like to use on my bum, just gently. Even Zoe had picked up my hairbrush, but she was biting her lip in doubt.

'Are you sure she can take this?' Zoe asked.

'They're her things,' AJ answered. 'If she didn't want them used on her, would she have bought them?'

Zoe shrugged.

'Makes sense to me,' Sam said, and struck a match.

They came in, surrounding me, all high on the joy of torturing me, each one of them tense with excitement. Mo lifted the tawse, Andrea poising her candle over my tummy. As Sam lit hers the others waited, until she had it posed over my chest. I watched, mouth wide in horror, as she tilted it. The flame touched wax, a bead forming, melting, growing, and falling, full onto one of my nipples. I screamed, jerking in my bonds at the sudden hot, stinging pain. The tawse cracked down on my bum and I screamed again, twisting as another drop of wax caught the side of a boob. More wax caught me, from Andrea, right in my belly button, and across my tummy. AJ's whip smacked down across my boobs, spattering hot wax across my neck and chest as it fell. The tawse fell again, on my thighs, an agonising prickling stabbed into me as Naomi ran her horrid toy along my side . . .

It was too much, far too much, all blending into one burning, dizzying pain as they laid in, whips, wax and spikes all over me, leaving me yelling and thrashing in my bonds, my vision red and blurred, my senses blank except for the torture, as I screamed over and over . . .

It stopped.

'For God's sake, someone shut her up,' Andrea said.

'Naomi,' AJ ordered, 'piss in your knickers. Gag her.'

I turned my head to the side, my eyes wide in shock and pain. Naomi was already undoing her trousers, and she pushed them down, over spotty blue and red panties, which made me giggle hysterically. She took her trousers off, her boots too, and she just did it, in her panties, right in front of everyone, and all over my bedroom floor. Mo laughed at the sight, AJ grinning approval.

She pulled them off, dripping pee, and mopped up some of the puddle, leaving them filthy and completely soaked. I opened my mouth in surrender as she leaned close, and they were crammed in, filling my senses with the acrid taste of her pee.

'That's better,' AJ said. 'We wouldn't want your neighbours to know what you're like, would we?'

As she spoke the first drop of hot wax landed on my bare skin, splashing over a nipple. I jerked, tensing. The tawse smacked in, Zoe's brush caught the side of one boob and it had started again. AJ laid in, Andrea lowering the candle, to an inch above my belly. Mo caught me, and again, getting faster, blow after blow. I screamed wordlessly into my gag, thrashing and bucking to the pain, my whole body burning, prickling, as the blows rained in, harder and harder, the wax spattering out across my skin.

Then Mo was hitting my pussy, full across the swollen lips, and it hurt so much, enough to make me lose my senses, to drive everything else out of my head. I just came, the orgasm rising from nowhere, exploding in my head as my back arched and every muscle in my body went tight. I felt fluid squirt from my pussy, splashing across my hot skin, and it had stopped once more, leaving me lying dizzy on the bed, mouthing slowly on the pissy panties in my mouth, my whole body aching and throbbing with pain, the skin of my bottom, legs and pussy inflamed and wet with sweat, by boobs encased in red wax, like a weird bra. They were staring down at me, all six of them, and not cruelly, but in frustration and amazement.

'You just came,' Andrea stated.

'Yeah, you came,' AJ echoed. 'That was supposed to be a punishment, a real punishment, you slut!'

'You're unbelievable, Jade, you soak it up like a fucking sponge!' Naomi swore.

'I know how to get to her,' Sam said. 'Have some fun with her. I'll be back in a minute.' .

She left, without explanation. They started on me again, not so vicious, but toying with me, just using me for their amusement. My gag was tied in to make sure I stayed shut up. Andrea went to the kitchen, for beer, and came back with the end of a cucumber as well, which she stuffed up my pussy. They put me in clamps, AJ and Naomi, grinning as they tightened the little screws, until my blood-stiff nipples were bulging out of the top, aching and purple with strain. My bumhole got greased with margarine by Mo, who had a fine time fingering my bottom before pulling the gag aside far enough to stick her dirty finger in my mouth.

That was when someone suggested giving me an enema, only jokingly, but when they caught the look of horror in my eyes they decided to do it for real. They used milk, two pints of it, from plastic bottles, with the wide, rough mouth of each plugged into my greasy bumhole before it was squirted up me, a bit at a time. Plenty went on the bed, but a good deal went in. I could feel it in my gut, the pressure growing, until my belly felt like it does just before my period, then worse, as if I was about to poo myself. They thought it was hilarious, particularly once they'd got my tummy bulging up, into a hard, round ball, swollen with milk. Even Zoe was thoroughly enjoying herself, her qualms forgotten in the sadistic joy of having another girl to torture.

The full two pints went up me, or most of it. I could hold it, just, fighting down the pain, determined not to give in, not on my own bed, not with the five of them gloating down at me, just hoping I'd lose control. They were loving it, which just shows how really cruel girls can be, and they had started to lay bets on whether I'd squirt if they frigged me off when Sam came back.

She had a feather.

I just looked at it, my eyes round with horror, knowing what was going to happen if she tickled me, exactly what was going to happen. She was grinning as she came towards me, holding it up, and twiddling it between her fingers. I began to shake my head, violently, trying to spit the gag out, desperate to beg off, to promise them anything, to be their toilet slaves for life, to let them have me as their property.

It was too well tied. I couldn't get it out. Panic was welling up inside me as she took my foot, gently, then hard as I tried to kick myself loose. My mouth went wide as the feather touched the sole of my foot. My leg muscles jumped, my insides twisting in torment.

She moved lower, tickling behind my knees, inside my thighs, up my side, in my armpit, all the while with me lurching on the bed, kicking in my bonds and struggling, desperately to keep my bumhole shut. I managed it, clenching my cheeks as tight as I could, fighting my own helpless reaction to that awful feather, even when she began to tickle the tuck of my bottom. Then she brought the feather down onto my pussy and trailed it slowly across my anus.

It happened, my gut going into spasm, my muscles twitching, beyond my control. My bumhole just opened. Immediately the contents exploded out, in a high arc of dirty milk, all over my bed, all over the floor, spraying out as my mouth closed tight in agonising shame, until Naomi's piddle was running down my throat.

Sam had stopped, gasping in shock as my anus erupted. The others laughed, uproariously, Naomi so hard she sank to her knees, Andrea clutching her sides, Zoe with her face scarlet, giggling behind one hand. My hole had closed, but I'd given up, and I let it open again, sending out a second spurt, and third, over my bum, to trickle back under my poor, beaten bottom. It died, to trickle and ooze from my hole, and I slumped down in the mess.

I lay there, my bottom in my filthy puddle, panting through my pig's nose, and trying not to choke on Naomi's panties, which where blocking my throat. Sam chuckled, and once more put the feather to my skin. My muscles tightened, my flesh writhing, my insides twisting as it was drawn over my belly. More mess spurted from my bumhole, the feather moving down, over my pussy-mound, onto my sex-lips.

At that my bladder went. I didn't really even try to stop it, just shutting my eyes in my shame as the pee spurted out, to splash over my tummy and thighs and add to the mess. My muscles had gone, completely, and I just did it on the bed, everything, all over myself, my belly jumping and pulsing uncontrollably as it came out. There was plenty of it, a golden fountain, rising almost vertically from my pussy, to patter down over my body and run into the open hole of my vagina. I was lost, my muscles jumping and twitching in an instinctive response that owed nothing to my mind.

Sam waited until my gushing pee had died down and carried on, teasing my pussy, mercilessly, ignoring the spurts of piddle coming out and the mess oozing from my bumhole. She just kept on teasing me, ignoring the mess, and tickling my pussy and my sloppy bumhole as I jerked and quivered in my bonds. More mess came out of my bottom hole, and I just let it, indifferent to their cries of pleased disgust as it squeezed out and dropped down into the crease of my bottom.

A moment later I'd sat in it, as Sam touched the feather to my clitty. I knew I was going to come immediately. I couldn't stop myself. She tickled, wriggling the feather over the little tight bud of flesh between my lips, tormenting me, bringing me up and up, until I was squirming, then thrashing crazily, my fat, piggy bottom splashing and squelching in the pool of milk and pee and mess, writhing, struggling, squirming, as it hit me. I'd been stripped, humiliated, tied, tortured, made to piss myself, to soil myself and now, finally, I was masturbating in my own filth, just like the filthy, dirty, brown-nosed little slut-pig I am . . .

I came, an orgasm totally and utterly out of my control, one to send me dizzy and blind, with my vision red and spots dancing before my eyes. It seemed to go on for ever, peak after peak with my bumhole pulsing and my pussy squirting pee, my bottom splashing in the sodden bedclothes, everything coming out, with no control whatever over my own body, just coming and coming and coming . . .

Then I'd swallowed the gag and I was choking, until AJ snatched it free, tearing the strap down over my chin and wrenching out the panties to leave me gasping for breath.

'Again!' Andrea exclaimed. 'She came again!'

'What a slut! Naomi added.

'I give up,' Sam said. 'I really thought she didn't like that.'

'I don't, I hate it,' I panted.

'Yeah, sure,' AJ slurred. 'Come on, I don't reckon she'll forget this in a hurry in any case. Come on, Naomi, get your kit on. Who's up for a drink?'

'Me, and I'm buying,' Mo answered. 'To say thank you for letting me in on this.'

'Any time,' AJ answered. 'After all, we've got to keep the sluts in order. Get on with it, Naomi, never mind your knicks, go bare. Coming, Andrea, Zoe?'

'Sure,' Andrea answered, Zoe responding with a shy smile.

'Hey? What about me?' I demanded.

'You can't come,' Andrea answered. 'They wouldn't let you in, not like that.'

'But . . .' I began.

'Shut it,' AJ answered. 'Or I'll have Sam mop up what's between your legs with the knicks, and you know where that'll go.'

I went quiet, watching as they cleared up, until they were actually starting to leave, when I could hold it no more.

'Hey!' I shouted. 'Untie me! Be fair!'

'You'll get out,' AJ said casually, 'in time.'

'I can't!' I pleaded. 'You've done me tightly! Please!'

'Just bite through the rope,' she said. 'It shouldn't take more than an hour or so.'

They just left, laughing together as they trooped out through the door, Naomi and AJ arm in arm, Andrea chatting happily to Mo. As Zoe left she turned, holding her nose and making a face at me. Sam went last.

'And let that be a lesson to you,' she said, shaking her finger at me. 'Bye, bye, Dumplings.'

'You ... you're not really cross, are you?' I managed. 'I'll see you again?'

She paused, took two quick steps back to me, kissed me and ruffled my hair.

'Don't be stupid,' she answered. 'How could we resist?'

NEXUS BACKLIST

This information is correct at time of printing. For up-to-date information, please visit our website at www.nexus-books.co.uk

All books are priced at £5.99 unless another price is given.

Nexus books with a contemporary setting

ACCIDENTS WILL HAPPEN	Lucy Golden ISBN 0 352 33596 3	☐
ANGEL	Lindsay Gordon ISBN 0 352 33590 4	☐
BEAST	Wendy Swanscombe ISBN 0 352 33649 8	☐
THE BLACK FLAME	Lisette Ashton ISBN 0 352 33668 4	☐
THE BLACK MASQUE	Lisette Ashton ISBN 0 352 33372 3	☐
BROUGHT TO HEEL	Arabella Knight ISBN 0 352 33508 4	☐
CAGED!	Yolanda Celbridge ISBN 0 352 33650 1	☐
CANDY IN CAPTIVITY	Arabella Knight ISBN 0 352 33495 9	☐
CAPTIVES OF THE PRIVATE HOUSE	Esme Ombreux ISBN 0 352 33619 6	☐
DANCE OF SUBMISSION	Lisette Ashton ISBN 0 352 33450 9	☐
DARK DELIGHTS	Maria del Rey ISBN 0 352 33276 X	☐
DIRTY LAUNDRY £6.99	Penny Birch ISBN 0 352 33680 3	☐
DISCIPLES OF SHAME	Stephanie Calvin ISBN 0 352 33343 X	☐